REDEMPTION

REDEMPTION

A NOVEL

MIKE LAWSON

Atlantic Monthly Press

New York

FIRST EDITION

Published simultaneously in Canada
Printed in the United States of America

First Grove Atlantic hardcover edition: April 2022

Library of Congress Cataloging-in-Publication data is available for this title.

ISBN 978-0-8021-5953-3
eISBN 978-0-8021-5954-0

Atlantic Monthly Press
an imprint of Grove Atlantic
154 West 14th Street
New York, NY 10011

Distributed by Publishers Group West

groveatlantic.com

22 23 24 25   10 9 8 7 6 5 4 3 2 1

REDEMPTION

1

Redemption, Illinois. Population eight thousand and dropping with each passing year. A drowsy, unremarkable town, home to neither industry nor academia. A place surrounded by corn and soybean fields, where a four-story building is the tallest structure within fifty miles that isn't a grain silo.

Jamison Maddox had been born and mostly raised in Manhattan, a city with a pulse, one with a throbbing, feckless heart. Manhattan was the center of the universe for finance, culture, and the arts. A mecca for the beautiful, the talented, the witty, and the rich. Manhattan was the only place Jamison had ever wanted to live and work—and yet here he was in Redemption, about to interview for a job he was certain he wouldn't want with a company that he'd never heard of.

He knew he'd fallen far—but had never thought it would come to this.

The unsolicited letter he'd received said the job paid only a hundred and twenty thousand annually—the amount wasn't negotiable—but if he was interested, he should come for the interview. The company would pay for his flight to Chicago, his rental car for the two-hour drive to Redemption, and one night in a motel. In his last job, Jamison made almost a million dollars a year, his base salary augmented by his annual bonus—and he always got a bonus.

For whatever reason the interview was not taking place at the offices of Drexler Limited, the company that had recruited him. It was instead being held in a small diner, one with Norman Rockwell prints on the walls and six red-topped stools in front of a lunch counter. He took a seat at a table near a window where he could look across the street at a hardware store, a pharmacy, and a barbershop. The name of the street was, of course, Main Street.

At two in the afternoon, the diner had only two other customers, a couple of men sitting apart at the counter. One of them wore a white lab coat; Jamison figured he probably worked at the pharmacy and was taking a late lunch. The other guy was wearing denim overalls and a green-and-yellow John Deere ball cap. A large blue handkerchief drooped from his back pocket.

An elderly man in a black suit carrying a briefcase stepped into the diner. His hair was white and full. He had bushy white eyebrows, thin lips, a prominent nose, and a blunt chin. His face was stern, hard, angular—what Jamison thought of as a Mount Rushmore face, one seemingly chipped from granite with jackhammers. He was a big, broad-shouldered old man, and not a kindly looking one.

He stood in the doorway for only a second before walking over to the table where Jamison was seated. He apparently knew what Jamison looked like, which wasn't surprising. Unfortunately, all it would have taken was a Google search to find a photo of him, one in which Jamison might have been wearing an orange prison jumpsuit. The old man moved as if his knees were bad and his back was somewhat bent, diminishing his height. Had he stood straight, he would have been at least six foot four. He must have been an impressive physical specimen when he was a young man.

Jamison smiled, stuck out his hand, and said, "Jamison Maddox. Thank you for inviting me."

The old man shook his hand; he didn't smile. His hand was larger than Jamison's, and although his fingers were swollen and gnarled from arthritis, he had a strong grip.

He said, "Claud Drexler. I'm glad you decided to come, Mr. Maddox."

The only waitress in the café—a slender blonde of nineteen or twenty—rushed to the table. "Can I get you anything, Mr. Drexler?"

"Just coffee for now, Cindy. I might have some of your mom's apple pie later."

Drexler studied Jamison, making a silent appraisal, and when he didn't say anything after a couple of seconds, Jamison pointed to a manila envelope lying on the table. "I brought my résumé with me since you didn't ask to see one before the interview."

Before Drexler could respond, Cindy brought him coffee in a white mug. He thanked her, took a sip, then said, "I don't need to see your résumé, Mr. Maddox. I believe I know everything I need to know about you. You're twenty-eight years old. You graduated from Yale with a three-point-seven grade point average; your GPA would have been higher had you spent more time studying and less time socializing. You did your postgraduate work at the London School of Economics after which you were employed by Goldman Sachs, where you remained until two years ago. I also know that following your trial you haven't been able to find suitable employment, and after paying your lawyer and the fines imposed on you by the court, you're almost broke. Right now, you're trying to sell your condo on Lexington for two million and not getting any offers and will have to lower the asking price by at least a quarter million to sell the place. You have to sell it because in a couple of months you'll no longer be able to pay your mortgage."

Jamison briefly closed his eyes. He'd been hoping that a company located in the flyover region of the American Midwest wouldn't know about what had happened in Manhattan. Obviously, he'd been wrong and naïve to have thought so. He said, even though he knew the answer, "So you know what happened at Goldman."

"Of course I know. Your legal troubles are a matter of public record and before we approached you, we examined all available records. As to your personal life, you've never been married. You were dating a woman named Amanda Nixon until ten months ago. Amanda is now engaged to a man who was your roommate at Yale and who you thought was your best friend. You're an only child. Your father died of cirrhosis of the liver when you were ten and you have what I guess could be called a distant relationship with your mother. Although I don't know this for a fact, I'm assuming you asked her for financial support during the last two years and she refused."

His relationships with his mother and his ex-girlfriend were not matters of public record. Drexler had obviously done a deep dive into his past. But seeing no point in lying—or in trying to make it sound as if he had a normal relationship with his mother—Jamison said, "Yeah, I did and yes, she did."

Two years ago, Jamison and three senior executives at Goldman Sachs were arrested for a virtual laundry list of financial crimes including insider trading, tax evasion, money laundering, and wire fraud. There was a total of forty-seven charges listed on the indictments of the four defendants. And the government did what it often does in complicated financial prosecutions: it made its case primarily by getting one of the four defendants—in this case, Jamison Maddox—to testify against the other three. It was over a year from the time he was arrested until his case was finally settled.

In return for testifying, Jamison wasn't sentenced to prison but he had to plead guilty and was fined an amount that equaled almost exactly ninety percent of all the money he had; the government obviously knew how much he had and wasn't going to allow him to profit from his crimes or even keep the money he'd made before he'd committed any crimes. The reason he was given the honor of being the government's sole witness was because he was less senior than the other three defendants and hadn't profited as outrageously as they had. The upshot of all this was that he was now a convicted felon and a pariah on Wall Street, and no reputable hedge fund or investment bank would ever hire him. Most of his friends had abandoned him and, as Drexler had noted, so had his longtime girlfriend.

Annoyed by the tactless way that Claud Drexler had laid bare his life, Jamison abandoned any attempt to act deferential. He said, "Why are you offering me a job, Mr. Drexler?"

"Because you're an intelligent young man and you have skills that can be useful to my company. I'm also sure that even though I'm offering you a much smaller salary than you used to make, the amount will be acceptable to you. The cost of living isn't high in Redemption, and although you won't be rich, you can have a comfortable life here. The fact that you're currently unattached also makes it more likely that you'd be willing to move to Illinois. Now I don't have any questions for you, Mr. Maddox. As I said, I believe I know everything I need to know about you. But I'm sure you have a number of questions for me, so ask them."

Jamison nodded. "To start with, I have no idea what Drexler Limited does. You don't have a website or any other online presence that I could find. You're not on LinkedIn or Facebook or registered with the Illinois Better Business Bureau. So I don't know what your company does, Mr. Drexler. I assumed, because you're offering a person with my background a position, that you do something in the financial sector. An investment company. A hedge fund. Maybe banking or venture capital. But I don't know for sure. What does your company do?"

"We're not a financial institution," Drexler said. "We do research for select clients."

"Research? What kind of—"

"A comparable company that I'm sure you've heard of is Fusion GPS."

"Are you talking about the guys connected to the Steele dossier?"

"Yes. Hardly anyone had ever heard of Fusion until the Steele dossier and the impeachment proceedings, and people assume it's a company that does opposition research to find dirt on politicians. But Fusion, like Drexler, mostly does financial and corporate research and not political work."

"What kind of corporate research?"

Drexler said, "Let's say Company A decides it wants to merge with Company B. Anyone who's not a complete fool knows that to really understand a company's finances you can't look at a website or a quarterly report or even at what the company has filed with the SEC. Companies lie to the SEC. So Company A will hire a firm like mine or Fusion to find out how much Company B is really worth and how much debt it's really carrying. Company B may have investors who are laundering money through it. Its income streams may have originated from shell corporations that are nothing more than post office boxes in the Cayman Islands. Its executives, the ones listed on corporate documents, may be secretaries who've been given fancy titles and told what documents to sign by the people who actually manage the company. And to do the required research on these companies you need people who understand complicated financial instruments and have contacts in the global marketplace. Some of Fusion's people are journalists—in fact Fusion was founded by two reporters who worked for the *Wall Street Journal*—and like journalists, they often rely on confidential sources to obtain information. They don't get their information from Wikipedia. And neither does Drexler Limited. Instead, we hire people like you."

Jamison started to ask a question, but Drexler continued. "We also do work for wealthy individuals. For example, say a woman is planning to divorce a husband who is worth several billion dollars. She knows he has money buried in offshore accounts and she'll ask us to find the money so her husband can't deny how much he has or move it and hide it before the divorce. We do some opposition research on politicians, but most often the research is of a financial nature. We don't hire private detectives to find out if a candidate is cheating on his wife or is really gay and pretending to be straight or anything unsavory like that. What we will do is make sure that a politician doesn't have ties to businesses that would constitute a conflict of interest if the politician were to be elected."

Drexler stopped to take a sip of coffee. "I'll also tell you what we *don't* do, Mr. Maddox. We don't do anything illegal. We don't hack into databases and we don't bribe public officials to obtain the information we need. We merely follow the breadcrumbs. We plow through documents that are available to the public if only the public knew where to look. We file FOIA requests. We look at material that's not online but can be found buried in the offices of county clerks. We talk to knowledgeable people. But to follow the breadcrumbs, we need people like you who know what to look for and how to interpret documents where the truth is often obfuscated by incomprehensible legal gibberish."

Drexler sat back in his chair and said, "So that's the job in a nutshell, Mr. Maddox. I want to hire you to do research on behalf of our clients. Does that sound like something that might appeal to you?"

It sounded fucking awful!

"Yes, it does," Jamison said. "It would be a good change of pace from what I used to do."

Jamison could almost see his soul leaving his body, rising like a wraith above Redemption as he said this.

"I'm glad to hear that," Drexler said. "But there are some things you need to know."

Before Jamison could ask what those things were, Drexler said, "There is nothing more important to me than protecting the identity of our clients and the work we do for them, and I do everything I can to keep Drexler Limited invisible to the media. I'll use Fusion GPS again as a point of reference. Once the media and the politicians learned that Fusion's client for the Steele dossier was the Democratic National Committee working on behalf of Hillary Clinton, the company had to spend millions to defend itself from lawsuits, and its employees spent countless hours giving depositions to lawyers and testifying before congressional committees. I don't ever want to experience what Fusion did. And to ensure that I don't, and to ensure the requisite degree of privacy for our clients, I've instituted a number of practices that you may find objectionable."

"Like what?" Jamison said.

Drexler said, "You'll be required to sign an NDA with a three-year non-compete clause."

Jamison shrugged. A non-disclosure agreement was pretty standard. A three-year non-compete clause wasn't, but since he doubted that any of Drexler's competitors—whoever they might be—would want to hire a convicted felon, he could live with that.

Drexler continued. "If you have a personal cell phone, which I know you do, you'll be required to relinquish it and use one provided by the company. Naturally, all your data and contacts would be transferred to the new phone. If we learn, however, that you've purchased a personal cell phone, you'll be terminated."

"Why do I have to use a company cell phone?"

"So we can see who you've been calling and who's called you if we wish to do so."

"You're kidding," Jamison said.

"I'm not. Since the phone you'll be given is a company phone, we'll have access to your phone records. On the bright side, we pay your phone bill."

"I see," Jamison said, not knowing what else to say.

"You will also not be allowed to conduct any company business or refer to company business on a personal computer. All business must be conducted on our computers. As we realize, in this day and age, that owning a laptop or an iPad is almost mandatory, you'll sign an agreement allowing us to scan your personal computing devices on a periodic basis."

"Scan them for what?"

"The scan will be looking for key words related to the work you've been assigned. We won't be reading your emails or looking at your search history unless the scan reveals that you've violated the privacy of our clients."

Before Jamison could respond, Drexler said, "You'll also agree to periodic polygraph testing."

"Are you joking?"

"I don't joke, Mr. Maddox. Not when it comes to my company. And there's nothing unusual about defense contractors polygraphing employees who hold top secret security clearances to prevent espionage. And we polygraph our employees for basically the same reason. Now you won't be asked any personal questions during the polygraph examinations, like who you've been sleeping with or if you watch pornography. I don't care about your personal life or your sex life provided you're not doing anything illegal. Basically, you'll only be asked one question when tested and that question will be: Have you disclosed any information about Drexler Limited or its clients to anyone outside the company?

"Now if you still think you're interested in the job after what I've just told you, I'll give you the paperwork to review today. We've booked you a room at a local motel and you can bring the signed papers to my office tomorrow if you choose to work for me. Or you can call me in the morning and say you've declined my offer. If you do agree to work for me, I'll expect you to start in three weeks—that'll give you time to sell your condo in Manhattan, once you've lowered the price—and we'll pay all reasonable moving expenses. A person on my staff will also help you find a house or an apartment here in Redemption, one compatible with your new salary.

"So what do you say, Mr. Maddox?"

Before Jamison could respond, Drexler swiveled his large head and said, "Cindy, I think I'll have that piece of pie now."

2

Drexler Limited was housed in a squat, unadorned, and nameless three-story redbrick building that had been erected in the early twentieth century and that at one time had been a factory that made starter motors for a budding automotive industry. There were wide-plank hardwood floors that had been sanded and stained a dark mahogany color but still bore the scars of boxes and equipment being dragged across them. There were massive exposed ceiling beams and twelve-by-twelve posts closely spaced to support the weight of the heavy machinery that had once rested on the second and third floors.

Jamison's office was on the second floor and he was surprised to see that he'd been given an actual office with walls and a door and not the cubicle that most modern companies assign to the lesser paid help. The wooden desk in his office was large and was either an antique or a good facsimile of one. It was beautifully made. He also had a wooden file cabinet that matched the desk as opposed to a typical sheet metal file cabinet purchased from somewhere like Staples. The computer on the desk was not an antique. It was an Apple laptop with a sixteen-inch screen and wasn't more than a year old. He even had a window with a view, the view in his case being a water tower with the name *Cornhuskers* painted on it in large red letters. He subsequently learned that *Cornhuskers* had been plagiarized from the University of Nebraska and was the name of the local high school's sports teams.

His enclosed office was not the only thing he found unusual about the building.

The first floor had only two occupants. When you entered the building through the main entrance, the first thing you saw was a desk where an armed guard was seated. Behind the guard was a wall that had a single locked door that provided access to the remainder of the first floor. Off to one side of the guard's desk was a wide staircase that led to the second and third floors and an ancient, slow-moving elevator for anyone unable to use the stairs. The guard's only function appeared to be making sure that the people who entered the building were people who worked there or who had an appointment. If he had other duties, Jamison had no idea what they could be. Nor could he guess why the guard was armed; Drexler Limited wasn't a jewelry store or a bank.

But other than the fact that the guard was armed, there wasn't anything unusual about him. He was in his fifties or early sixties and had the look of a retired cop or ex-military. He didn't look like an active-duty Navy SEAL.

The first floor contained the building's operating systems. In addition to heating and ventilation components, there were banks of servers and the heart of the building's security system. Jamison found the building's security impressive: locks on all the doors that required a key card and a six-digit code to open them; cameras in half a dozen places on the exterior of the building, and internal cameras in every hallway on the upper floors. Also on the first floor was an industrial shredder. All the documents disposed of by the people who worked in the building were put into ordinary wastebaskets and every night a janitor, under the watchful eye of the security guard, emptied all the wastebaskets and ran their contents through the shredder.

Other than the armed guard, only one other person dwelled on the first floor and this was Drexler's HR director, who was also in charge of security. Security directors that Jamison had encountered on Wall Street had always been men, and they'd often been former, high-ranking cops. When he'd worked at Goldman Sachs, the man in charge of security had been a perpetually skeptical, always serious, retired CIA officer. He'd been expecting someone along these lines at Drexler Limited—and he was miles off the mark.

Drexler's HR/security director turned out to be a plump, pleasant, very talkative woman in her fifties with a short gray perm and twinkling blue eyes. Her name was Mary White and a producer would have cast her as Mrs. Claus, or as the grandma in a commercial baking cookies for her grandkids.

Mary was the first person he met after he started with the company, and before getting down to business she offered him coffee and a pastry and told him about nearby shops and restaurants; the pastry she served him came from a bakery down the block that was highly recommended. She had him fill out a standard W-2 form and went over the company's health insurance, sick leave, and vacation policies. While he was munching on a second pastry, she went over the NDA he'd signed, making sure he understood the legal liability of violating it. She also reminded him of the unusual protocols that Claud Drexler had already told him about—the random polygraph testing, the need to give up his cell phone, and the fact that his personal computing devices would be periodically scanned—but she did this in such a way that made all these things sound perfectly normal. As she efficiently transferred the data from his old iPhone to his new company iPhone, she told him about a farmers' market that was held in the town square on Saturdays and the wonderful fresh, organic produce that came from nearby farms.

Lastly, she gave him a security badge that also functioned as a key card and would allow him entry to the building and access to the office area on the second floor. Her parting words to him were: "Jamison, I'm so glad you decided to join our little family."

And it was a small family. As best Jamison could tell, the company employed only about twenty people. About half of those people were on the second floor with him. The other half were on the third floor and Jamison learned that his key card wouldn't open the doors on the third floor; in fact he was not permitted to be on that floor at all unless escorted by someone who worked there.

□ □ □

As Jamison came to know his coworkers, he began to think of the second floor, the floor where he worked, as the Island of Misfit Toys.

One employee was a Pulitzer Prize–nominated journalist who'd been fired for making up one of the sources in a story. The story had been accurate; it was just the source that had been invented. One of the lawyers he worked with had left a white-shoe law firm after being permanently disbarred for an act of misconduct. Not all of his coworkers had check-ered pasts, however. They were instead people who simply struck Jamison as lacking the social skills or the ambition to fit in well or advance in a big-name company; they were extremely good at analyzing data but seemed incapable of forming relationships or making small talk at a cocktail party.

As for the people on the third floor, they would all say hello or nod pleasantly to him when he encountered them entering the building or going up the stairs, but he'd only been introduced to one of them. The one he'd met was a man named Steven Lang, a humorless, taciturn man only a few years older than he was. Steven was his immediate supervisor and the one who gave him his assignments.

◻ ◻ ◻

"You want another beer?" Ralph asked.

Ralph Finney was the friendliest person Jamison had encountered at Drexler and on a Friday, after he'd been there for a week, Ralph invited him for an after-work drink. Ralph was short and dark and the most hirsute individual that Jamison had ever met. Wearing shorts and sandals, his hairy legs and feet made Jamison think of hobbits.

"Sure," Jamison said. He and Ralph were sitting in a pub called the Shamrock, an unimaginative name that graced hundreds of pubs and bars across the United States. It had a large, varied stock of beers on tap and offered appetizers and sandwiches from a limited menu. Its chief attractions were that it was a block from Drexler Limited, had an outdoor seating area with tables shaded by umbrellas, a dozen television sets constantly tuned to sports—and cute waitresses.

Ralph returned to their table with two beers. (Although the waitresses were cute, they were extremely slow and it was faster to go up to the bar and order.)

Ralph said, "So how do you like the job so far?"

"I like it," Jamison lied.

The truth was that after only a week, Jamison was bored by both his job and the town but didn't see any point in saying so. On the other hand, the hours were reasonable—no seventy-hour workweeks like he'd experienced at Goldman—and he would be getting a steady paycheck and be able to pay his rent. He even had a little money in the bank after selling his condo in Manhattan. Not a lot of money, but a little. He'd found a roomy, two-bedroom apartment in Redemption in a building that had only six tenants and was just a mile from his office; had the apartment been located in Manhattan the rent would have been five or six thousand a month. In Redemption, he paid twelve hundred.

"What do they have you working on?" Ralph asked.

Jamison hesitated. "I was told not to talk about my assignments—even with the people I work with. This isn't my idea of a dream job, but I'd just as soon not get fired after only a week."

Mary White had told him that discussing his assignments with anyone outside of Drexler was strictly forbidden and anyone who did so would be terminated immediately. But she'd also said that discussing assignments with coworkers was "strongly discouraged." It occurred to Jamison then that maybe the reason all the people who worked on the second floor had individual offices instead of being clustered together in a cube farm was that you couldn't overhear what people were saying on the phone. Cubicles also encouraged the free exchange of ideas, gossip, and socializing, apparently activities not embraced by Drexler Limited.

Mary had explained that Drexler's practices all had to do with protecting the privacy of its clients and that the company operated on the *need-to-know* principle. That is, if you discussed a job with people who didn't have a need to know, the greater the likelihood that a leak would occur. She'd quoted the adage that the only way two people could ever keep a secret was if one of those people was dead. She'd smiled when she said this, but Jamison noticed that the smile didn't reach her eyes. For just a moment, he'd found plump, maternal Mary White somewhat chilling.

"You can't talk specifics," Ralph said. "If you do and Mary finds out, like during your polygraph test, she'll wag her finger at you and tell you that you've been a bad boy, but that's all that will happen. I mean, as long as you keep it vague. They know it's impossible for people who work together not to bitch about their jobs."

As Jamison had been there for only a week, he hadn't been polygraphed yet.

Answering Ralph's question, he said, "They gave me a softball assignment just to ease me into things, I guess. I'm doing an analysis of . . . of some companies."

Jamison had been told to analyze five construction/demolition companies all located within a hundred miles of Detroit, Michigan. He was also to provide a financial profile of the companies' owners. All the companies were small, independently owned, and none had more than forty full-time employees; they would take on temporary employees if business was brisk. They were all profitable—a couple of them just barely—and they experienced the normal cycles that most construction companies did, work ebbing and flowing depending on the weather and the economy in general. None of the companies were carrying a lot of debt. Although they frequently needed loans to make their payroll when business was slow, the loans were always repaid.

Four of the five owners were typical, successful, small businessmen. They paid themselves adequate but not outrageous annual salaries and carried affordable mortgages on upper-middle-class homes. They owned or leased decent vehicles but not luxury cars. A couple of them owned vacation homes in addition to their primary residences, but the second homes were affordable because the owners were frugal.

The fifth owner stood apart. He was a man named Douglas Crane, whose company was located in Dearborn, Michigan. Crane was swimming in a deep sea of personal debt. He had been divorced twice and a good chunk of what he made went for alimony and child support. Nonetheless, he lived in a massive home with a pool and a large dock on

Lake Erie, owned a forty-two-foot pleasure boat, drove a Range Rover that retailed for ninety thousand, and spent lavishly on himself and his girlfriends. To make matters worse, Crane was a regular at the MGM Grand Casino in Detroit and was one of those gamblers who didn't know when to walk away from the craps tables. Basically, Crane was the guy in the circus act who had a dozen plates spinning on a dozen long poles and he was currently running from pole to pole to keep all the plates aloft—but he wouldn't be able to manage it for much longer.

Jamison didn't know who the client was or why the client wanted information on these five companies. He assumed the client was interested in acquiring one or more of them. So Jamison was in the process of ranking the companies from best to worst, analyzing the likelihood of them remaining in business if times got tough, identifying their major assets, their weaknesses, and their strengths—the sort of analysis he'd do if the companies were publicly traded and he was considering buying stock. Altogether it was a mundane assignment made somewhat difficult only because he didn't know the client's objective. Was the client interested in buying one or more of the companies as Jamison suspected, or was he instead interested in driving them out of business and acquiring their buildings and other assets? Two of the companies sat on valuable real estate that could be developed. Whatever the case, he hoped his future assignments would be more challenging.

"How 'bout you?" Jamison asked Ralph. "What are you currently doing?"

"Oh, just a review of a software system that some state is looking into."

Jamison knew that Ralph had worked for Cisco Systems for five years developing cyber security software to protect databases that contained sensitive information. Corporate and government databases had been breached so many times by foreign and domestic hackers that Jamison could understand that there might be clients interested in acquiring the next generation of software to protect information. If a state was the client, the software could have to do with public employee information or voting systems or programs like Medicaid, which had significant issues when it came to fraud.

Jamison had asked Ralph why he'd quit Cisco and come to work for Drexler and Ralph's honest answer had surprised him. Ralph said that he'd had a nervous breakdown. His boss at Cisco had been a prick who'd pressured him relentlessly and he became an insomniac, developed an eating disorder, and gained fifty pounds. His girlfriend—the only one he'd ever had—eventually dumped him, and then, the last straw, like a bad country song, his dog died. That pushed him over the edge. He became a full-on basket case, refused to leave his house, stopped bathing, started drinking heavily, and began making bizarre phone calls to people in the middle of the night. Finally, his mother forced him to get treatment and he spent a month in what he called an insane asylum, which of course hadn't been an insane asylum but a standard rehab facility. After he got out of treatment, he spent a couple of months living with his mom, mostly playing video games as he tried to decide what to do next, and that's when he got a letter from Claud Drexler. Ralph had told Jamison that he loved working at Drexler and he loved Redemption. He'd been raised in Los Angeles and had worked in San Jose and had never lived in a small town like Redemption, and he didn't ever want to leave it.

As it was a warm June day, Ralph and Jamison were sitting outside and they noticed a woman wearing white shorts and a yellow tank top walk past the low fence surrounding the pub's patio. The woman was tall, had short blonde hair, toned arms and legs, and a loose, athletic stride. Had Jamison been sitting in a bar in Las Vegas instead of a pub in Redemption, he might have assumed that she was a showgirl reporting for work; she certainly had the legs of a dancer. But she wasn't a dancer. She worked on the third floor at Drexler Limited. Jamison had seen her once before entering the building but had never been introduced to her.

Ralph said, "God, she's gorgeous. I'd give my left nut . . . Well, maybe not a nut, but definitely a kidney to spend one night with her."

"What's her name?" Jamison asked.

"Gillian Lang."

"Lang? Is she related to Steven Lang?"

"She's married to him."

"Oh," Jamison said—and the fantasy he'd been having about becoming involved with Gillian Lang burst like a bubble.

"Do you know what she does?" Jamison asked.

"Nope."

"So what do the people on the third floor do? I mean in general. The only contact I've had with anyone who works there is with her husband and all he does is give me my assignments."

"Nobody knows what the people on the third floor do."

"How can that possibly be?" Jamison asked. "We all work in the same company."

"In case you haven't figured it out, Claud Drexler is paranoid when it comes to security. The people on the third floor are, I guess you'd say, his inner circle and they're the only ones who interact with the clients. They find out what a client wants, give assignments to the worker bees like you and me, and then take what we give them and present it to the clients. But who the clients are and why they want the information they want is only known to those who work on the third floor."

"That's unbelievable," Jamison said.

"Not really. When I was at Cisco, I sometimes worked on classified systems for the DOD. These were top secret systems and they were compartmentalized. That means that I would be shown only enough to understand part of the system but not the entire system. By compartmentalizing information, only those at the very top had a complete picture of what the system did, which was most likely something related to espionage. Claud Drexler operates the same way. He allows us to see part of what's going on but not everything that's going on so we can't spill the beans to whoever cares about spilled beans."

"Are the people on the second floor forbidden to mingle with those on the third?"

"Oh, hell no. We have a company Christmas party every year. A Fourth of July bash, too. Claud, who's a big Cubbies fan, will spring for seats at Wrigley Field once or twice a summer, and we'll take a bus together to Chicago to see a game. People mingle socially all the time. There's a guy on the second floor who's the bridge partner of a gal on the third floor who's a bridge fanatic, and they're always traveling to tournaments together. One of the third-floor people is into drones and he and Wally—you've met Wally—fly their drones together. In any company there's a certain amount of separation between management and the workers and Drexler isn't any different. The only real difference is that when we get together, we don't talk about our jobs."

Gillian Lang walked into the pub's outside seating area, looked around briefly, then walked over to a table where another woman was seated. The other woman appeared to be a few years older than Gillian and wasn't as striking as she was. But then no one in the pub was. The other woman stood up and hugged her.

"Who's she sitting with?" Jamison asked Ralph. "If she works at Drexler, I've never seen her before."

"That's her sister-in-law. Her name's Agnes Pine and she doesn't work at Drexler but her husband does. She's the mayor of Redemption."

At that moment, maybe sensing that she was being stared at, Gillian looked over at Jamison. Their eyes connected for a long moment, Gillian smiled slightly and nodded—Jamison thinking the acknowledgment was probably because she recognized him from the office—then she turned back to her friend the mayor. But the look she'd given him . . . Jamison had gotten that look from women before. It was the look of a woman who was interested. It was just his luck that she was not only married, but married to his boss. His luck hadn't been good since he was arrested two years ago.

3

Claud was on the phone when Mary White entered his office. He was wearing one of the dark suits he always wore to work, a white shirt, and a red-and-blue striped tie. Why he wore a suit had always puzzled Mary; everyone else in the company dressed casually. Maybe he wore the suit because he was the boss. Or maybe it was a generational thing. Men of his generation believed that a man who worked in an office should wear a suit.

He made a just-a-minute gesture at her and went back to talking to whomever he was talking to. It sounded as if he was having a problem with the air conditioner at his house and needed someone to come out and take a look at the unit. Mary had known as soon as she saw him on the phone that he wasn't talking about company business; he'd never make a call about anything having to do with the company on an ordinary landline. There was a special room on the first floor that he used for making business calls.

Although Claud ran Drexler Limited there was nothing remarkable about his office. He had a large but rather ordinary wooden desk and an old, but comfortable, tilt-back black leather chair behind the desk. In front of the desk were two uncomfortable wooden chairs and against one wall was a dusty, black leather couch long enough to accommodate Claud's large frame should he choose to take a nap. Claud didn't care what his office looked like because he never met there with anyone other than his employees and he felt no need to impress them. Mary did wonder, however, why he'd never hung a couple of pictures on the walls to add some color to the space.

On his desk was a state-of-the-art laptop computer that Claud rarely used. He didn't trust computers. He'd thought about insisting that everyone at Drexler Limited use typewriters—you couldn't hack a typewriter—but his employees convinced him that typewriters were impractical and that the company's cyber security protocols made it almost impossible for anyone to get into their machines.

Other than the computer and the phone, there were only two other objects on Claud's desk: a baseball signed by Sammy Sosa and a photo of Claud's late wife. Claud had actually caught the ball at Wrigley Field when Sosa hit a home run, then, like an excited boy, he'd hung around after the game to get Sosa to sign it. Why Claud had become such a baseball fanatic was a mystery to Mary. As far as she knew, he'd never played baseball in his life. As for the photo of his late wife, it showed an attractive woman in her forties with long dark hair and sad brown eyes. Claud's wife had been forty-two when she committed suicide.

Mary wondered how much longer Claud would be able to manage the company. He was eighty-one now, and although mentally he seemed okay—there'd been no short-term memory problems or any other evidence of senility or dementia—he couldn't stay in charge forever. Physically, he appeared to be as fit as a man twenty years his junior. He'd had his prostate removed ten years ago before the cancer could spread to any other organs and he was cancer free. He had arthritis and took pain meds for that, needed pills to manage his blood pressure, and got indigestion if he didn't watch what he ate, but other than those small issues, he appeared to be in excellent health. And as he liked to remind people, he came from good stock. His father had lived to a hundred. At some point, however, he'd have to make a decision on a successor and groom whoever it was going to be.

Claud got off the phone and aimed his dark eyes at her. Despite his age, the intensity in his eyes hadn't dimmed.

Claud's routine was to spend the first couple of hours each morning talking with the people on the third floor individually to make sure he was up to date on where all the various projects stood. His last appointment was usually with Mary to make sure there were no brewing security issues.

Today he started by asking, "How's our new employee Mr. Maddox doing?"

Maddox had now been with them for a month and had been given a couple of simple assignments, which he'd performed satisfactorily. He'd yet to be polygraphed, something Mary intended to do tomorrow.

"He appears to be settling in fine. I had one of the kids break into his apartment to do a search and scan his laptop. There was nothing in the apartment out of the ordinary and nothing on the laptop at all concerning. He rarely emails anyone. He stopped corresponding with most of the friends he had in New York over a year ago, after his trial. He emails his uncle occasionally but all he's told him about his job is that he'd landed something in Redemption, something low stress that didn't pay particularly well, but that he was happy. When his uncle asked what he was doing, all he said was, and I quote, 'some boring analytical stuff.' "

When Mary said "one of the kids" broke into Maddox's apartment she meant one of *her* kids. She had a daughter and two sons and they did most of the company's security-related legwork, although there'd been a few times over the years when outside experts had to be called in. Claud called these outsiders "consultants," which made them sound benign. They weren't.

"I've also chatted with Ralph Finney a couple of times. He's become Jamison's closest friend here in town. Ralph's assured me that Jamison hasn't been overly curious about the company or the assignments given to other employees. The biggest problem with Jamison is that he's bored. He misses Manhattan, the night life, the bars. And the women. I really need to find him a girlfriend. The problem with Redemption, as you well know, is that there aren't a lot of unattached good-looking women his age."

Mary paused, then said, "I think you should give him an assignment where he gets to travel to someplace fun, someplace where he could spend a few days on a beach and go to bars packed with girls. The boy needs to get laid. A little break from Redemption would be good for him and getting away once in a while will keep him interested in his job. I'd have one of the kids accompany him, of course."

"I'll think about it," Claud said. "Now what about the Connor boy?"

Mary shook her head. "No improvement. Since his father died, he's turned into a truculent pain in the ass. His father was able to control him; his mother can't. He's a corrupting influence on his cousins, calling them brainwashed sheep and things like that. He's determined to leave when he's eighteen and says that if anyone tries to stop him, he'll reveal everything he knows. And him leaving would be fine if he could be trusted not to talk, but I don't think he can be."

"So what do you recommend?" Claud asked.

"I don't know," Mary said, shaking her head again. "But we're having to spend an abnormal amount of energy keeping tabs on him. The good news is that he doesn't have any outsiders that he's close to. He's not close to anyone. He spends most of his time holed up in his room playing his guitar, listening to music, and looking at weird Internet sites. But so far he hasn't called or emailed or texted anyone and said anything that's a problem. He's just one of those strange, gloomy kids, like those Goth kids you hear about, the ones all dressed in black."

Before Claud could respond, Mary said, "I tried to get him hooked up with the Pine girl. If he had a girlfriend in the family, then his attitude might change. And Carol Pine's a good girl and she's willing to make the sacrifice, but Dennis has rebuffed all her overtures. Plus, as much as I hate to say it, Carol isn't what you'd call a bombshell. She's pretty enough but she needs to lose some weight. Whatever the case, Dennis is not into her, as the kids say."

"Is he suspicious about his father's death?"

"No, thank God. He still believes it was an accident and so does Alice. They both knew Fred drank too much, so they weren't really surprised by the way he died."

Fred Connor had died when his car was struck by a train and the police couldn't understand how he'd ended up on the train tracks. One possibility was that he'd parked there deliberately, which would have made his death a suicide. A second possibility was that the engine had died while the car was crossing the tracks and Fred hadn't been able to restart it. A third, and the most likely possibility, was that Fred hadn't even realized that he'd stopped on the tracks and had probably been unconscious at the time of his death. The police favored this possibility as Fred's blood alcohol level had been a staggering .29 and Fred had gotten two DUIs in the last five years. What the police didn't realize was that one of Mary's sons had held a gun to Fred's head, told Fred that he was going to kill Fred's wife and son, and then forced Fred to consume an entire bottle of the cheap bourbon he favored. And it was Mary's son who'd parked the car on the tracks and then placed Fred in the driver's seat.

Mary said, "But if something were to happen to Dennis, so soon after Fred passing, Alice might go completely off the deep end. And who knows what she might do."

"Maybe the boy and his mother both need to go," Claud said quietly, almost as if he was thinking out loud.

"Jesus, Claud. You can't be serious. Alice hasn't done anything wrong and she does her job. I realize she's not the sharpest knife in the drawer but losing her would leave a gap someone would have to fill, and we're shorthanded as it is."

"So, Mary, let me ask again. What do you recommend? His attitude isn't improving, his mother can't control him, you're spending too much time watching him, and your attempt to get the Pine girl to seduce him failed. What's next?"

Mary sat there a moment, head down, staring into her ample lap. "I guess he has to go. But I need to find a way to do it where his mother won't be even the least bit suspicious. If something were to happen to her son, so soon after what happened to her husband, she has to be absolutely convinced that we didn't have anything to do with it."

Mary left Claud's office feeling depressed. Dennis Connor was only seventeen years old and his failure to conform was a collective failure, a family failure, just as the family had failed to deal with the boy's father's alcoholism. And Claud knew, even if he wouldn't admit it, that he, too, bore some responsibility for Dennis Connor. God, he was a cold, hard, old son of a bitch. She supposed if he hadn't been, the family would never have survived for these past sixty years. But a seventeen-year-old boy? Sometimes Mary just hated her job.

4

The polygraph test was anticlimactic.

Mary had Jamison sit in a comfortable chair with armrests, wrapped a couple of black straps equipped with sensors across his chest, put a blood pressure cuff on his left arm and cups on two of his fingers that he learned measured skin conductivity, which apparently changed when a person was lying. All the devices were connected to a laptop computer on Mary's desk. The whole time she was hooking him up, she asked how he liked his new apartment and if he needed any pots and pans or Tupperware. She said she had *scads* of extra Tupperware containers.

When everything was ready to go, she took a seat at her desk where she could see his face and the laptop screen. He couldn't see the screen. She said, "Now I'm just going to ask you a few questions to establish a baseline. I want you to answer yes to all the questions. Do you understand? Say yes to every question until I tell you otherwise."

"Got it," Jamison said.

"And relax, for crying out loud," she added with a laugh. "Now, is your name Jamison Maddox?"

"Yes."

"Were you born in New York City?"

"Yes."

"Did you go to Yale?"

"Yes."

"Did you play second base for the Yankees? No, don't laugh. You'll mess up the test. Did you play second base for the Yankees?"

"Yes."

"Did you used to work at Goldman Sachs?"

"Yes."

"Can you bench press four hundred pounds?"

"Yes."

"Is your mother's name Vera?"

"Yes."

"Did you date Lady Gaga?"

"Yes."

"Okay. That was great. Now I want you to answer the next set of questions truthfully but limit your responses to yes or no unless I tell you otherwise."

"All right."

"Have you told anyone outside the company about any of your assignments at Drexler Limited?"

"No."

"Have you bought a personal cell phone?"

"No."

"Have you talked to anyone in the company about your work?"

"Yes."

"Who?"

"Ralph Finney."

"What did you tell him?"

"Only that I was analyzing a few companies."

"Did you tell him the companies' names?"

"No."

"Well, okay. And I'm glad you were truthful with me, Jamison. But don't do that again. If Ralph or anyone else asks what you're working on, you just say you can't discuss it. Are we clear?"

"Yes, ma'am."

Mary got up and removed all the sensors from him. As she was doing this she asked, like a mother would, "Have you met any nice girls since you've been in town?"

"No, unfortunately not."

"Well, I'm sure you will, a young man as handsome as you."

◻ ◻ ◻

As Mary had noted, Jamison *was* a handsome man, so handsome that when he was in his teens he was stopped twice on the streets of Manhattan by agents and offered a job as a catalog model. He had a lanky build, curly dark hair, and a glint in his blue eyes that always made it seem as if he was amused. His most notable feature was that when he smiled, dimples formed in both cheeks. The girls loved those dimples.

Jamison's own mother, however, hadn't asked if he'd found a girlfriend in Redemption. His own mother hadn't called him since he'd moved to Redemption—which wasn't the least bit surprising.

Jamison had been sent to a boarding school in Connecticut at the age of ten, six months after his father died due to complications from alcoholism. His mother had never wanted a child and only had Jamison to please his father. He was fortunate that his mother, thanks to his father, had enough money to enroll him in a good school and that his father's brother turned into a doting uncle who became a surrogate dad.

When he'd been at boarding school, he usually spent his Christmas vacations with his uncle Jed because his mother was rarely in New York in December. She preferred to spend her Christmases in places like Hawaii or the Caribbean—she didn't like cold weather—but it never occurred to her to invite her son to spend his Christmas vacations with her. His summers were usually spent at some expensive, well-supervised camp in the Adirondacks where he would hike and paddle canoes and learn how to rock climb.

Before he'd graduated from college, he'd called his mother occasionally, but usually only when he'd exceeded his allowance or needed to get her to sign some document she was required to sign, like when he spent a quarter in Florence, Italy. She rarely called him. Since college, he might speak to her two or three times a year and he was almost always the one who initiated the calls.

She did call him when she read in the *Times* that he'd been arrested. The only thing she'd said was: "Is it true?" And when he'd said yes, she said, "Well this is humiliating." She never asked if he needed help or offered any sort of emotional support.

His father had left his mother over a hundred million dollars, as well as some pricey real estate she could sell whenever she wished, and his mother treated herself well with his father's money. She didn't spend it on outrageous things—there were no gold bathtub faucets in her apartment, and she didn't own a private jet or a two-hundred-foot yacht—but she didn't scrimp either. Her apartment in Manhattan was worth fifteen million. She'd bought a hundred-acre ranch in New Mexico and a couple of horses when she decided to take up horseback riding. She traveled extensively—traveling seemed to be her primary hobby—and she had a multitude of wealthy friends across the planet that she visited. She'd had a series of handsome boyfriends since his father's death—Jamison had seen pictures of some of them in the *Times* when she attended some charity event or the opening of a play that she'd invested in—but she'd never married any of them. Jamison suspected she was incapable of loving another person and didn't want to face the possibility of a man taking some of her money if the marriage ended up in divorce.

The one thing his mother didn't do was spend her money on her son. She'd supported him until he graduated from college then made it clear that he was on his own from that point forward. Which had been fine with Jamison when he'd worked at Goldman and made an outrageous salary, but it would have been nice if she'd offered to help with his legal costs after his arrest. He wondered if he was mentioned in her will. In fact, he wondered if she even had a will. A narcissist like Vera Maddox probably thought she'd live forever.

Jamison did feel obligated to call her when he left New York to move to Redemption. He figured that she should at least know where he was living even though he knew she didn't care. So he'd phoned and said, "I'm leaving New York. I've got a job in Redemption, Illinois." Her response had been, "Where on earth is Redemption, Illinois?" Then before he could answer, she said, "Oh, I have a call coming in that I have to take. I'll talk to you later." She never called back.

Jamison had seen a television show one time where a crocodile laid a hundred or so eggs on the bank of a river, and after the baby crocs burst from their shells the mother crocodile pretty much abandoned them. Some survived, although many were eaten by fish or birds or other crocodiles—but Mama Crocodile had already moved on. Vera Maddox was that lady crocodile.

5

Mary spent the morning shopping, wandering in and out of stores, thoroughly enjoying the experience although the only thing she purchased was a pair of expensive running shoes. She didn't jog but the shoes provided the kind of support she'd come to need as she'd gotten older. She'd had a terrible case of plantar fasciitis a couple of years ago and didn't want a repeat of that experience. But whether she bought anything or not, it was always fun to go shopping in Chicago, although she certainly wouldn't want to live there. Chicago was too crowded, too noisy, too dirty—and much, much too violent. It wasn't at all unusual for a dozen people to be shot in a single day.

Her last stop was a bookstore where she flipped through the cookbooks. She didn't need another cookbook—she probably had twenty in a bookcase in her kitchen—but she liked to look at the pictures in them and sometimes just couldn't stop herself from buying another one. She glanced at her watch. One thirty. She'd better get going. She was scheduled to meet the consultant at two and didn't want to be late.

She parked her car a couple of blocks from Grant Park and strolled over to the Buckingham Fountain. The Buckingham Fountain is constructed of Georgia pink marble. It's one of the largest fountains in the world and is modeled after a similar one at the Palace of Versailles. It's built in a rococo wedding cake style, spits water a hundred and fifty feet into the air, and is guarded by eight angry-looking bronze seahorses, the bronze green with verdigris. Mary thought the fountain was hideous and symptomatic of Chicago's tendency to go overboard.

The consultant—a woman, as she'd insisted—was seated on a bench on the west side of the fountain. Mary knew she was the consultant because she was wearing a pink breast cancer awareness baseball cap. The woman was in her early thirties. She had a nice figure but a rather plain face—and plain was good. Mary didn't want journalists taking an interest in the woman after she'd completed the job, which could happen if she was photogenic.

Mary sat down beside her and said, "Did you know this fountain was dedicated in 1927?"

"Yes, and designed by the architect Edward H. Bennett."

The password nonsense out of the way, Mary said, "Have you visited the school?"

"Yes. Last Wednesday, and he behaved exactly as you said."

"Where are you living?" Mary asked.

"An apartment in Evanston."

Evanston was a Chicago suburb.

"I signed a one-year lease. I'm a website designer looking for a job in the Chicago area but haven't yet found one I like. I have some savings and my mother sends me money."

"And what reason will you give for passing through Redemption?"

"I was tired of job hunting, needed a change of scenery, and decided to go for a day trip in the countryside."

"Good. Keep it simple. You just went for a long drive. It was a spur of the moment decision. You didn't have plans to meet anyone. You didn't have any particular destination in mind. We'll have to hope the weather is decent that day, although if it's a little rainy that would be okay—in fact it could be advantageous." Mary meant that a little rain would be a good excuse for poor visibility, but too much rain would discourage a normal person from going on a long drive.

"The car you'll be driving. Do you own it or is it a rental?"

"I own it. A permanent resident wouldn't rent a car. I bought it when I first arrived in Chicago."

"Is your driver's license up to date?" Mary asked.

"Of course. All the paperwork—auto insurance, registration, etcetera—is valid and current."

"And is the car in good working order? I mean, no defects like headlights that are burned out or brakes in need of repair, anything at all that the police might consider a factor that contributed to the accident?"

"The car's perfect."

"And you understand that you'll have to stay here for several months, even if you don't go to jail. The family won't file a lawsuit but there will be some sort of trial and you'll probably have to return to Redemption several times to be questioned by lawyers and the police."

"I'm aware of that and I'm prepared to stay as long as necessary."

"And you know that you can't have any alcohol or drugs in your system that day."

"I don't use drugs and, of course, I understand," the woman snapped, making no attempt to mask her annoyance.

Mary could see that she was becoming irritated with the questions and understandably so. She wouldn't have been selected for the assignment if she'd been a fool and didn't appreciate the potential consequences of what she had been sent to do. Nonetheless, it was Mary's job to make sure.

Then the young woman said, "And I hope you understand that depending on who's around, and how close they are, I may not be able to reach him first. That's the one part of your plan that is out of my control."

"I realize that," Mary said. "Just do your best, and if he survives, we'll deal with him in the hospital. The main thing is that his mother has to see it happen and that you're prepared for the legal ramifications that will follow."

"I'm prepared."

"Great," Mary said, and rose from the bench. She patted the consultant on the shoulder and added: "We'll expect you in Redemption on Wednesday."

6

Jamison was sitting on the beach in a short-legged lawn chair, dressed only in swim trunks and a baseball cap, drinking a beer, sunning himself, looking out at Chesapeake Bay and the bikini-clad women around him. He'd be happy to stay in Virginia Beach until the end of the summer, even though he realized that wasn't going to happen. He'd stretched out the job as long as he could but knew he'd have to leave in a day or two.

A few days after his second polygraph test, Steven Lang came to his office and gave him a new assignment. That was another odd thing about Drexler Limited: his boss always came to Jamison's office and never told Jamison to come to his. He'd never even been in his boss's office.

Jamison couldn't figure Steven Lang out. Or to be accurate, he couldn't figure out why a woman as stunning as Gillian Lang would have married him. Steven wasn't a bad looking guy—tall, slim, dark complexion, appealing if you liked mysterious, brooding Heathcliff types—but he was a serious asshole with no sense of humor whatsoever. Jamison couldn't recall the guy ever smiling and he'd made no effort at all to make Jamison feel welcome in the company.

Jamison's assignment had to do with a manufacturing company located near Virginia Beach. Most people know that developing a vaccine to prevent various diseases is incredibly complicated, time consuming, and expensive, but little thought is given to how the vaccine gets into those little vials and disposable syringes that hold it. Well, what the company in Virginia Beach did was manufacture the machines that fill the vials and syringes. The machines were mechanical marvels that contained hundreds of complex parts that moved the vials and syringes along a conveyor belt, spritzed the vaccine into them, and then sealed them. This entire process, of course, had to be accomplished in a manner that was completely sterile.

This manufacturer in Virginia Beach was already a successful enterprise that produced vaccine-vial-filling machines for a number of pharmaceutical companies, but what made it particularly attractive from an investment standpoint was that the U.S. government—the Department of Health and Human Services—had just signed an agreement with Merck Pharmaceuticals to produce a hundred million doses of a measles vaccine that would be given to low-income children. In order to meet the demand, Merck contracted with the company in Virginia Beach to provide additional machines and replace some of its older, existing models.

A Drexler Limited client apparently wanted to buy into the company and wanted to know the company's value, its assets and liabilities, its production capabilities, and the likelihood of it staying in business after the new contract was fulfilled. The client also wanted research done on the men who owned the company. It was owed by three men. One had a fifty-one percent interest; the other two had the remainder, equally divided between them. If the company looked viable, the client wanted Jamison to persuade the man who had the controlling interest to sell his share, but he wasn't allowed to reveal the client's name—which Jamison couldn't have done anyway as he didn't know the client's name.

So he'd come to Virginia Beach and had taken his time carrying out the assignment, doing a lot of the research online in a bar near the beach and stopping early each day to soak up some sun. A couple of nights ago, he met a teacher from Roanoke who was vacationing with a girlfriend and Jamison spent the night with her. They had a date tonight and he was looking forward to it; it seemed as if it had been forever since he'd had a date with an attractive young woman.

As he was sitting there drinking his beer, he pulled out his phone to glance at the day's headlines. One article caught his eye. It was about the FBI busting a terrorist cell that had been planning to blow up the McNamara Federal Building in Detroit with an Oklahoma City–style truck bomb. And similar to Timothy McVeigh, these were homegrown terrorists, a group of Michigan-based white supremacists. They'd targeted the twenty-seven-story building in Detroit not only because they didn't like the federal government but also because it housed Michigan's only immigration court. The FBI learned about the group thanks to an informant, and when the terrorists purchased the detonators needed to set off the bomb, the Bureau arrested them. But what got Jamison's attention was that the guy who'd sold the detonators to the terrorists was Douglas Crane, the man who owned the construction/demolition company in Dearborn that Jamison had previously researched for another unknown Drexler Limited client.

"Holy shit," Jamison muttered. His first thought was that Crane may have decided to sell detonators to terrorists because he was drowning in debt, although maybe he didn't know they were terrorists. His second thought was to wonder if Claud Drexler was aware of the situation and if the client who'd asked him to research Crane could be involved in any way in the aborted terrorist attack.

He sent a text message to Steven Lang. The text included a link to the story and said: "Boss, did you see this article?" Fifteen minutes later,

Steven responded: "Yes. Will discuss when you return. Focus on the job you've been given."

Asshole.

Thirty minutes later, Jamison picked up his beach chair and returned to his rental car. He needed to get back to his motel and shave and take a shower. He was meeting the majority partner in the vial-filling-machine company for a drink in an hour to discuss buying his interest in the company. After that, he'd be heading off for his date with the pretty teacher.

◻ ◻ ◻

The majority owner in the company was a mechanical engineer named Don Steward. Jamison had called him, said he represented a client who was interested in buying into his company, and would like to meet with him. Steward had said he wasn't interested in selling but Jamison said, "Why don't you at least listen to what the offer is? It's a good offer."

Steward agreed to meet him at a golf course, saying they could talk after he finished playing with some of his buddies.

Jamison walked into the clubhouse bar, dressed in casual clothes: beige Dockers slacks, a Tommy Bahama shirt, and top-siders sans socks. He figured his attire would be suitable for a golf course meeting. Also for his date after the meeting. He saw Steward sitting at the bar. Steward was in his mid-fifties and appeared to be in good physical shape. He was one of those guys with a deeply tanned face except for his forehead, which was bone white because he always wore a baseball cap. He was wearing a blue golf shirt with a Nike swoosh and cargo shorts. He still had his golf shoes on.

Jamison had learned from his research that Steward could do just about anything: weld, operate a lathe or a milling machine, fix cars if they needed fixing. An article published in a local magazine said he'd built his own house—had operated the backhoe to dig the foundation, poured the concrete, erected the structure, installed the plumbing, and did all the electrical work. He could have easily hired someone to build the house but building it was his idea of fun.

Jamison introduced himself and Steward offered him the seat next to him at the bar. Jamison asked if he could buy Steward another beer and Steward accepted. While waiting for their beers to arrive, Jamison gestured out the window facing the eighteenth green and said, "Nice looking course."

"Yeah, but they had the pins positioned where Tiger Woods couldn't have two-putted them. I lost four strokes putting. And on the fifth hole . . ."

And blah, blah, blah. Typical golfer whining.

The beers arrived, but before Jamison could say anything, Steward said, "I don't mind having a drink with you, but like I told you on the phone, I'm not interested in selling my share of the company. I like what I do, and I like my business partners. So you're probably wasting your time."

"Mr. Steward, you're fifty-five years old and you pay yourself two hundred and fifty thousand a year as the controlling partner in the company. Let's assume you work ten more years, which means you'll take home two and a half million by the time you're sixty-five, the age when most folks like to retire. But just for the sake of argument, let's say that you decide to bump up your salary to three hundred grand now that you've got this new contract with Merck. That means you'll make three million in a ten-year period, not counting what you make off your current investments."

"You seem to know a lot about me and my company."

"I just did the necessary due diligence on behalf of my client, who is willing to offer you five million for your share in the company."

"Five million?"

"Yes. I'd say that's a pretty generous offer and guarantees that you'll make five million regardless of the future success of your company. If you sold your interest in the company to your partners right now, they might be willing to pay that much, but they'd stretch the payments out for at least ten years. My client will pay you the total in one lump sum immediately."

Steward turned and looked out at the golf course for a moment, watching a fat man on the eighteenth green sink a long putt and pump his fist. Finally, he turned back to face Jamison and said, "Nah, I think I'll pass. I'm already worth five million and I don't need another five. I live a pretty simple life and have no desire to own a mansion or buy a yacht or anything like that. But the main thing is, I like what I do and I'm too young to retire. If I sold my stake in the company I'd just get bored and start another one making something else. So thanks for the beer but I'm gonna pass."

"What if the offer was seven million, Mr. Steward?"

"Seven?"

"Yes. And that's as high as I'm authorized to go."

"Why in the hell would someone offer me that much?"

"To be frank," Jamison said, "I have no idea. And if it was my money, I certainly wouldn't. Even with this new contract you've got, the overall value of your company isn't going to increase significantly, and that's why it seems to me that you might want to take the bird in hand. And if you get bored in retirement, seven million will give you a lot of options when it comes to doing other things."

Steward sipped his beer, thought for a moment, then said, "I'm still gonna pass. And I have to tell you there's something off about someone offering that much. I don't know what, but . . ." Steward got up and said, "I need to get going. We're having some friends over for dinner tonight and I'm barbecuing and my wife will get pissed if I don't get home on time."

Jamison watched Steward depart after stopping briefly to say hi to a couple of other golfers; he appeared to be a popular guy. He walked away without looking back and had left Jamison's business card sitting on the bar. But Jamison was thinking that Steward was right. There *was* something off about someone offering the guy so much, particularly in a one lump payment, and Jamison couldn't figure out what would motivate another businessman to do that. But he wasn't going to waste any more time thinking about it. Tonight, he was going to enjoy his date with the pretty teacher and tomorrow he'd text Steven Lang to let him know that Steward had turned down the offer.

There was no way Jamison could have predicted how his bosses at Drexler Limited would react.

7

On Wednesdays young Dennis Connor took a guitar lesson from a man who lived on the outskirts of Redemption. Playing the guitar was one of the few things that made the surly teenager happy. So every Wednesday at four p.m., Alice Connor would pick up her son at the high school, where he was taking summer classes to make up for two he'd failed the previous semester. The classes actually ended at three thirty but his mother picked him up at four because he liked to practice for half an hour before meeting with the guitar teacher. The half-hour delay was good for Mary's plan as that meant that fewer students, teachers, and parents would be around when Alice picked him up.

Alice always parked across the street from the school, her car facing east, the direction she would go to get to the guitar teacher's house. To reach her car, her son would cross the street illegally, meaning he didn't use the crosswalk. Instead, Dennis would walk directly to Alice's car, which was parked about halfway down the block. A bus stop used by the school buses prevented her from parking closer to the crosswalk.

At exactly four p.m., Alice arrived at the school and parked. Dennis came out of the school approximately ten minutes later. It was typical of him to keep his mother waiting. He crossed the street, holding his guitar case in his left hand, looking down at the phone in his right hand, moving slowly.

The consultant was in her car, parked at the corner, and she saw him start to cross the street. She stepped on the gas pedal, turned the corner, increased her speed, and struck Dennis when he was halfway across the street. The speed limit near the school was twenty miles per hour; she was driving approximately forty when she struck him. When she hit the boy, he flew up in the air and landed with his head hitting the windshield, after which he slipped off the hood of the car and fell to the pavement. The consultant immediately slammed on the brakes, her car skidded to a stop, and she threw open her door and ran to the boy.

Alice Connor saw the accident and screamed. She was in such a state of shock that she had a hard time undoing her seat belt, but she eventually did so and rushed over to her son. The consultant reached the fallen boy first. While pretending to see how badly Dennis was injured, she pressed the auto injector she was holding in her right hand against the boy's bloody right arm. The auto injector was a spring-loaded syringe, like the ones army medics use to inject morphine into wounded soldiers. In this case, the auto injector contained a chemical that almost instantly stopped Dennis Connor's heart. There was no concern that an autopsy would find the chemical in the boy's bloodstream, assuming an autopsy would even be performed. The cause of death was obvious. It helped that the boy's neck appeared to have been broken when his head hit the windshield.

A teacher, who had walked out of the school after Dennis, saw the accident and immediately called 911. He would be one of the witnesses interviewed by the police. Alice was now kneeling next to her son, sobbing as she cradled his head in her arms. She knew that he was dead, although she wouldn't admit it to herself. The consultant was also crying.

(The consultant turned out to be a better actress than Mary could have imagined.) She kept saying, "Oh, my God, I just looked down for a moment. I didn't see him. I didn't see him."

The police and an ambulance arrived almost simultaneously, about five minutes after the accident. One of the good things about living in a small town was that the police responded quickly. Even though it was obvious to the medics that the boy was dead, they transported him to the hospital in an ambulance, and allowed his mother to accompany him. There he was declared DOA by the doctor on staff.

The police interviewed the consultant. She said she was driving through Redemption, just sightseeing, and looked down at her phone, at the map app, just before she hit the boy. She hadn't been talking on the phone or sending text messages or anything irresponsible like that. She'd just glanced down momentarily at her phone, which had been sitting in a cup holder. When asked how fast she was going she said probably about thirty. She hadn't realized she was in a school zone. She agreed to take a breathalyzer test and to give blood to look for any other drugs that might have affected her ability to safely drive a car. She did point out that the boy hadn't used the crosswalk.

Ultimately, because the driver had not been impaired, Dennis Connor's death was determined to be a tragic accident and not felony vehicular homicide. The consultant was charged instead with negligent driving and second-degree vehicular homicide, a misdemeanor, not a felony. The judge sentenced her to three hundred hours of community service, which she would be allowed to serve in the Chicago area, and a ten-thousand-dollar fine. The people who had sent the consultant to Illinois to assist Drexler Limited had to spend a few thousand more to pay for her lawyer and would lose the use of her services for at least six months—which was acceptable to all parties involved and considered a small price to pay to preserve the secrets of Drexler Limited.

Alice Connor accepted that her son's death was accidental. She'd seen the accident, after all, and because she knew exactly what had happened, there was nothing to be suspicious of. Also, the woman who'd killed her son hadn't tried to run; had she eluded the police that would have definitely made Alice doubtful. But the driver stayed at the scene, allowed the police to question her, was clearly devastated by what had happened, and returned to Redemption for her court appearances. In the end, Alice came to the conclusion that she was just a woman who had terrible luck. First her husband, being the drunk he was, passed out in his car on a train track and now her poor, unhappy child is fatally struck down crossing a street.

Mary White genuinely felt sorry for Alice and she was committed to doing everything she could to help her get through the difficult times ahead of her. She'd have her over for dinner frequently; would make sure other women in the company included her in things to get her mind off her sorrows; she'd have her own kids—including the son who had killed Alice's husband—help Alice if she needed anything done around her house.

Alice was family after all.

8

When Jamison returned from Virginia Beach, Steven Lang came to his office to discuss what had happened with Don Steward.

Steven said, "I can't believe he'd turn down seven million. There must have been something you could have said to persuade him."

Jamison said, "I'm telling you the guy just isn't motivated by money. He's already pretty rich and he likes what he does. I got the impression that his company was almost like a hobby for him. He just likes engineering and tinkering with shit. The other thing is, he told me that he thought there was something off about anyone offering that much. It made him suspicious."

Steven said, "What? Why would he be suspicious?"

Jamison noted that, for the first time since meeting him, Steven showed some actual emotion, as if Steward being suspicious about the offer was alarming or significant. Normally, Steven displayed about as much emotion as a paving stone.

"I don't know," Jamison said. "He never said. He just thought it strange that someone would offer so much. Maybe he was worried that somebody was planning to launder money through his company." He paused before saying, "You know, maybe if I'd been able to tell him who the client was, that might have made a difference. Then he would have known that a drug cartel wasn't trying to buy into his business."

"A drug cartel? Are you trying to be funny, Maddox?"

"No, I'm not trying to be funny. I'm just saying I might have been able to convince him to sell if I'd been able to tell him that the client was somebody legitimate, somebody he'd heard of, maybe somebody he admired and might have gone to work for after the sale."

"Well, the client didn't want his name known too early. If you'd been able to close the deal, then of course the name would have come out. Anyway . . ."

With that, Steven rose to his feet, saying: "I'll pass on what you said to Mr. Drexler. He's going to be very disappointed."

Jamison almost shrugged, then decided not to. Steven, the prick, might take that as a sign that he didn't care about Mr. Drexler's disappointment. Which he didn't.

Steven turned to leave Jamison's office but Jamison said, "Hey, wait a minute. What about that guy Crane who was arrested for selling detonators to those skinheads?"

"Oh, yeah, him," Steven said. "I don't know anything more about what happened other than what the papers said. Mr. Drexler talked to the client, of course. He didn't want the company associated in any way with someone who'd conspired with white supremacists, but the client said that he never approached Crane. As you know, the client was looking at several companies and after he got your report, he just scratched Crane's off his list. He never even spoke to the man. End of story."

After Steven left his office, Jamison sat for a moment mulling over what Steven had told him. He supposed Steven was telling him the truth;

why would he lie? But what were the odds of Drexler Limited being asked to research the one guy in America who ends up selling detonators to domestic terrorists? Oh, well, not his problem.

□ □ □

Mary White and Steven Lang took seats in the uncomfortable visitors' chairs in Claud's office, Mary wishing the man would buy some decent furniture. The damn wooden chairs made even her well-padded backside ache.

Getting right down to business, as he almost always did, Claud said, "So. What are we going to do about Mr. Steward? The client wants into that company and he's demanding that we make it happen."

When Claud said "the client" Mary and Steve, of course, knew who he meant. Drexler Limited had only one client—although the people on the second floor thought there were many. Claud also insisted that when discussing the client, even privately, they use no other nomenclature. It was a matter of discipline and developing communication habits that were consistent with Drexler Limited's purported function as a research company. You could never tell who might be listening.

It was for this reason, too, that the term "consultant" was applied to outside experts brought in to deal with problems when the words *operative* or—as in the case of Dennis Connor—*assassin* would have been more accurate.

Mary said, "I think Steward's wife will do what we want."

While Jamison Maddox had been in Virginia Beach so had two of Mary's children, her daughter and her eldest son. And while Jamison had been researching Don Steward and his company, Mary's kids had spent part of their time watching Jamison to make sure he stuck to the assignment he'd been given and didn't talk to anyone who might be law enforcement. The rest of their time was spent checking out Don Steward's wife. Steward's wife had always been Steven's backup plan if Jamison failed.

Steward didn't have any children and his current wife was his second wife. He'd divorced his first wife ten years ago. His wife was twenty years younger than he was, in her mid-thirties, an attractive woman but not terribly bright. She was from Savannah, Georgia, where she'd been born and raised and where most of her friends and family still lived. She tended to spend lavishly on herself when it came to clothes, jewelry, and the car she drove. Don Steward was a fairly wealthy man and didn't seem to mind how much she spent—within limits. Steven's intuition told him that Mrs. Steward would like the limits to be higher.

What all this meant was that if Don Steward were to die, Mrs. Steward would inherit his share of the company and would be more than happy to sell it to the highest bidder and move back to Savannah. The client would have preferred to buy his way into the company. Killing Steward and buying it from his wife would be slower and more complicated because his estate would have to go through probate, and there might be issues with Steward's partners. Unfortunately, Steward's refusal to sell had made this new course of action necessary.

"Do we need to bring in a consultant to deal with Mr. Steward?" Claud asked.

"No," Mary said. "The kids can take care of him."

A consultant had been necessary for Dennis Connor as his death couldn't be connected to anyone in the family. But when it came to Steward, Mary's children could easily handle the task.

"Okay, then, let's get on with it," Claud said, his tone indicating they were dismissed.

Steven said, "Before we adjourn, one more thing. Maddox brought up Crane again. I told him that the client who'd hired us to research Crane never followed through with Crane or had any contact with him. Maddox seemed satisfied with the explanation, but my gut tells me we need to keep a close watch on him."

"I am," Mary said, offended by Steven's comment. Mary's job was keeping a close watch on all the employees of Drexler Limited, including Steven.

Steven said, "I know, but I'd suggest you monitor his calls for the next several days and get into his personal computer again as soon as you can. We need to know if he's making any inquiries when it comes to Crane."

"I'll do that," Mary said. To Claud she said, "Crane hasn't been connected to the client in any way, has he?"

"Of course not. The client's person never dealt with Crane directly. He dealt with one of the men who bought the detonators from Crane, and those bumbling fools had no idea who he represented."

What Claud meant was that the client's operative had pretended to be sympathetic to the white supremacists' cause and had steered one of them to Crane, a man over his head in debt, as a possible source for acquiring detonators. What the client hadn't known was that the FBI had an informant in the neo-Nazi group.

That was just the way it went sometimes. The client couldn't win them all.

◻ ◻ ◻

Mary had dinner that night with her sons and her daughter.

Her sons—Sam and Matt—were both married but their wives hadn't been invited. They were good women and trusted employees of Drexler

Limited, but they didn't meet the *need-to-know* criterion when it came to Don Steward.

Her daughter, Judy, wasn't married and Mary was beginning to doubt that she ever would be. She'd thought for some time that Judy might be a lesbian. She'd only had one boyfriend, when she was eighteen, and he hadn't lasted long and she'd never had another one after that. She wore her hair short, spiking it up with some sort of gel, and Mary thought the style was cute but a bit mannish. Mary couldn't remember the last time she'd seen Judy in a skirt or a dress. Well, if she was a lesbian, Mary didn't care as long as Judy was happy. She loved her daughter deeply, as she did all her children.

The other thing about Judy was that even though she was the youngest, she was the brightest and most creative of her three kids, and when they worked together, Judy was the one who took charge. Judy came across to outsiders as a brash, fun-loving young woman; they had no idea how driven she could be, or how ruthless if a situation required it.

Judy and her brothers had inherited their looks from Mary and not their father, Mike, Mary's late husband. They all had dark hair and all were of medium height, stocky, but not overweight. Mary had looked almost identical to her daughter when she was Judy's age and before she'd gained weight. And all her kids were in excellent shape and jogged and lifted weights to make sure they stayed that way; like soldiers— which they essentially were—they had to be physically able to meet the demands of their profession. Also, like soldiers, they were very well trained, having spent their summers at various places when they were in their teens and early twenties learning the skills of their trade. Their friends in Redemption had thought they were enjoying summer camps or were away at college when they were actually attending training sessions that the client had arranged.

During dinner, they gossiped about people in the family and folks in Redemption. Most of the time was spent talking about Mary's grandkids, Sam's two boys, Bobby and Randy, and Matt's daughter, Carly. Carly was the apple of Mary's eye. The girl was just delightful and so incredibly bright and talented. Mary's vision of the future was that Judy would one day replace her at Drexler Limited and Carly would replace Judy.

While they were eating dessert—a cherry pie that Sam's wife had baked—Mary got down to business.

"We need to deal with that Steward fellow in Virginia Beach," Mary said. "Any ideas?"

"Yeah," Judy said. "Carjacking."

Before anyone could ask her to explain, Judy said, "Steward's company gets a part made by a small company in Richmond, some kind of precision casting, and Steward visits the company at least once a week. The company in Richmond is this minority-owned business located in this god-awful neighborhood. Every house and store in the area has bars on the windows and security cameras. Well, Richmond has recently had a spate of carjackings. Like more than a dozen. Some gang of thugs is jacking high-end cars and Steward drives a 2020 Benz."

Judy scooped up another piece of pie before she continued. With her mouth half full, she said, "The way the gang works is two people, both wearing ski masks, will drive up next to the car they want to jack. Then one of them gets out and points a gun at the driver. They make the driver get out of his car and give them his cell phone so he can't call the cops right away, and then the jacker with the gun drives away in the stolen car with his buddy following. Three people have been pistol-whipped because they mouthed off or were too slow to get out of their cars. So far no one's been killed, but a murder wouldn't be a surprise.

"I figure we could do it near this casting shop in the shitty neighborhood the next time Steward goes to Richmond. We'll be seen on surveillance cameras so we'll have to steal a car. We'll also have to go down there to check out the area more thoroughly to figure out escape routes and someplace to dump the cars. You know, all the details, but it's easily doable."

Before anyone could speak, Sam said, "Can you and Matt handle it, Judy? Bobby and Randy both have baseball games this week and I'd like to make 'em since I missed the last few."

"Sure," Judy said.

"Fine with me," Matt said.

"Okay," Mary said. "Who wants another piece of pie?"

9

Jamison and Ralph, as had become their custom, were drinking beer at the Shamrock on a Friday evening after work. Ralph was going on and on about some movie possibly starring Brad Pitt that was based on a weird documentary called *Tiger King*. Jamison was only half listening to him because he was looking over at Gillian Lang, his boss's wife. She was again having drinks with her sister-in-law, the mayor, and as it was a warm summer day, she was again wearing shorts that showed off her long legs. On her feet were thin sandals and around her left ankle was a thin, gold chain, which for some reason Jamison found erotic.

Ralph said, "Well, I gotta get going. I promised the old lady next door that I'd fix her television. This old gal, about once a week, hits some button on her remote that fucks up the entire system and she can't figure out how to reset it. The good news is, she'll feed me dinner and she lets me take home everything we don't eat."

After Ralph left, Jamison ordered another beer. He was in no rush to return to his empty apartment. He glanced over at Gillian again and this time she caught him looking. Embarrassed, he picked up the dinner menu and pretended to study it. Sadly, after more than three months in Redemption, he knew every item the Shamrock offered on its menu.

A moment later a voice asked, "Can I join you?"

He looked up and saw Gillian Lang smiling down at him.

She was breathtaking. She had a summer tan making the freckles dusting her high cheekbones more visible. Her short, blonde hair was lighter in a few places thanks to the sun. Her eyes were a pale blue color and radiated intelligence. When she smiled, she displayed a slight Lauren Hutton gap between her two front teeth, this small imperfection somehow making her even more perfect.

"Sure," he said. "Can I get you a drink?"

She held up the glass she was holding in her right hand, which he hadn't noticed. She said, "I'll finish the one I already have." She sat in the seat where Ralph had been sitting, crossed her tanned legs, and Jamison again noticed the thin gold chain around her left ankle.

Quit staring at her legs, you idiot!

Jamison glanced over at the table where she'd been sitting and said, "Did the mayor leave?"

"Yeah. Had to go home and fix dinner for her husband. Since my husband's out of town I don't have to worry about that, not that I cook dinner for him all that often anyway. He does most of the cooking."

"I didn't know he was gone. Where did he go?"

Gillian patted his hand, sending a tingle up his arm, and said, "Now you know better than to ask a question like that."

"Yeah, sorry, I just—"

"I have to ask you something, Jamison. You seem like a decent guy—not one of those greedy Wall Street thieves—and you were making an incredible salary at Goldman. What on earth possessed you to do what you did?"

"So you know what happened with me at Goldman."

"Yeah. I was curious about you—"

Now that was good to hear.

"—and I took a peek at your personnel file. You're lucky you're not in jail."

"Luck didn't have anything to do with it," Jamison said. "I agreed to be the government's star witness to keep from going to jail. If I hadn't taken the deal I was offered, one of the other guys would have and I'd be in a cell right now instead of sitting here talking to you."

"So why did you do it?"

Jamison shook his head, a wry expression on his face. "One night me and three guys I worked with—the three guys who went to jail—were sitting in a bar in Manhattan getting drunk. One of the guys was my boss and the other two were senior players in the company. We were celebrating a deal that I'd just negotiated. The funny part is, the bonus I got on that deal was almost twice as much as I made off the insider trading scheme. Anyway, while we're sitting there, a guy comes over to our table to say hi. He was my boss's ex–brother-in-law and sat on the board of Eli Lilly. He was also a Goldman client."

"Eli Lilly?" Gillian said. "The pharmaceutical firm?"

"Yeah. Anyway, this guy was so drunk he could barely stand, and he lets it slip that Eli had just made a major breakthrough on a drug for treating prostate cancer. He said the company's lawyers had convinced the FDA to bypass some of the clinical trials, which would mean that the drug would be on the market in just a couple of months and a lot sooner than anyone expected.

"After this drunken fool left, me and the three guys I was with just looked at each other. We all realized that we had the inside dope, no pun intended, on something we could make a small fortune on. We knew it was wrong, but we talked ourselves into it. The only good news is that I didn't make as much as the other guys did because I wasn't as greedy as they were, and I didn't do a bunch of outrageous things to evade taxes. I knew it was a dumb thing to do, but I went along because one of the guys was my boss and the other two could help me advance at Goldman."

Jamison took a sip of his beer and looked at Gillian; she was smiling slightly, seeming more amused than shocked by what he'd done. Jamison said, "There's nothing about this story that makes me look good and I don't have any excuse for what I did. I was weak—and I've never thought of myself as a weak person—and I did something stupid to make a little bit of money that I didn't need and it cost me my career." He paused then added: "Is there anything else you'd like to know about my criminal past?"

"I guess not," Gillian said. "But I am curious as to why you decided to come here of all places. Even if you have a record, there must have been something you could have found closer to home."

"I'm sure I could have gotten some kind of job in New York, not doing what I used to do, but something that would have probably paid about as well as this one. I have an uncle who's quite wealthy and he has a lot of friends, and I'm sure one of his friends would have found a spot for me. But the truth is that I was ashamed of what I'd done and I didn't want to take advantage of my uncle. He's like a father to me. And I just needed a change of scenery. The people I used to think were my friends had all started avoiding me and I felt like the village leper whenever I encountered people I knew in public." Jamison sighed. "Redemption frankly isn't my idea of an ideal place to live, but it'll do for a while until something else comes along, and I'm at least doing something that takes advantage of my skills."

After that, they chatted about life in Redemption, Jamison getting the impression that she was as bored with the little town as he was. She told him that she didn't have kids and spent her free time playing golf and tennis. When she mentioned tennis, Jamison said that he played, too. Then he added, "Maybe I can play with you and your husband one of these days if I can find myself a doubles partner." To which she responded, "Steven doesn't play tennis. His idea of sport is killing things. He's a hunter."

He knew he couldn't talk to her about what she did at Drexler Limited but he found she was also evasive about other aspects of her personal life. When he asked where she'd attended college and what she'd majored in, she made a dismissive gesture and said, "Oh, one of the Seven Sisters where I got a master's in partying." Then she immediately switched the topic, asking him about the London School of Economics. When he asked her why she went to work for Drexler, she said, "I suppose it was because I had to do something, and it was the best thing I could find here." Her answer sounded off; she didn't strike him as a person who would settle for a job that didn't fully engage her or fulfill her. Which made him ask, "I know you can't talk about what you do, but do you *like* what you do?"

While they'd been chatting, they'd both had a couple more drinks. Jamison was drinking beer; she was drinking gin and tonics, heavy on the gin. She was a bit tipsy but not so drunk that she wouldn't be able to drive home. So he didn't think that alcohol contributed to what she said next.

Instead of answering his question about liking her job, she looked into his eyes and said, "Why don't we go to your place?"

He sat back, stunned, not knowing how to respond. He wanted her, there was no doubt about that, but he'd never been a man who slept with married women, and certainly not a woman married to his boss. Also, he may not have enjoyed working at Drexler, but the idea of having to hunt for another job so soon after finding this one was not appealing. He stammered, "I, uh, I would—"

Reading his mind, she said, "If you're worried about my husband, don't be. He couldn't care less who I sleep with."

Jamison doubted that was true—but it was all he needed to hear.

10

As Claud Drexler had told him during his initial interview, Drexler Limited occasionally did some financial research with political ramifications. Jamison's current assignment had to do with a congressman named John Corcoran, a Republican from Ohio. Corcoran had been a member of Congress for thirteen years, was a rising star in the GOP, and was considered a potential future vice presidential candidate. He was currently the ranking Republican on the U.S. House Committee on Appropriations, which had its fingers into almost everything: defense spending, military construction projects, homeland security, financial services, energy development, and so forth. His congressional district voted overwhelmingly Republican.

Jamison had no idea who the client was, but he assumed it was some super PAC backing a long-shot Democratic contender for Corcoran's seat. His job was to figure out how John Corcoran had managed to amass a small fortune in the time that he'd been in the House of Representatives. Thirteen years ago, before being elected to Congress, Corcoran had been a high school wrestling coach and his net worth had been less than half a million bucks, almost all of that being the equity in his small house in Dayton. Today his net worth was approximately seven million, even though his annual salary as a congressman was only a hundred and seventy-four thousand.

Jamison learned that Corcoran had made some money off a book deal. He was given a two-hundred-thousand-dollar advance on a book that sold only about twenty thousand copies, but thanks to its publication he now made five thousand dollars per speaking engagement on the conservative lecture circuit. He sold his small home in Dayton to a Republican multimillionaire for twice as much as it was worth and purchased a much larger one in Ohio and another one in Arlington, Virginia, for half of what they were worth. The interest on his home loans was two percent because he borrowed the money from a Republican billionaire. He made a killing by purchasing stock in Lockheed Martin, Northrop Grumman, and Raytheon—all defense contractors—right before they were given multi-billion-dollar contracts from the Pentagon. These stock purchases were clear-cut cases of insider trading—the crime Jamison had been convicted of—but members of Congress were allowed to play to a different set of rules. Or knew how to get around the rules. The bottom line was that Corcoran became rich the same way most longtime members of the House and Senate did, both Democrats and Republicans, and there really wasn't anything noteworthy about his financial story.

Jamison passed on what he'd learned to Steven Lang. As best Jamison could tell, Steven had no idea that Jamison was sleeping with his wife. Or if he did know, it wasn't evident in his attitude toward Jamison. He acted the way he'd always acted: cool and aloof and not the least bit interested in Jamison's personal life.

What Jamison didn't realize was that he was not the only employee at Drexler Limited doing research on Congressman Corcoran.

□ □ □

Because of the number of attendees, the meeting to discuss the status of ongoing efforts related to Congressman Corcoran was held in a small conference room near Claud's office. There were six people present: Claud; Steven Lang and his wife, Gillian Lang; Mary White and her daughter, Judy; and a man named Edward Pine, who was the husband of Redemption's mayor.

Claud started the meeting by saying: "The client is not happy with our lack of progress when it comes to Mr. Corcoran. Let's review where we are and what can be done next. Steven, please begin."

Steven said, "On the financial side, unless Gillian's found something new, there's really nothing useful. Maddox found a few things that would embarrass him but nothing illegal or significantly damaging from a political perspective. Next week, Corcoran and a few other politicians are meeting at Christian Montgomery's estate to discuss federal subsidies to companies that Montgomery and some of his rich pals control. Maybe something will happen at an after-hours event that will be helpful, but I don't think Corcoran would be that stupid and I doubt that Mary or Gillian can infiltrate Montgomery's security."

Christian Montgomery was worth billions, although no one knew how many billions because he hid his money in a lot of different places and in myriad ways. He was also a sexual deviant who had a fondness for underage girls, some as young as fifteen. He held parties with these girls in attendance on an island he owned and would invite some of his clos-est friends. Among his close friends were Saudi crown princes, Russian oligarchs, and members of British royalty. Montgomery, however, had never been arrested thanks to a law firm with over two hundred lawyers that he retained to defend his interests, and money he gave to politicians to make an arrest even more unlikely. What Steven was saying was that maybe Corcoran would be invited to participate in one of Montgomery's orgies—but it was doubtful that Corcoran would accept the invitation. Furthermore, security at Montgomery's place was almost impossible to penetrate; his physical and cyber security systems were as secure as the president's.

"Gillian, what about you?" Claud asked.

Claud had told Jamison that his company didn't do things like hack into databases. Claud had lied to Jamison. Gillian had told Jamison that she'd attended one of the Seven Sisters and majored in partying. She'd also lied to Jamison. She'd attended Northwestern and majored in computer science.

Gillian said, "I've been inside Corcoran's personal computers, his laptop and the desktops he has in his homes in Dayton and Arlington. I didn't try to get into the computers in his office in D.C. because, like Steven said, the man isn't stupid. There's nothing in any of his machines that's useful, and he isn't smart enough when it comes to computers to hide something from me. He doesn't visit child porn sites, he doesn't have a girlfriend he emails, he doesn't have a secret file containing incriminating information. We've spent hours listening to his cell phone conversations. We've recorded a number of things he's said that would be politically embarrassing to him but nothing so bad he wouldn't survive if the recordings were made public. His wife, by the way, is having an affair with her gynecologist but I don't see how that helps us. He wouldn't protect his wife; he'd divorce her."

Claud shook his head. "Mary, do you have anything to add?"

"Not really. The kids have spent weeks following him, and so far nothing. He doesn't visit hookers, and like Gillian said, he doesn't have a girlfriend on the side. Or a boyfriend. But Judy's noticed one thing that might be worth pursuing."

Turning to her daughter, Mary said, "Go on, Judy, tell him."

Judy said, "I think he's got a thing for black chicks. I mean, if Corcoran's daughter was to date a black guy, he'd probably disown her. Without a doubt, based on some of his phone calls, he's a flaming bigot. But I've spent a lot of time watching him and I've seen the way he looks at some black women. They're all the same type: very dark, tiny waists, big asses, and big tits."

Seeing Claud wince at her language—Claud was a bit of a prude—Judy said, "Hey, I'm just sayin.'"

"Go on," Claud said.

Judy said, "There's a restaurant on Capitol Hill where he goes for lunch about three days a week and one of the waitresses there is his type. He makes a point of always sitting in her section of the restaurant and he can't take his eyes off her. So it's just a gut feeling on my part, but I think it might be worth trolling a girl in front of him. The problem would be figuring out how to get the girl next to him in a setting where he might make a move. He's never hit on this waitress because a restaurant's just too public, not to mention he's a snob and probably thinks a waitress would be beneath him."

Mary said, "But how would we get a woman into his orbit?"

"I don't know," Judy said, but Ed Pine said, "I might be able to do that." Then added, "Through Cooper & Cooper."

Mary's expertise was security; Steven's was finance and logistics; Gillian's was technology. Ed Pine's specialty was politics. The client had people in a lobbying firm on K Street in D.C. called Cooper & Cooper. Its operation was completely separate from Drexler Limited, but Pine was Drexler's liaison with the firm.

Pine said, "We could bring someone into Cooper & Cooper and find a way to put her in contact with Corcoran. But she'd have to be someone who's not only physically appealing to him, but also very bright.

A dummy wouldn't be able to pull it off. I think I'd start by looking at high-end escort services, probably on the West Coast. We wouldn't want to hire someone in the D.C. area or even New York. I could just imagine her bumping into some politician who's used her services before. But this will take some time. We'd have to find the right girl, train her, develop a background story with the necessary documentation, and then come up with a lobbying job for her at Cooper & Cooper where she'd have access to Corcoran."

No one asked what the girl would do if she was able to seduce Corcoran. That was obvious: she would take Corcoran to bed in a place where their liaison would be videotaped. Also no one asked what would happen with the girl after she'd done her job. The answer to that question, too, was obvious.

"We're not up against a hard deadline, so we have some time," Claud said. "I mean, sooner would be better than later but Corcoran is going to be elected next year and he'll keep his seat on the Appropriations Committee. Since Judy knows the sort of woman he likes, you can work with her on this."

Judy said, "Uncle Claud, you understand that I can't guarantee he'll fall for her. It's just a feeling."

"Well, it's better than anything anyone else has been able to come up with," Claud said. "Meeting adjourned."

11

It happened a second time—and Jamison didn't like it.

He had set up a Google alert for Don Steward, the Virginia Beach engineer. He set the alert on his office computer, of course, as he would have gotten into trouble if he'd set it on his laptop at home. And he didn't set the alert for any sort of underhanded reason.

A Drexler client had wanted to buy into Steward's company and Steward had rejected the client's seven-million-dollar offer. Keeping tabs on Steward and his company via the Internet might allow Jamison to discover something that would be beneficial to his employer. For example, if the company had some sort of setback, such as a costly lawsuit or a problem with one of its suppliers, that could make the client's offer more appealing to Steward. Whatever the case, if Jamison had learned something that might change Steward's mind when it came to selling his interest in the company, he would have passed the information on to Steven Lang and earned an atta-boy.

But when his computer chirped that he had an alert and he saw the headline on the article he was stunned. *Virginia Beach Man Killed in Carjacking.*

The article said that the city of Richmond had been having a rash of carjackings, all apparently committed by the same gang of thieves. It appeared as if Steward and his expensive Mercedes had simply been in the wrong place at the wrong time. The article noted that other carjacking victims had been beaten and Steward was the only one who'd been killed, but the Richmond cops said they weren't surprised that the violence had escalated to murder, that it had only been a matter of time.

The article troubled Jamison in part because he'd genuinely liked Don Steward. He'd seemed like a decent guy. But what really concerned him was that this was the second time something out of the ordinary had happened to a person that he'd researched for a Drexler Limited client. The coincidence of two people he'd investigated both making the news in ways involving criminal activity—one conspiring with criminals, the other being the victim of a crime—was hard to imagine. Fortunately, there wasn't anything that Jamison had done—or that Drexler Limited had done—that was criminal. The last thing he needed, considering what had happened in New York, was to be involved in anything illegal.

Jamison glanced at his watch. It was five and time to leave. He was meeting Gillian at his place at six. Since he didn't cook, he needed to stop someplace and find something someone else had cooked for their dinner. That, and a couple bottles of wine.

◻ ◻ ◻

Jamison lay in bed, enjoying the sight of Gillian Lang. They'd been sleek with sweat after they'd had sex and she decided to take a shower before going home to her husband. She was now standing, peeking out his bedroom window, wearing a towel she'd wrapped around her waist, leaving her small breasts uncovered.

Jamison was fascinated by the woman and not just because of her beauty. He'd been with a lot of beautiful women. His last girlfriend, Amanda, had been younger than Gillian and, if he was being objective, just as beautiful. But he realized now that there hadn't been anything extraordinary about Amanda. She'd been like most of the women he'd dated, born into wealth, pampered all her life, and although she'd been fun to be with, she now seemed insubstantial and immature when compared to Gillian. If he was being honest about it, Jamison supposed he could say the same thing about himself.

Gillian intrigued him more than any woman he'd ever known and partly because she shrouded herself in mystery. Not only wouldn't she talk about her job, but she also refused to discuss her upbringing or her parents or much of anything about her past. But he knew, even though he didn't have any facts to support his conclusion, that she'd experienced things that he hadn't, serious things, difficult things, that had made her who she was. And he wanted to know who she really was.

There was also a vulnerable side to her, an ineffable sadness—he could see it in her eyes—and he got the impression that the cause was more than just being trapped in a bad marriage. She'd once mentioned that she'd never been outside of the United States and would love to see Europe, but when he'd asked what was stopping her from traveling, she brushed the question aside. Once he bluntly asked her why she'd married her husband; she just shook her head and offered nothing.

She reminded him of a blue-eyed lioness in a cage, looking out through the bars at a world she yearned to join—and he wanted to set her free.

But as long as he stayed away from personal topics, she was a pleasure to be with. She was quick-witted and had a dry, cynical sense of humor that he enjoyed. She was well-read, more so than he was, and she liked talking about books, movies, and television shows. They didn't have serious political discussions, but she liked to point out the foibles of

politicians, which she mostly gleaned from late night television come-
dians. He also liked that she was athletic and much more so than his last
girlfriend. He'd played tennis with her twice and although she wasn't
quite as good as he was, she was close. He was thinking about taking up
golf, although he'd never found golf appealing, so he could play with her.

He asked, "What are you looking at out there?" The only view from
his bedroom window was a tree-lined residential street filled with old
houses.

Without turning around, she said, "A little girl playing jump rope."

She sounded wistful when she said this, and he'd noticed before that
she became a bit melancholy when she saw young children. He got the
impression that she'd like to have kids but when he'd asked her once if
she wanted children, she'd looked away and didn't answer. Another topic
that was out of bounds.

He said, "I wish we could go someplace. You know, get out of this
damn town for a couple of days, like maybe spend a long weekend in
New York."

He'd noticed that she had no problem in getting away from her husband to spend time with him. Often Steven was out of town and even
when he wasn't, they got together a couple of times a week. She was
discreet about their affair. They didn't dine alone in local restaurants or
have drinks together at the Shamrock. They always came to his place.
He got the impression that she didn't really care if her husband knew
she was sleeping with someone but, at the same time, she didn't want to
embarrass him. But since she refused to talk about her relationship with
the man she'd married, he had no idea what she was thinking when it
came to Steven Lang.

She turned to face him, a wide smile on her face. "I'd really like that,"
she said. "Maybe in a couple of weeks. I can't right now, there's just too
much going on at work, but say the week after next."

"I can always say it's time for me to visit my mother." Gillian laughed; Jamison had told her about his relationship with his mother.

She said, "You don't have to make up an excuse. You're allowed to go wherever you want when you're not working."

That was true. No one at Drexler had ever said that he needed to get permission to leave Redemption and he'd gone to Chicago a couple of times on weekends, one weekend spending the night in a hotel. He'd just needed a break from Redemption and wanted to feel the energy of a big city again. The odd thing was that on the Monday after his weekend stay in Chicago, Mary White sprung one of her random polygraph tests on him. She didn't ask anything about what he'd done in Chicago, however; all she'd asked was the standard question—if he'd spoken to anyone outside of Drexler about the company's business. The timing of the polygraph test had bothered him, though; it was as if Mary had known that he'd been out of town.

"But what excuse will you give for spending a few days away from home?" Jamison asked.

Again, the I-don't-want-to-talk-about-it head shake. She dropped the towel she had around her waist on the floor—she wasn't the neatest girlfriend he'd ever had—and looked for her clothes, which were scattered around the bedroom. "I need to get going," she said. "But I really like the idea of going to New York, Jamison. Do you think you could get tickets for *Hamilton*? When it played in Chicago, I wasn't able to see it."

"Piece of cake," Jamison said. He wasn't a Wall Street player anymore, but he knew how to acquire hard-to-get tickets to Broadway plays. He immediately started thinking about where they'd stay in New York and where they'd eat and what they'd do when they weren't lying in bed.

12

When Gillian arrived home, she saw that Steven was there. He'd taken a trip to D.C. with Ed Pine where they'd met with a VP in the lobbying firm of Cooper & Cooper. The objective had been to decide on a suitable role in the firm for the woman they planned to use to seduce Congressman John Corcoran.

Judy White had found an acceptable candidate in L.A. Her name—or at least the name she used on the escort service's website—was Heather Fine. Heather came to L.A., as so many beautiful young girls do, in hopes of becoming a star. It was not to be; she waited tables for a year and never got a single audition. But she had no problem at all finding work as an escort who charged three hundred per hour if she *didn't* sleep with a client; the price for her companionship escalated significantly if sex was involved—and it almost always was.

Heather was bright; bright enough to play the role of a lobbyist. She'd completed two years of college at San Diego State before she'd decided to head north to Hollywood. Steven and Ed were currently working on a legend for her. They doubted that Corcoran, if he became enamored with her, would run a background check on a woman employed by a reputable K Street firm—but he might. So Gillian stole the identity of a woman named Maria Alverez in Miami who bore a strong resemblance to Heather. Maria was single, had graduated from Florida State with a BA, had no criminal record, and a satisfactory credit rating. Consequently, if Corcoran were to call up a pal in the FBI and ask him to do a record check on a Maria Alverez, formerly of Miami, the check wouldn't reveal anything that should alarm Corcoran. Heather would have to memorize a background story that matched the real Maria's but that also shouldn't be a problem.

The client had authorized Judy to offer Heather three times her average annual income, not a small amount. And Heather understood that she'd be involved in blackmailing a politician—although she didn't know his name yet—and she didn't have a problem with doing that. Heather's goal was to amass a large amount of money while she still had her looks, and then retire to someplace where the cost of living would make working unnecessary. If she could find a wealthy man to marry, that would be the cherry on her sundae.

So Heather was in, and the planning regarding Corcoran was moving forward. What hadn't been decided was what Heather's specialty would be in the lobbying firm. She had to become a subject matter expert in some field that would give her a reason for meeting with Corcoran in his leadership capacity on the Appropriations Committee. Thus, Steven and Ed Pine's trip to D.C. Because of Claud's paranoid nature, these were discussions that had to take place face-to-face and not on a phone.

When Gillian walked into the house, she found Steven in the kitchen looking at plans an architect had drawn up to expand and modernize the kitchen. Steven wanted new cabinets and more counter space. He wanted a gas stove instead of an electric one, gas being the energy source preferred by chefs.

Steven and Gillian lived in a stately, redbrick Tudor that was about eighty years old. The lawn was manicured and the flower beds were immaculate and Steven did almost all the yard work. The house, however, wasn't what Steven really wanted. He wanted a place with a scenic view, one with a library and a swimming pool and a wine cellar, one with grounds featuring century-old oak trees and a sweeping driveway made of hand-laid stones. But he knew he'd never be able to own such a place. Claud paid Steven and Gillian adequate salaries but not salaries large enough to own a grand home. The client's money was mostly spent on operational matters—like Heather's payment for seducing the congressman.

So Steven, to his credit, did the best he could to make the home he and Gillian owned in Redemption as attractive and unique as possible and did most of the work himself. Over the years, he'd become an excellent carpenter and an above-average plumber and electrician. He'd installed hardwood floors, retiled the two bathrooms, and built a screened-in back porch that was a pleasant, bug-free place to sit on hot summer nights. Apparently, he was now ready to tackle a kitchen remodel.

Steven had a number of interests. He liked to cook. He'd become somewhat of an expert on wines and although he didn't have a wine cellar, he'd converted one closet into a temperature-controlled space where he could store thirty bottles. He also liked to hunt, and a couple of times a year would go hunting with another man in Redemption, one not associated with Drexler Limited. Steven's primary passion, however, was his job. Even though he was only thirty-six, he appeared to be the most likely candidate to replace Claud if Claud ever retired.

Yes, a lot of things interested Steven. The one thing that didn't interest him was his wife.

◻ ◻ ◻

Steven and Gillian's marriage had been arranged—arranged in the same way that medieval princes were married to princesses to maintain control of dynasties. Gillian had known she was going to marry Steven from the time she was seventeen. Looking back on her life, Gillian couldn't believe how *malleable* she'd been. But she was the norm in the family, not the exception. The exception was Dennis Connor—and look what had happened to him.

In most ways, her indoctrination into the family's business wasn't much different than what happened in other closed societies. Like the Amish. Amish elders had such a strong hold on the next generation that young men and women living in the twenty-first century were content to go without television, sewed their own clothes, and commuted in horse-drawn carriages—and then passed on their beliefs to the following generation.

Religious organizations were more adept than any when it came to programming the young. Little Catholics would be handed over to the nuns and priests when they were five or six and completely immersed in the catechism of their faith. The brainwashing they were exposed to stuck with many for their entire lives—and they then passed on their beliefs to their children. There was nothing at all unusual about cults and religious organizations and militant groups molding their young into their own image. Mormons, Catholics, Muslims, and Evangelicals had beliefs that defied logic, science, and common sense—yet their children followed in their footsteps like lemmings. White nationalists produced white nationalists. Polygamists bred more polygamists. Seventy-five people perished with David Koresh in the flames at Waco. Over nine hundred drank the Kool-Aid. If you got them young enough and if the leader of a group was charismatic and the message was amplified by faithful followers, you can get children to believe almost anything—some for a while and some forever.

In Gillian's case, it wasn't a religion that had its grip on her; it was instead the family's reason for existence. She'd been taught to believe that she was a member of a unique clan and the needs of the clan were paramount and came before those of any individual. The problem was, at the age of thirty-two, that her desires no longer matched the family's and Claud Drexler's hold on her had weakened. She was the Catholic who still attended Mass but no longer truly believed the priest was changing bread into the body of Christ. She had no desire to spend the rest of her life—and risk her life—doing the family's work.

But how would she ever get free? You didn't walk away from Drexler Limited.

◻ ◻ ◻

Steven said to her, "Let me get your opinion on something. I'm trying to figure out where to put the microwave. Ideally, it would go over the stove, but I really want a vent hood over the stove and the ventilation systems that come with most microwaves aren't all that good. I don't want to put it on the counter because that takes up counter space. I was thinking I might build a small pantry near the door, on the other side of the refrigerator, and put the microwave on the top shelf of the pantry, but that would mean you'd have to open the pantry door every time you wanted to microwave something."

Gillian shrugged. "I don't know," she said. "Like you said, it would be a lot more convenient if it was over the stove. Do they make a custom microwave with better, uh, suction?"

"I haven't found one yet," Steven said and went back to studying the kitchen plan.

She knew Steven would eventually do whatever he wanted and it would be acceptable. She said, "Well, I'm going to bed. I'll see you tomorrow."

"Goodnight," he muttered, not looking at her.

They were normally pleasant and polite to each other, although they could go for days without talking about anything that wasn't work related. The only thing they really had in common was their jobs.

Gillian went to her room and closed the door. She felt languid after sex with Jamison. She undressed and put on one of the extra-large T-shirts she typically wore to bed, then flopped down on the bed, turned on the television in her room, and started clicking through the channels for something to watch.

She and Steven slept in separate bedrooms and had been doing so for the last five years. They both agreed that they got a better night's rest if they slept alone. And it was about five years ago that she'd last had sex with him.

When they first got married, when she was twenty-two and he was twenty-six, they'd had what she imagined was a normal married couple's sex life. Frequent, almost daily sex the first year, gradually tapering off to once or twice a week, then maybe once a month, until it finally stopped altogether. Gillian, who'd had several lovers while in college, found Steven better than some and worse than others, but sex with him hadn't been terrible. The problem, she supposed, was that they'd never truly loved each other; there'd never been any passion, any spark, any chemistry. She liked sex and she needed it, and she'd had a couple affairs in the last five years as well as a number of one-night stands when she'd traveled out of town, but Steven, as best she could tell, could do without sex. She was pretty sure he wasn't gay and she supposed he must occasionally have sex with women when *he* went out of town. She was almost positive he wasn't involved with anyone in Redemption; she was certain she would have heard if he was. She wouldn't be surprised if he was celibate. Steven's passion was his job; he was like a monk devoted only to his god. Whatever the case, he didn't care who she slept with as long as her sex life didn't interfere with her work.

Certainly, Mary White and her children knew that she was sleeping with Jamison—it was Mary's job to know—but she wasn't sure that Steven did. Mary would have told Claud, of course, but she may have elected not to tell Steven. Mary might think that Steven would be jealous of Jamison, although Gillian knew he wouldn't be, and Mary and Claud may have been concerned that if there were hard feelings between Steven and Jamison the situation could negatively impact productivity.

Jamison. She wasn't in love with him—she didn't think she'd ever been in love with anyone—but she liked him enormously and more than any man she'd met in some time. He was not only a beautiful physical specimen, he was also good in bed and fun to be with. Most importantly, he made her laugh and she trusted him. She knew he'd never do anything to harm her. But what she couldn't tell yet was whether he loved her enough to risk his life for her.

She had to make Jamison Maddox fall head over heels in love with her. She had to.

13

Jamison told Steven that he'd like to take the upcoming Friday and Monday off because he wanted to spend a long weekend in New York. He said he hadn't seen his mother or his uncle in quite a while, and more than anything else, he missed the city and needed a break from Redemption.

Steven said, "How's the cannery project going?"

"Good," Jamison said. "I'll be done next week, no later than Wednesday even if I go to New York."

The cannery project was another odd assignment. Jamison had been told to do an analysis of five canneries in the United States. The canneries all canned vegetables, mostly corn and beans. The client, however, wasn't particularly interested in the financial health of these companies; the only thing the client wanted to know from a financial standpoint was if any of them were likely to go out of business in the near future. None of them were.

What the client was interested in was the "efficiency" of the canneries, meaning he wanted a comparison of how many cans were produced a day, how widely those cans were distributed, and where they were distributed.

The client also wanted to know about the kind of machinery that was used and Jamison was expected to produce a synopsis of the canning process, including a flow chart, from the time the vegetables arrived at the cannery until the cans were sealed and placed on a truck. This aspect of the job required a considerable amount of research on Jamison's part as he didn't know a damn thing about canneries; he was a finance guy, not a fucking engineer.

Lastly, the client was interested in ten people who worked in the five canneries. Jamison learned that none of the ten people held senior positions; they weren't executives. They were all midlevel managers, basically foremen, who supervised the production process and each of them had ten to fifteen years of experience. What the client wanted to know was which of these ten people would be most amendable to relocating.

As best Jamison could figure, the client was foreign—either a foreign individual or a foreign corporation—and was looking to set up a canning operation in his country, so he needed a person with hands-on knowledge of the production process. The thing that surprised Jamison was that someone had obviously done some pre-screening of the ten men and they all had one thing in common: indebtedness. Some had two mortgages on their homes; one had a lien against his house for failure to pay a contractor. All of them had a substantial amount of credit card debt. This made Jamison think that maybe the client wanted to establish a cannery in some godawful place in Africa or the Middle East, and to incentivize an experienced man to move there, the client would be willing to pay off his debts.

Further research showed that although the ten men knew the business, they had a number of flaws. A couple were possibly alcoholics based on the number of DUIs they'd collected. Four were divorced and domestic violence appeared to have contributed to two of the divorces. Two of the divorced men were behind in child support and alimony payments. One man had been arrested for assault, something related to a neighbor's dog. Another had been arrested at some Second Amendment demonstration, where he and several other men had entered the state capitol packing AR-15s, violating a prohibition against guns inside the capitol building.

Again, Jamison could only assume that what made these people attractive was their experience combined with the debts they owed, which might make them willing to move if their debts were paid off—but the client apparently hadn't done much research when it came to their personal lives. The truth was that Jamison wouldn't have hired any of them. Nonetheless he produced a profile for each of the ten candidates. For example:

William Hubbard. Fifteen years experience. Combined debt (home, cars, credit cards) approximately two hundred thousand. He was born and raised in Alabama but as he's currently living in Minnesota, he might be willing to relocate to somewhere warmer. He's one of only two candidates that has no children and therefore wouldn't have issues related to relocating kids. His wife appears to have a gambling problem and a large part of his personal debt is due to her behavior as opposed to his own. He got a DUI ten years ago, but hasn't gotten one since then.

Robert Coolidge. Twelve years experience. Combined debt, one hundred eighty thousand. He's missed his last two mortgage payments. He separated from his wife for issues related to domestic violence but is involved in a bitter child custody dispute with his ex for their seven-year-old son. His attachment to his son might make him less willing to relocate but if he doesn't get some immediate financial relief, he's soon going to be homeless.

Jamison felt like putting a note at the bottom of the profiles saying: *You got ten bad apples here, all of them slightly rotten. Good luck.*

But Jamison didn't care who the client picked. The only thing he cared about was spending a long weekend in New York with Gillian—and fortunately Steven agreed, if somewhat reluctantly, to let him have Friday and Monday off.

□　□　□

The weekend in New York with Gillian was everything Jamison had hoped it would be.

He met her at JFK. He flew in from Chicago and her plane from D.C. arrived an hour later. He had no idea what she'd been doing in D.C. and he didn't ask. Nor did he ask what excuse she'd given her husband for spending the weekend away from Redemption.

Even though it meant dipping into his savings, Jamison got them a suite at the Plaza, which cost about eight hundred bucks a night. The weather was perfect and they spent the first afternoon strolling through Central Park, returned to their room at four, made love, and showered. They had dinner at a decent but modestly priced Italian place in the theater district. (The next night, they would dine at Eleven Madison Park where dinner would cost Jamison almost as much as his monthly rent for his apartment in Redemption.) Following dinner, they saw *Hamilton*. The seats had cost Jamison five hundred bucks. They would have been more expensive but Jamison knew a guy who knew a guy. Gillian loved the show.

Gillian had never spent much time in New York and she wanted to do the things that most tourists did. They rode to the top of One World Trade Center where they were treated to a panoramic view of the city; they took the ferry to Staten Island because Gillian wanted to see the Statue of Liberty from the harbor; they had drinks in bars that were known to be watering holes for celebrities; they walked across the Brooklyn Bridge and strolled past the bronze Wall Street Bull on their way to

Battery Park, Jamison regaling her with stories of the unindicted crooks he used to work with.

Their last night in New York, as they were finishing dinner in a place that Jamison claimed made the best paella outside of Madrid, Gillian grew pensive. The sadness was back in her eyes. Seeing she was troubled, he asked her what was wrong. She said, "I don't want to go back to Redemption."

"Neither do I," Jamison said.

"Yes, but you can leave any time you want. I can't."

"Why not," he said. "What's keeping you there? Your husband?"

"Hardly," she said.

"So divorce him, quit Drexler, and go someplace else."

"I can't do that."

"Why not?" he asked again.

"I can't tell you why not."

"You're not making any sense. Are you saying you're afraid to leave your husband? Is Steven one of those assholes who will try to harm you if you do?"

"It has nothing to do with my husband."

"Come on, Gillian, then what's the problem? Your husband can't stop you from divorcing him and Drexler can't stop you from quitting. You're not an indentured servant. If you're miserable, and I know you are, why not pick up and start over? You're only thirty-two years old. You don't have kids. Leave if you want to leave. Hell, I might even leave with you."

"Would you really leave with me?"

"In a heartbeat," Jamison said.

Jamison had answered her question without thinking—in a heartbeat—but he knew, in that instant, that he was being sincere. He didn't want to spend the rest of his life working for Claud Drexler or living in sleepy Redemption, but he knew he wanted to be with her. If she wanted him to go with her, he would.

"My only problem," he said, "would be finding a job where a felony record wouldn't matter. But I know I could find something. The rub is that I don't have enough money saved up to spend a lot of time job hunting. But if you want to go, and want me to go with you, I'll do it."

Gillian studied his face for a moment, then took his hand and said, "Let's go back to the hotel. I want to make love to you, and I don't want to talk about this anymore. Maybe sometime in the future, but not now."

Gillian had succeeded.

Jamison Maddox was head-over-heels in love with her.

14

They weren't traveling back to Redemption together. Gillian had an eleven a.m. flight to Chicago out of LaGuardia. Jamison was flying out of JFK and wasn't leaving until four in the afternoon. They had breakfast together, Gillian mostly silent, which Jamison attributed to her reluctance to return home. Before she got into the cab taking her to the airport, Jamison said, "Don't worry. We'll figure something out. You can't spend the rest of your life being miserable." He kissed her lightly on the lips then stood on the curb watching the cab depart—and decided at that moment to do something that he'd been thinking about for some time, the decision now driven by what Gillian had said last night.

He went back to his room, packed, and checked out of the hotel, arranging with the front desk clerk to leave his luggage at the hotel until two, at which time he'd return to catch a cab to the airport.

He knew when he got back to Redemption, ol' Mary White would most likely ask him what he'd done and who he'd visited with in New York. She would ask in a casual way, as if she was just curious, and Jamison would mostly tell her the truth. He wouldn't say he'd spent the weekend with Gillian, but that he had spent it with a woman he knew. Regarding what he was planning to do next, he'd also be honest, saying that on his last day in the city he decided to visit the only family he had, namely his mother, his uncle Jed, and his cousin, Naomi. He doubted his mother would see him, which was fine. He didn't really want to see her. As for his uncle, he was looking forward to seeing him but the person he really wanted to see was his cousin.

Before attempting to flag down a cab, he checked to see if his flight was still on schedule, and when he did, the little message popped up on his iPhone screen asking if it was okay for Google to use his location. It occurred to him just then—and he wondered why it hadn't occurred to him before—that if Mary White wanted to know where he'd been, all she'd have to do was check his company-owned iPhone. Yes, thanks to fucking Google, she'd be able to track his movements if she wanted to, but that was okay. There was no reason to hide the fact that he'd visited relatives.

While still standing on the street in front of the hotel, he called his mother. It was just after nine and he suspected she'd still be in bed or, if not, had just arisen. She was not a morning person, and when she answered the phone, Jamison got the exact response he'd expected.

"My God, Jamison, what are you doing calling at such a god-awful hour. I haven't even had a cup of coffee yet."

Jamison lied, saying: "I figured you would have been up for hours by now."

"So what is it?" his mother said.

"I'm here in New York and my flight back to Chicago doesn't leave until four. I thought as long as I was in town, I'd pop in and see how you were doing. You know, maybe we can go out for brunch or something."

"Well, you should have given me some advance notice. Today's impossible. I've appointments from ten thirty on."

"Well, okay," Jamison said. "Maybe I'll see you next time I'm in town."

"Yes, that would be, uh, good," his mother said. "Now I have to go. I need to get my makeup on."

Jamison wondered if one of these days his mother would have some sort of epiphany. Maybe lying on her deathbed she'd conclude that she'd made a horrible mistake by remaining so distant from her only child and she'd regret not having spent more time with him.

Nah, that would never happen.

The call to his mother out of the way, a call he'd made only so his cell phone records would show that he'd called her, he flagged down a cab and proceeded to his uncle Jed's apartment. He didn't bother to call his uncle first because he had no doubt that he'd be home. Uncle Jed was a creature of habit. He was officially retired now but he spent every weekday morning until lunchtime checking on his investments, poring over the financial news, making calls to friends, politicians, and lawyers on business-related issues. After lunch, he would play.

Jed Maddox was an avid golfer. He played poker with a number of people as rich as he was, the irony being that he and his poker buddies played for peanuts; the big winner in his uncle's weekly poker game might take home a hundred bucks or, at worst, might lose a hundred bucks. He owned a forty-foot sailboat he moored on Long Island; because he knew he was a lousy sailor and a danger to others, he usually had a more competent man go with him to pilot the boat. Evenings he would meet friends for drinks, eat in the best restaurants in the city, go to comedy clubs and jazz clubs and plays. He had several girlfriends, mostly women his own age; he liked all of them but had no desire to marry any of them. His first wife had died when he was fifty—he was sixty now—and he'd told Jamison that he had no desire to wed again.

Jed had been his father's younger brother and also his business partner in the hedge fund they'd founded. Together they'd amassed the fortune that Jamison's mother was now spending. Jamison had no idea how he would have survived childhood had it not been for his uncle Jed.

The doorman at his uncle's building had been there for as long as Jamison could remember, which meant he'd been there for at least twenty years. He smiled broadly when he saw Jamison and said, "I'll let your uncle know you're on your way up. He'll be delighted to see you."

Jamison took the elevator to the seventeenth floor. There were only two apartments on the floor, his uncle's and one belonging to a reclusive writer. The writer had only written three novels but had made a staggering amount of money off them, then stopped writing altogether and rarely left his apartment. His uncle had told Jamison the writer was crazier than a bedbug but a nice guy, nonetheless.

His uncle flung the door open before Jamison had a chance to ring the bell and enveloped him in a hug. His uncle looked just like his father—or the way his father would have looked if he'd lived to sixty. He was tall, taller than Jamison, about six foot four. He was thin thanks to good genes, not his diet. His hair was gray and thinning; his eyes, like Jamison's, were bright blue. And like Jamison and Jamison's father, when he smiled, which was often, dimples appeared in both cheeks.

When Jamison had been arrested, the hardest thing he'd had to do was tell his uncle. His uncle could tell how ashamed he was and didn't spend any time telling him how foolish he'd been. Unlike his mother, Jed had asked if there was anything he could do. His uncle's lawyer, one of the best (and most expensive) in Manhattan, had represented him. His uncle had offered to help pay his legal fees but Jamison refused. He would have accepted help from his mother but was too ashamed to do so from his uncle.

Jed held him at arm's length and said, "You look good. In fact, you look great." He cocked his head to the side and said, "Have you got a new girlfriend?"

Jamison said that he indeed had a new girlfriend and had just spent three days in the city with her. He saw no reason to tell Jed that his girlfriend was not only married but married to his boss.

Jed's apartment had a multimillion-dollar view of Central Park and the city's lights at night, but after living in the place for so long, his uncle had become oblivious to it. He took Jamison into the kitchen, a kitchen suitable for a master chef. His uncle liked to cook but when he hosted dinners or parties, he would bring in students from New York's Institute of Culinary Education—one of the finest culinary schools in the world—and pay them an outrageous amount to cook for his friends.

His uncle set out a plate of pastries and poured them cups of coffee and they sat there and chatted. Jamison intentionally steered the conversation toward his uncle's many activities. He learned that Jed had a new golf coach, an LPGA tour winner who was not only a fantastic teacher but fantastic to look at, too. Also, that he'd be taking part in a sailboat race next month, Jamison commenting that he just hoped Jed didn't run the boat aground. (He'd done that before.) Eventually, however, just as Jamison had anticipated, Jed asked him how he liked his job—and Jamison lied.

"I'm happy," he said. "I never thought I'd like living in a small town, but it's grown on me. As for the job, it's low stress."

"Yeah, but what do you do exactly?"

Now it was time to come up with an answer that would pass Mary White's next polygraph test. He said, "Mostly I just produce standard financial profiles of companies that clients use to make buy or sell decisions on. Pretty boring stuff."

"Well, like I've told you before, if you want to get back into the game here in the city, I'm sure I can help you find a way."

Jed *had* told him this before. Jed was sure that with his connections he could get his nephew back into a Wall Street firm in *some* capacity, although not in a role that was as prestigious or as lucrative as his former Goldman job. Jamison doubted, however, that even Jed's influence would be sufficient; it had been only a year since he'd been on the front page of the *Wall Street Journal* dressed in orange coveralls, his hands cuffed behind his back. And as he'd told Gillian, he'd been so humiliated by what had happened that he'd just wanted to get out of New York, maybe not forever, but for a while.

"Thanks, Uncle Jed, but I'm good for now. Plus, I like this lady I'm dating and she lives in Redemption."

After forty minutes, Jamison said he had to get going because he wanted to drop in on Naomi before he had to leave for the airport.

"She'll be so happy to see you," his uncle said.

□ □ □

Naomi.

Jed's daughter, Naomi, was five years older than Jamison, but Jamison thought of her as a younger sister, not an older cousin. She was autistic and had difficulty with social interactions. She wouldn't look most people in the eye—Jamison was an exception—and *hated* to be touched, Jamison again being an exception. She had an IQ that went off the charts and was able to read by the time she was three. She got an almost perfect score on the SATs, which she took just for fun, but she didn't have a high school or a college degree. Jed had enrolled her in several different schools as she'd been growing up, but the stress of attending a formal school had been too much for Naomi. Naomi's late mother had homeschooled her some, but Naomi had learned mostly on her own.

Naomi had an apartment in Tribeca. She didn't like to interact with people, but she did like to watch them—and Naomi said you couldn't beat Tribeca for people watching. She also had a job—she was very proud that she was able to support herself—and the job was one she could do without leaving her apartment. She worked for a polling company. Some polling companies, like FiveThirtyEight, are managed by statisticians such as Nate Silver, but many others are run by political types who develop the questions but can't begin to comprehend the mathematics of statistics. Naomi understood the math.

Jamison rang the bell outside of Naomi's apartment building. She answered through the intercom, saying: "Who is it?"

"It's Jamison."

"Okay, I'll let you in," she said in a neutral-sounding voice. You had to know Naomi as well as Jamison did to know that she was excited and delighted that he was visiting.

He knocked on her apartment door and when she opened it, she said, "Hello, Jamison," her face expressionless. Jamison wasn't fooled. He knew that *Hello, Jamison* was Naomi shrieking: *Oh, my God, I'm so glad to see you!*

He hugged her—Naomi responding by standing there stiffly, her arms down at her sides—but the fact that she allowed him to touch her at all was an indicator of how much he meant to her.

He stepped back and looked at her and said, "You look great."

"Thank you," Naomi said.

Naomi took after her mother, not her father. She was short, no more than five foot one, had dark hair and dark eyes, an upturned nose, rosebud lips, and a flawless, pale complexion—pale because Naomi never went outdoors without a hat and an application of sunscreen, having read about the relationship between skin cancer and the sun. Her hair was cut in a short pageboy. It was a practical and unremarkable hairstyle except for the fact that the person who cut her hair was his uncle Jed because Naomi didn't want a stranger touching her. Jed had become an accomplished stylist but Jamison always wondered if Naomi would ever have her hair cut again after her father died. He could imagine her as a dark-haired Rapunzel, her untamed locks hanging to the floor. Jamison also thought that his cousin would be considered a pretty woman if her face ever showed the least bit of animation, which it never did.

Naomi said, "Would you like a cup of coffee?"

"No, I just came from seeing your dad and I'm coffeed out."

Seeing Naomi didn't know what to say next, Jamison said, "Can we sit and talk for a moment."

Naomi's apartment was a small, one-bedroom unit, the kitchen and the living room all in the same space. There was a kitchen table that would seat two but there was only one chair. On the table were stacks of paper and a laptop; the table was Naomi's office. The furniture in the living room consisted of a brown corduroy couch, a matching armchair, a coffee table, two mismatched end tables, and a couple of lamps. The furniture was spotless, not a stain or a mote of dust, but inexpensive and possibly even secondhand. There was no television or audio system in the apartment; Naomi's computer served as her entertainment center.

Jed would have been happy to buy his daughter any apartment in Manhattan and furnish it like a palace, but Naomi insisted on living in a place she could afford on her salary. What she didn't know was that Jed had cut a deal with the building's owner to charge Naomi the rent he charged, while Jed paid the remainder himself. When Jed died, Naomi was going to be a multimillionaire and Jamison was certain that Jed had some plan for managing her money and watching over her when he passed. Jamison also imagined that he'd be part of the plan.

They took seats in the living room, Jamison on the couch, Naomi sitting on the armchair on the edge of the seat, her feet planted firmly on the floor, her heels touching.

Jamison knew it would be pointless to attempt to make small talk with Naomi, so he came straight to the point. He said, "Naomi, I would like you to do something for me."

The reason Jamison had come to see Naomi was that a few years ago she became interested in genealogy—although with her OCD personality, the word *interested* meant *obsessed*. She produced a chart that took up an entire wall, tracing the Maddox family's lineage back to, as best Jamison could tell, the Dark Ages. Naomi had been disappointed to learn that her ancestors didn't include a single person of historical note. There was no king or queen or famous scholar, politician, or artist. It appeared as if the twenty-first-century Maddoxes had descended from the commonest of folk: foot soldiers, farmers, laborers, and a couple of small-time thieves. But Naomi spent a couple of months on the project, working on it practically nonstop. She did most of her research online but when she needed to, she corresponded fearlessly with historians and visited libraries and did whatever else people do to learn where they came from. She wouldn't let anything stop her.

"What do you want?" Naomi asked, meaning *I'll do anything for you.*

"I want you to find out everything you can about some people I work with in Illinois."

Jamison had been curious about the people on the third floor of Drexler Limited for some time, but after last night, after Gillian said it was impossible for her to quit, he really wanted to know more about them. What was there about Drexler Limited, or the people who worked there, that would make her think she couldn't ever leave?

Jamison took out a piece of paper torn from a notepad in his hotel room and handed it to Naomi. On the paper were the names of all the people he knew who worked on the third floor.

"I'll get started on it right away," Naomi said.

"No, you don't need to do that. Just work on it when you have time. It's not urgent."

"I'll get started on it right away," Naomi said. "I'll email you what I find. But I need your email address."

"No, you can't email it to me."

"Why not?"

"You just can't." He couldn't tell Naomi that his computer was periodically scanned by his employer. "I want you to mail me a paper copy of whatever you learn. Okay? Just stick the results in an envelope and mail them to me. I put my address at the bottom of the list."

As best Jamison could tell, no one had ever tampered with his mail.

"Okay," Naomi said.

"Now, would you like to go get some lunch?"

"No, I'm not hungry and it's too early for lunch."

15

Gillian was the last person to arrive for the meeting; she was two minutes late, which earned her an annoyed look from Claud. Seated around the table in the conference room outside Claud's office were Claud; Mary White; Mary's three children, Sam, Matt, and Judy; Sam's wife, Sarah; Steven Lang; and Ed Pine, the husband of Redemption's mayor. Steven Lang, Gillian Lang, and Ed Pine were involved with the project to compromise Congressman John Corcoran. Sarah White, Sam's wife, was spearheading the cannery project, the one Jamison had worked on. Gillian didn't know why Mary's children were there, but if they were, it meant that there was probably a security issue of some kind.

Claud said, "We have a problem. As some of you know, we've been working for some time on a project involving a number of canneries. As is always the case, the exact nature of the project has been limited to only those who have a need to know—which in this case is Steven and Sarah—but in general the client's objective was to gain access to one of these canneries by convincing an employee to assist us. Sarah, tell them what happened."

Sarah White—a cheerful, energetic, small blonde woman—was heavily involved at the school her two boys attended. She was vice president of the PTA, a volunteer teacher's aide, and chairman of the committee raising funds to install lights and build a new set of bleachers for a baseball/soccer field. The other moms with grade school children in Redemption liked her enormously and thought they knew her well. Had they known about the cannery project they would have realized that they didn't know Sarah White at all.

Sarah said, "For this project, we had to bring in a consultant—and the consultant screwed up. Big time."

Gillian wasn't directly involved in the cannery project. What she did know, however, was that if a consultant had been brought in for the project, and if it was ultimately successful, then the law enforcement reaction was going to be substantial.

During the sixty years the family had resided in Redemption, there had been a number of close brushes with the law but due to luck and skill, none of its members had ever been arrested. The jobs they did were often risky; risk couldn't be avoided. There was, however, a rule: if a job was likely to involve a large law enforcement response, particularly a federal response, they used outside operatives whenever possible to minimize the likelihood of the family being exposed.

For example, and in spite of the precautions they took, Judy and her brother Matt took a risk in killing the engineer Don Steward in Richmond. Murder is always risky. They didn't leave evidence behind and they made sure they weren't caught on a security camera in a way that they could be identified. But you can never tell when simple bad luck or bad timing can cause a job to go wrong. Some armed citizen—and God knows there were enough of them in Virginia—could have intervened during the carjacking and they could have been shot or arrested. Or a cop might have driven by at precisely the wrong moment, saw them execute

Steward, and given chase. No matter how many precautions are taken, no matter how well a job is planned, there is nothing that can be done to avoid simple bad luck. But when it came to killing Don Steward, one thing was certain: the only law enforcement organization that would be involved was the Richmond Police Department—which has fewer than a thousand cops to serve and protect a population of more than two hundred thousand.

But assisting white supremacists to blow up the McNamara Federal Building in Detroit was a whole different story. Had the terrorists been successful there would have been an overwhelming federal response. Not only would hundreds of agents from the FBI, the ATF, and Homeland Security have been engaged, all the power and technology available to the federal government would have come into play. The NSA would have monitored phone calls; satellites would have been repositioned; the footage from every camera in the area would have been examined; the entire city would have been locked down to prevent the terrorists from escaping. Gillian had no doubt that had the terrorists succeeded in blowing up the building and killing hundreds of people, they would have been caught eventually, just as the Boston Marathon bombers and Timothy McVeigh had been caught. And the terrorists being caught was acceptable to the client. But Drexler Limited's only involvement in the failed plot had been to identify a person who could provide detonators, and no member of the firm went near that person or the terrorists. Apparently, the cannery project was similar.

Sarah continued. "As Claud said, the consultant's job was to find the employee we needed and convince him to help us. The family's primary role was providing the names of likely employees, funding, and some logistical support. The consultant settled on one man, became friends with him, and spent a lot of time working on him. The guy was not only in debt but extremely bitter about almost everything. He didn't get a promotion he thought he deserved. He was a vet who thought the country had abandoned him. He had some PTSD issues and was also an alcoholic, which we thought would make him more malleable. In other words, the consultant thought this guy was perfect—and it turned out he was wrong.

"Last night, the consultant finally got around to telling the cannery worker exactly what we wanted him to do and the man went berserk. I mean, *literally* berserk. He attacked the consultant, and the consultant was forced to kill him, but the consultant was badly injured. He was stabbed. He was able to drive himself to a hospital; if he hadn't done so, he would have bled to death. Last night, after they stabilized him, he borrowed a phone from a nurse and called me."

"Oh, Jesus," Mary said.

"Yeah, not good," Sarah said. "Anyway, he told me what happened. He also said they were going to have to remove a kidney that was damaged when he was stabbed. So right now, the consultant is in a hospital awaiting surgery. As far as I know, the police haven't linked him yet to the dead cannery worker. But I have no idea if this man left evidence behind that can connect him to the murder or if anyone saw him leaving the man's house after he was injured. The murder wasn't planned. We can assume that he won't talk to the police, but we have no idea what he might say if he's sedated or what he might do if the police arrest him."

Claud said, "I spoke to the client's man this morning. He has decided, and I concur, that the consultant has to go."

Turning to Judy, Claud said, "I want you and your brothers to deal with this immediately. The cannery worker lived alone and it's Sunday so his absence from work hasn't been noticed. But before his body is discovered, you need to take care of the consultant. If he was in a state to travel things would be different, but in his current condition, he has to be eliminated. Do you understand?"

"Yeah, sure," Judy said. "Where's he at?"

"Kansas City. Saint Luke's Hospital," Sarah said. "I'll give you the details on him after this meeting."

"Is there any way this consultant can be linked to the client?" Mary asked.

"Only if he talks," Sarah said.

"But can he be linked to us?" Mary asked.

"I don't think so," Sarah said. "I'm the only one who dealt with him directly, but we never met in person and we communicated with burner phones and encrypted emails."

Claud said, "All right. Judy, you and your brothers go with Sarah and get whatever information you need. The rest of you remain here."

Mary's kids and Sarah left the conference room, Mary's children making Gillian think of a pack of hunting dogs about to be taken off the leash. They all looked eager, particularly Judy, whose thin lips were curved upward in a small smile.

Claud said, "Gillian, I want you monitoring the police response to the cannery worker's murder in Kansas City. We need to know when they find the body and any leads they might be pursuing. Get together with Sarah right after she briefs Mary's children. As for the rest of you, I want to know where the other projects stand and if you'll need any help from Mary's kids or Gillian. Ed, how are we progressing with Congressman Corcoran?"

"Good," Ed Pine said. "We put Heather into Cooper & Cooper as we'd planned. She's now supposedly representing a company involved in cyber security that is pushing for contracts on military bases. Cyber security is an area under the purview of Corcoran's congressional subcommittee that deals with military construction projects. She's had two meetings with Corcoran where she was one of several people present but she said she could tell that Corcoran was definitely interested in her, and she's a woman who would know. She'll be attending a fundraiser at the May-flower Hotel in a few days and Corcoran will also be there. She'll find a way to let Corcoran know she's staying the night at the hotel because she doesn't want to drive home afterward. We don't know if Corcoran will take the bait or not. We've told her not to push, to take her time reeling him in, but if he does decide to go back to her room, we'll be ready."

"So you don't need Judy or Gillian at this point?" Claud said.

"No," Ed Pine said, and Steven Lang nodded to indicate that he agreed.

"And the Virginia Beach company?"

"Everything's on track and, in fact, moving faster that I'd expected," Steven said. "Steward's widow has accepted the offer, we've overcome the objections from Steward's partners, and we've started to bring in the people we need. I'm planning to head down there tomorrow morning to check on things."

"And you don't need any help from Gillian or Mary's kids?" Claud said.

"Nope. Everything's under control."

◻ ◻ ◻

Gillian met briefly with Sarah, discussed how she would monitor police activity in Kansas City, then headed to her office.

She had no intention of doing anything to monitor the cops in Kansas City.

She was thinking that, with Mary and her lethal children completely occupied with killing the consultant in Kansas City, this was the perfect time to leave Redemption.

It was time to set herself free.

It was time for her and Jamison to run.

Jamison Maddox was in love with her and she was convinced that he'd do anything she wanted. But there were drawbacks to including him. He might eventually decide that going to the law was a better solution than running and she'd have to talk him out of this. The law wouldn't help her; the law would get her killed.

Were it not for one thing, she would have run on her own. She'd be safer on her own. She didn't need Jamison to protect her; she could protect herself far better than he could. She wanted companionship and he was a perfect companion—but companionship was a luxury she could forgo if need be. And she could always find another companion. But Jamison had access to the one thing she didn't have, and it was for this reason she needed him, and she doubted another person would come along any time soon who would both fall in love with her and be able to give her what she had to have.

16

Jamison let Gillian into his apartment, smiling, delighted to see her. He was holding a bottle of wine in his hand that he'd been about to open.

Oddly, she didn't return his smile or kiss him hello. She said, "We need to talk."

Oh, oh, Jamison thought. In the past, when a woman had said *we need to talk,* that usually meant the relationship was about to change or advance to some new level, like breaking up or moving in together or getting engaged—the last two not likely when it came to Gillian. He wondered if Steven had found out about their affair.

He held up the bottle in his hand and said, "Would you like a glass of wine while we talk."

"No."

They sat down at the kitchen table and she was silent for a long time, just looking into his eyes. She said, "I'm going to leave Redemption. I can't bear it here any longer. Do you still want to come with me?"

It had been three weeks since they'd taken the trip to New York where she'd first spoken about her desire to leave. He'd brought up the subject a couple of times since then, but she'd always said that she wasn't ready to talk about it—until now.

Jamison smiled. "Yes, without a doubt. I'll give notice tomorrow."

"No, Jamison, you won't give notice. You can't tell anyone we're leaving. And I mean no one." Before he could say anything, she said, "It's time for me to tell you the truth about myself. And it's time for you to know that leaving with me could get you killed."

"Killed?"

"Yes," she said. "I'm not exaggerating."

She took a deep breath, as if about to dive into an icy pond. "Drexler Limited is a criminal organization. I'm a criminal."

Jamison stammered, "What, what kind of criminal organization?"

"Drexler Limited works for a syndicate."

"A syndicate? Do you mean the mafia?"

"The word 'mafia' gives you the wrong impression. The syndicate isn't a bunch of Tony Soprano wannabes, hijacking trucks and extorting money from mom-and-pop grocery stores."

"Then what—"

"The syndicate is controlled by a few wealthy, powerful, connected men. At least I think they're all men and there are four of them. One lives in Chicago and he's Claud's main contact. Claud takes the train to Chicago a few times a month to see this man, but he'll sometimes use couriers, people on the third floor, to send information because he doesn't trust phones and email. Anyway, these men own successful, legitimate businesses and their businesses provide a plausible explanation for their wealth, which avoids complications when it comes to the IRS. Claud knows who the men are, but for security reasons, no one else in the company does and Claud is the only one who has any direct contact with them. Inside the company, the syndicate is only referred to as *the client* and it's involved in sophisticated crimes on a massive scale. Like I said, they're not hijacking trucks. They're involved in Medicaid and Medicare fraud, identity theft, insurance fraud, contract fraud, and the amounts of money they've stolen over the years is in the realm of hundreds of millions of dollars."

"Jesus," Jamison said, not able to wrap his head around what she was telling him. "But what's your role in all this?"

"The people at Drexler assist the syndicate in a number of ways. We help with money laundering and tax evasion. In case you didn't notice, one of the lawyers on the second floor is an expert on tax law. We obtain information the syndicate needs, such as information about large government programs, like Medicare and Social Security and military construction projects. One of the people you work with is an expert on government procurement programs. And you've been a part of these schemes even though you didn't know it. Like the company you researched in Virginia Beach. The syndicate wanted into it because it opened up doors related to a large government contract with HHS. *Legitimate* government contractors inflate their bills and pad their expenses. Can you even imagine what an illegitimate contractor might do, one who won't hesitate to break the law and has no intention of remaining in existence once he's stolen all he can? And there's something else you need to know when it comes to the Virginia Beach company. The people who killed Don Steward weren't a couple of carjackers as the newspapers said. He was killed by two of Mary White's children."

"Her children!" Jamison said. "Are you shitting me?"

Gillian ignored his outburst. "When you first joined the company, you did research on some companies in Michigan. That had to do with gaining access to a state construction contract."

Jamison said, "What about that guy Crane, the one involved with those white supremacists?"

"Steven actually told you the truth when it came to him. After the client got your report, he decided he wanted nothing to do with Crane's company and the syndicate had no involvement whatsoever with the terrorists. Why would it? There's no money in terrorism."

"Actually, there's a *lot* of money in terrorism," Jamison said. "Not for the terrorists necessarily but for all the people who make money trying to stop the next terrorist attack, like companies in the security industry. The U.S. government spent *billions* to increase security after 9/11."

"That may be, but as far as I know—and unless Steven lied to me—Crane's association with the terrorists was just a bizarre coincidence. The terrorists used him to provide detonators because they found out, like you did, that he needed money. But right now, and using some of the information you provided, the syndicate has taken over one of the construction companies that will be involved in an upcoming Michigan transportation project, which they can milk for millions."

Jamison said, "You talk like this syndicate is, hell, I don't know, like SPECTRE in a damn Bond movie."

"This isn't a movie, Jamison. This is real. This is my life. And the syndicate isn't a group of cartoonish super villains seeking world domination. It's just a few very smart people who are very good at committing fraud."

"You didn't answer my question, Gillian. What's your role in all this?"

"I lied to you when I told you I had a liberal arts degree. And I swear I'll never lie to you again. I actually have a degree in computer science, and I hack into corporate and government databases when the syndicate needs information. I've hacked into the computers of politicians to find things to use to control those politicians. Like one of Claud's current projects, that you also worked on, involves a congressman who sits on the House Appropriations Committee. The plan is to blackmail this congressman and force him to steer certain green energy projects toward syndicate-controlled companies."

"Is everyone at Drexler involved in this stuff?" Jamison asked.

"Yes. But the people on the second floor are people like you, people who are experts in certain areas and who can assist us, but are never given the complete picture as to *why* they're assisting us. Your friend Ralph, for example, researched a cyber security system used by some states for Medicaid allocations but he didn't know how the research was going to be used. It was ultimately used to assist the syndicate in a Medicaid fraud scheme that netted approximately fourteen million dollars. And most of the time, when people on the second floor are asked to research something, they'll be told to research a lot of extraneous things that have nothing to do with the job in order to hide the one piece of information that the client really wants."

"What about the research I did on those guys working in canneries?"

Gillian said, "I don't know anything about that job. I haven't been involved in it at all. But I think it might be related to SNAP."

"Snap?"

"The Supplemental Nutrition Assistance Program, what they used to call food stamps. Vendors, like farmers, and for all I know canneries, provide food for the program and I'm assuming the client has some scheme to make money off of that. But I don't really know. I do know there's a lot of fraud associated with food stamps."

"But how exactly is the fraud committed? How does the syndicate work?"

"In a lot of different ways. It depends on the program and the circumstances. Like Medicare fraud. Medicare fraud often involves nursing homes, so the syndicate will get control of a nursing home and a crooked doctor, and the doctor submits bills for patients that don't exist and for treatments that were never given. When it comes to insurance fraud, there was a ring in Cincinnati that the syndicate put together. Five or six guys would buy old cars and intentionally get rear-ended in accidents, and the drivers and the passengers in the cars would sue and submit medical claims for nonexistent back and whiplash injuries. In Cincinnati, they racked up two million in false claims before the group moved on."

"What I'm trying to find out is if I've done anything illegal," Jamison said. "I'm already a convicted felon. The last thing I need is to be associated with something criminal."

"No, you haven't done anything illegal, although I suppose a zealous prosecutor could make the case that, wittingly or not, you've been an accomplice."

"Jesus Christ," Jamison said, and got up from the chair where he'd been sitting and began to pace his small kitchen. His hands were pressed to the sides of his head as if he were trying to prevent it from exploding.

"Calm down. You can walk away any time you want. No one is going to try to stop you or kill you. I mean, if they knew what I just told you, they'd try to kill you, but no one is ever going to know that we had this discussion. So go to the office tomorrow and tell them you're quitting and going back to New York. You can do that. But I can't. If I leave—if I run—they'll try to track me down and if they find me, they'll kill me because they can't take the risk of me talking."

Gillian sighed. "So now you know the truth," she said. "I'm going to run because I can't keep doing what I'm doing. I can't stay married any longer to Steven and I don't want to end up in jail, which might eventually happen. I want to be free. I want to be free of my husband and Claud Drexler and my life in Redemption. I want to start over. But you don't have to leave with me. I'll find a way to survive on my own."

"I want to leave with you. I don't want to lose you and I want to help you."

She said, "Jamison, that's your heart talking, not your head. And I don't think you've really grasped what leaving with me means. Not only will you be in danger, you'll have to change your identity. You'll not be able to have any contact with people you know, like your uncle Jed in New York. Because what you don't realize is that the syndicate has connections in law enforcement and the government, and they'll have the ability to track us if we leave any sort of trail. If you call your relatives, if we use a credit card in our real names, if we fill out the paperwork to take out a loan to buy a house, they'll find us. To survive, Jamison Maddox and Gillian Lang have to disappear as if they never existed. You need to decide if you're really ready for that."

Jamison started to speak but she said, "Wait. There's something else you need to think about."

It was time to plant the seed.

"You need to understand that if you go with me, we're going to be poor, at least for some time to come. I don't have any money, just a few thousand dollars I've managed to hide from my husband. You have only about a hundred and fifty thousand in your bank account. I know because I've looked. I can move the money you have in a way that it won't be traced but how long can two people who can't provide résumés or references or college transcripts survive on a hundred and fifty thousand? We're going to have to get jobs and they probably won't pay very well." She gestured at Jamison's small kitchen with its outdated appliances. "This apartment you're living in right now? It isn't anything special but it's likely to be better than any place we'll live in the near future. You've never been poor, Jamison. You need to decide if you can stand being poor."

She stood up. "I'm leaving now. I don't want you to make a decision without taking a few days to really think about it."

She had no intention of giving him a few days.

"But I'm telling you that as much as I love you, and as much as you love me, the best thing you can do for yourself is to let me leave without you."

With that she headed for the door.

He said, "Damnit, wait a minute."

"No. You need to think about what I've told you."

And with that she was out the door, leaving Jamison looking poleaxed.

17

His father having been an alcoholic, Jamison rarely drank hard liquor, but this occasion called for something stronger than wine or beer. He splashed an ounce of bourbon into a glass, drank it in one swallow, poured a second drink, this time adding ice, and sat back down at the kitchen table.

He finally understood the walking mystery that was Gillian Lang and why she'd always been so secretive and evasive about her life. He also now understood why the people at Drexler Limited weren't allowed to discuss their work, why employees' computers were scanned, and why they were given polygraph tests. All those things made sense if the people on the third floor were engaged in criminal activities and wanted to ensure that their crimes would never be disclosed.

He also now fully comprehended why Gillian wanted to leave Redemption. It wasn't just because she was tired of living in a small, decaying town and married to a man she didn't love. She was a fundamentally decent person and no longer wanted to be part of a criminal enterprise. She also feared, and rightfully so, that if she stayed she might be arrested one day and spend the best years of her life in prison.

Jamison had been terrified of going to prison and he imagined that Gillian was too.

What he didn't know was if this syndicate she'd talked about was really as powerful and dangerous as she seemed to think it was. Did these four men, whoever they were, actually have the ability and the connections to track them if they fled Redemption and would they really try to kill them to preserve their secrets? He had no way of knowing, but it was obvious that Gillian believed what she was saying and considered them to be formidable.

Then there were Mary White's children. He was certain Gillian hadn't been lying about them having killed Don Steward. Why would she lie about that? But the idea of Mary's kids being killers was mind-boggling. He'd met them at the company's Fourth of July picnic. He didn't know what they did in the company as he'd never had any work-related contact with them, but they'd seemed like ordinary people—not hit men—and there wasn't anything the least bit sinister about them. Mary's sons were married and had grade-school-aged kids and he remembered Sam tossing a Frisbee to his boys. And Mary's daughter. He'd gotten a kick out of her. At the picnic, she'd been Jamison's partner in a badminton game against her two brothers and he remembered her calling them a couple of "lame-ass pussies" when they lost the game. She was a bit crude—she swore a lot—and was incredibly competitive, but a lot of fun and he'd enjoyed playing with her. He couldn't imagine her killing anyone.

But whatever the future held, he really didn't have to think hard at all about going with Gillian, even knowing the truth about her and what leaving with her meant. In fact, if anything, he wanted to go with her more than ever because he wanted to protect her. It occurred to him that he'd spent his entire life helping only one person—himself—but for Gillian he was willing to make whatever sacrifices were required.

◻ ◻ ◻

The one question he hadn't asked Gillian was *why* she had become part of a criminal organization. He hadn't asked the question because he thought he already knew the answer—thanks to Naomi.

That day when he got home from work, just before Gillian had arrived, he found an envelope in his mailbox. It was from his cousin.

He was surprised that it had taken so long for Naomi to get back to him. He knew she hadn't forgotten about his request to research the people on the third floor because Naomi never forgot anything. But when he didn't hear from her for three weeks, he'd figured that the reason for the delay was that she'd gone overboard in her research as she had a tendency to do, just as she'd done when she became interested in the history of the Maddox family. All Jamison had wanted was a little background information on the people he worked with. He could have done the research himself, but he obviously couldn't do it on the company's computers, nor could he do it on his own laptop, which was periodically scanned. So he'd figured that if Naomi had done three weeks of research she would have sent him *boxes* of information—not a business envelope that held only a few sheets of paper.

The envelope contained a one-page letter, what looked like a genealogy chart, and brief bios on the people he worked with. The bios gave only basic information such as birth dates and marital status and addresses and schooling. The sort of information that could be found online and in public records, but there was nothing in the bios that pointed to the people at Drexler Limited being criminals. None of them had a criminal record.

He noticed when he'd read Gillian's bio that it said she got a degree from Northwestern and not from one of the Seven Sisters as she'd said, but he'd thought that either Naomi had made a mistake or maybe Gillian had done her undergraduate work at Northwestern and then had finished at some other university.

But it was Naomi's letter that was most shocking.

It began with: *Jamison, I'm sorry it took me so long to get back to you, but I kept going until I reached a dead end.*

Jamison hadn't initially known what that meant.

She wrote: *The thing that I learned is that all the people whose names you gave me are related!*

Naomi was overly fond of exclamation marks and she was more animated when she wrote than when she communicated verbally.

In 1961, five young, married couples settled in Redemption, Illinois. The couples were: Claud and Vivian Drexler, John and Cynthia Lang, Robert and Joan Connor, Douglas and Sheila White, and Aaron and Gloria Pine. They arrived within a few months of each other; they didn't arrive at the same time and they didn't live together in some sort of commune. And I didn't find anything to indicate that these couples knew each other before they settled in Redemption.

Anyway, four of the five couples had children and their children all married children born to the five couples named above. It didn't surprise me that the children of people living in a small town would mostly marry people who lived there. What did surprise me was that they were all relative newcomers to Redemption and their children didn't marry anyone who had been settled in the area for a long time and that none of them, not a single one, married anyone who lived outside of Redemption. What are the odds of that happening?

Then it got really strange! The children of the second generation produced a third generation—and the third generation again married people related to the five original couples! See the attached chart.

Of the first generation, the only one alive today is Claud Drexler, who is eighty-one. All the others are now dead. Most of them died of natural causes— heart disease, cancer, etc.— and most of them lived into their seventies. Two, however, committed suicide, Claud Drexler's wife, Vivian, and Aaron Pine, who's the father of second generationers Mary (Pine) White and David Pine.

Jamison had never spoken to David Pine, other than to say hello to him when he entered the Drexler building. David Pine was the security guard on the first floor, but the significant thing about him was that he was Gillian's father, which Jamison hadn't known until he'd seen the chart. He looked nothing like Gillian—he was a hulking, dark-haired, brown-eyed man whereas Gillian was blonde, blue-eyed, and lithe—and she'd never even *hinted* that David was her dad. Although she'd never said so specifically, she'd given Jamison the impression that both of her parents were dead.

Looking at the genealogy chart, Jamison saw that the second genera-tion originally consisted of ten people but only three were alive today. Two had died in their late teens, one in a drowning accident, the other due to a drug overdose. Two had died in a car accident together after they were married and when they were in their forties. Two others died of cancer while they were fairly young, one of those being Mary White's husband, Mike. And one, Fred Connor, had been struck by a train. The living members of the second generation, now all in their late fifties or early sixties, consisted of Mary White, her brother David Pine, and Fred Connor's widow, Alice, who Jamison had met. He met Alice when he'd attended her son's funeral, some poor kid named Dennis who was hit by a car near his high school.

The third generation consisted of nine people: Gillian and Steven Lang; Mary White's children, Matt, Sam, and Judy; Sam and Matt's wives, Sarah and Connie; and Ed and Agnes Pine. Agnes was not only the mayor of Redemption, she was also Steven Lang's sister. Agnes's husband, Ed Pine, worked on the third floor but Jamison had never had any contact with him at work. Connie White, Matt White's wife, was Steven Lang's other sister and Sam's wife, Sarah, was the much older sister of Dennis Connor, the kid hit by the car. Jamison had met Sam's and Matt's wives at social events but didn't know anything about what they did at the firm or if they even worked at the firm.

The fourth generation at this point consisted of a girl named Carol Pine, the teenage daughter of Ed and Agnes Pine; Sam White's two boys, Bobby and Randy; and Matt White's daughter, Carly, who Mary White always talked about when Jamison was polygraphed.

It occurred to Jamison that the five first-generation couples hadn't exactly populated the earth in a grand fashion. A genealogy chart is usually like a pyramid: small at the top and larger at the base, but because so many people had died over the years, some dying when they were very young, today the family consisted of only seventeen people, of which thirteen were adults.

He went back to Naomi's letter.

She wrote: *Now the fact that these people are all related is somewhat shocking but I suppose if you looked at other close-knit groups, like maybe a tribe of nomads or people in some odd religious sect, like the Mennonites or the Amish, you'd find the same thing.*

But here's the big news and the reason it took me so long to get back to you. For all the people in the second, third, and fourth generations I could find the usual data that's available in public records if you know how to dig: birth and death records, where they went to school, when they were married, who they married, previous addresses, etcetera. All that information is contained in their bios. But for the first generation I couldn't find anything prior to 1961.

Now that's really weird, Jamison, and I dug like crazy—that's what took me so long—but I couldn't find any record of these people before they arrived in Redemption. No former homes, no criminal records, no military service, no information on their parents. The only thing I was able to conclude is that these people changed their names before arriving in Redemption. That's the only thing that makes sense. I could understand if maybe one, or even two couples had changed their names, but five? Who these five couples really are and why they all settled in Redemption is a mystery I wasn't able to solve.

Jamison hadn't asked Gillian about her family's history because, for one thing, she hadn't given him a chance to ask. But the other reason was that he'd read Naomi's letter just before she'd arrived at his apartment and he hadn't fully digested it and had wanted to think about it before discussing it with her.

Naomi's research, however, did explain one thing: it explained *why* Gillian had gone to work for a criminal enterprise. Naomi had compared the family to a tribe, and it was a tribe, a tribe that committed crimes. And Gillian, born and raised in the tribe, had had no choice but to take an active role in the tribe's activities.

Something else occurred to him just then. Gillian had said that she didn't have any money and his initial thought had been that her husband most likely controlled all the money they earned. But now he could imagine a different scenario. Maybe all the money the family made went into one big pot and Claud Drexler controlled the pot and doled out the money sparingly.

The family being a criminal enterprise also explained something that had puzzled him ever since he'd gone to work for Drexler Limited. He hadn't been able to understand how a company located in a small town, a company that didn't advertise and had no online presence, remained profitable. But now he did. The company survived off the large amounts of money generated by the syndicate's criminal activities.

But that raised another question. When he thought about the people who worked on the third floor of Drexler Limited, none of them appeared to be wealthy. He'd seen some of their homes, the cars they drove, the way they dressed. Everything about them struck him as middle class. Not even Claud Drexler, the man in charge, appeared to be wealthy. The suits he wore were a decade old. If the syndicate that Gillian had spoken of had made millions, wouldn't some of that have been passed down to their partners at Drexler Limited? Although maybe it had been. Maybe the money was socked away in a Swiss account and Claud had decided that an ostentatious display of wealth could shine a spotlight on his criminal activities.

It also occurred to him that maybe the reason Naomi had not been able to trace the first generation any further back than 1961 was *because* they were all criminals and that's why they'd changed their names. They'd all been running from the law.

Whatever the reason, he now understood why Gillian wanted to get away from these people, and regardless of the risk and the sacrifices he would have to make, he was going to help set her free.

18

Gillian was waiting outside the building when Jamison arrived for work the next day. She couldn't talk to him in his office because, unknown to Jamison, there was a bug in his office that recorded everything he said. She didn't care, however, if other people saw her talking to him outside. Not at this point.

Jamison saw her standing near the entrance, nodded to her as he normally would have, and started to go up the steps to enter the building. He had no idea that Mary White knew about their affair and when he was at work, he kept up the pretense that they were merely coworkers.

She said, "Jamison, come here. I need to talk to you."

He walked over to her and said, "I've thought about what you said last night and—"

"Jamison, something has happened and I'm leaving Redemption today. I wanted to give you some time to think, but—"

"What happened?" he asked.

Gillian had no intention of telling him her reason for leaving today was because Mary's kids—the ones who would be sent to find her—were occupied in Kansas City. She shook her head, feigning impatience. "It doesn't matter what happened. The only thing that's important is that if I'm ever going to have a chance at a different life, I need to run today. I wanted to give you a few days to think about—"

"I don't need a few days. I've made up my mind. I'm going with you."

"Jamison, your entire life is going to change if you go with me. Nothing will ever be the same. Are you absolutely sure?"

"Yes."

She took a breath, acting relieved. Well, actually she wasn't acting; she was relieved.

"Okay," she said. "Here's what you need to do. In an hour say you're sick and going home. Steven's not here, so tell Mary. One of the reasons I'm leaving today is that Steven left this morning to go to Washington and he won't be back for a couple of days."

Steven was actually going to Virginia Beach to see how things were proceeding with Don Steward's old company.

She took a folded piece of paper out of a pocket and slipped it into Jamison's hand. She said, "On that paper is the routing number for a bank account. As soon as you leave the office, go to your bank in person and have the bank move the money you have in your account to that one. Don't move the money online, using your own computer. Get ten thousand dollars in cash. They'll eventually find out where you moved the money to, but by then I'll have moved it to someplace where they'll never find it."

"Okay," he said.

"After you go to the bank, drive to the truck stop outside of town and put your cell phone on a semi, one with out-of-state plates. Wedge it into someplace on the truck so it won't fall off."

"Why?

"Because they'll try to track us with our cell phones and putting yours on a truck might mislead them for a while. After you've done that, go home and pack a suitcase, enough clothes for a week. Don't pack more than that. We have to travel light."

"So where are we going?"

"We'll talk about that later. We don't have time right now. I'll swing by your house as soon as I can to pick you up and we'll take off."

She squeezed his hand and said, "I love you so much."

□ □ □

Jamison followed Gillian into the building. He noticed that she passed the security guard, David Pine—her father—without even glancing at him. Obviously, they didn't have a good relationship and he wondered what the story was.

As he'd noted before, Gillian didn't bear any resemblance to the man and Jamison suspected that David—unlike his daughter—wasn't very bright. Had he been, he most likely would have been given some other job in the company. Which made him wonder what Gillian's mother had been like. The information Naomi provided had shown that her mother had been a woman named Susan and that she'd passed away from breast cancer when Gillian was twenty-three.

Jamison sat in his office for an hour mostly thinking about what he was going to pack. It was September and the weather in most parts of the country was warm to hellishly hot, but as he didn't know where they were going, he figured he should pack a sweater and one warm jacket. And maybe a suit, a dress shirt, and a tie; at some point in the future he might need a suit for a job interview.

Oddly enough, he didn't feel apprehensive. He could tell that Gillian was nervous and clearly believed that the people in the syndicate would try to kill her, but he was inclined to think that she was overstating its ability to track them. People went off the grid in a country the size of the United States all the time and even the federal government couldn't find them. And for all he knew, Gillian might be considering someplace overseas as a final destination.

Whatever the case, he didn't feel frightened or apprehensive. Instead he felt excited, like a man about to leave on a grand adventure. He felt the way he did on his first day at college or on the day he went to work for Goldman Sachs: his whole life had been ahead of him then and he'd been looking forward to it. He felt the same way now: he was leaving a town that he'd never wanted to be in in the first place, and he was leaving with his lover to begin a new life. And he was confident that they could make it a good life.

He was somewhat concerned about finding a job to support them. Gillian had said that they'd have to assume new identities to be safe, so his experience and college degrees wouldn't help and getting a job that didn't involve manual labor might not be easy. But he knew he'd figure something out.

As for being poor, that was a possibility and one he could live with if he had to, but maybe there was a way around that, too.

◻ ◻ ◻

Gillian went to Sarah White's office. She needed to find out where things stood with the Kansas City consultant. Or to be accurate, she needed to find out how long Judy and her brothers would be occupied.

Sarah was on a cell phone, most likely a burner, and she made a just-a-minute gesture when Gillian stepped into her office. The focal point of Sarah's office was one wall that held half a dozen photos of her two sons dressed in baseball uniforms, posing with the family dog, sitting on Santa's lap. They were cute, mischievous-looking little guys who resembled

Sam. Gillian couldn't help but wonder if they'd eventually grow up to be thugs like Sam and Matt.

Sarah finished her call and Gillian said, "I just wanted to get the latest on Kansas City. There's nothing on the Internet about the cops finding the body of the cannery worker or about any strange deaths at Saint Luke's Hospital. I have one of my machines monitoring police communications and there's nothing there either."

Gillian actually *had* checked the Internet to see if any bodies had been found or if any recent murders had been reported, but that's all she'd done.

Sarah said, "Judy and her brothers arrived in Kansas City last night about midnight. Judy told me the consultant's in a room with another person, which complicates things a bit, but she's planning on dealing with him tonight. Sam drove by the cannery worker's house, and so far it appears as if no one knows he's dead. Anyway, by tomorrow morning the problem should be taken care of."

"Good," Gillian said. "I'll let you know if I pick up anything."

◻ ◻ ◻

An hour passed and Jamison took the stairs down to the first floor, to Mary White's office. She didn't notice him standing in her doorway as she was squinting at something on the screen of her computer. He rapped on the door frame and she looked up, frowned, and said, "Yes, what is it?"

Now that was different. Mary usually greeted him with a smile and asked how he was doing.

He said, "I'm not feeling well. Got some kind of bug and I'm heading home. Steven isn't around and since I didn't know who else to tell, I thought I'd tell you."

She looked at him for a moment, still frowning, then said, "Fine, but before you go, we need to do an exam. You're overdue."

What the hell? Had she picked up on something that made her suspicious? Was it possible that she knew what he and Gillian were planning?

He said, "Right now? I'm really not feeling—"

"It'll only take a minute," she said. "Sit down."

"Sure," he said, then clutched his stomach. "Oh, shit. Where's your bathroom?" Then he covered his mouth and gagged, pretending he was trying to keep from vomiting.

"There," she said, pointing at a door across the hall from her office. Jamison ran to the door, flung it open, stepped inside the small bathroom, and slammed the door shut.

He sat down on the toilet and texted Gillian.

◻ ◻ ◻

Gillian's phone beeped that she had a text message. It was from Jamison.

Mary is going to polygraph me.

When?

Right now! I'm in the restroom across from her office, pretending to be sick.

Stall her as long as possible. I'll screw up her computer.

"That bitch," Gillian muttered. "Why today of all days?"

She quickly navigated her way through the company's intranet and into the computer that Mary used for the polygraph tests.

◻ ◻ ◻

Jamison heard a rap on the bathroom door. Mary said, "Are you all right in there?"

"No," he said. "Just give me another minute."

He didn't know what Gillian was planning or how long it would take. He did know that there was no way he was going to be able to pass a polygraph test. He waited a couple more minutes, flushing the toilet several times, then opened the door and walked slowly back into Mary's office. He said, "You might want to wait awhile before going into that bathroom."

"Just sit down and let's get this over with," Mary said.

"Are you okay, Mary?" Jamison asked. "You seem a little out of sorts today."

"I'm fine," she said. She hooked him up to the machine, which took another couple of minutes. He'd been hoping to slow her down by starting a conversation but, surprisingly, she wasn't in a talkative mood. She moved to take the seat behind her desk and all he could do was hope that he'd delayed her long enough for Gillian to do whatever she had to do.

Mary said, "I'll do a baseline as we usually do."

"Yeah, sure," Jamison said. "But you better hurry. My stomach—"

"Be quiet. Now is your name Jamison Maddox?"

"Yes."

"Were you born in New York City?"

"Yes."

"Was your father the president of the United States?"

"Yes."

"Have you discussed any—" She stopped and rapped on the side of the laptop screen. "Damnit, what's wrong with this machine?"

She tapped a few keys then said, "Let start over. Is your name Jamison . . . Goddamnit!" She tapped on the keyboard futilely for a moment then said to Jamison, "Unhook yourself. There's something wrong with this damn computer. We'll do this tomorrow."

"Yeah, whatever you say," Jamison said.

□ □ □

Gillian's phone rang. It was Mary White.

Mary said, "Gillian, my computer is on the fritz. Can you come down here and take a look at it?"

"What's going on with it?"

"I have no idea. It keeps locking up on me."

"Have you tried restarting it?"

"Yes."

"Okay, I'll be down in a minute," Gillian said.

Gillian took the stairs down to Mary's office and took a seat in Mary's chair so she could operate Mary's computer. Mary went and sat in the chair where Jamison had been sitting. As Gillian was tapping on the keyboard to correct the problem that she'd created, Mary said, "Anything coming out of Kansas City?"

"No," Gillian said, pretending to focus on the computer. "But I talked to Sarah and everything seems to be proceeding as planned."

"Yeah, I talked to Judy just a bit ago and she told me she should have everything wrapped up by tomorrow."

Gillian had been hoping that it would take Judy longer in Kansas City. She should have known better; Judy was such an efficient little killer.

"Okay," Gillian said. "I think it's all right now, but it might not be a software problem. Your hard drive could be going bad."

Gillian got up to leave but Mary said, "Hold on a sec. Let's see if it's working. Sit down in the hot seat and hook yourself up."

"Mary, I don't have time right now. I need to—"

"This will only take a minute," Mary said.

Gillian thought about telling Mary to go to hell—she wasn't one of the people on the second floor Mary could push around—but she didn't want to make Mary think that anything was wrong. And it wasn't like Mary was going to ask if she was planning to run, and if she did ask something that Gillian had to lie about, then she'd say that Mary's computer was obviously still having problems.

She said, "Fine," took a seat, put the bands around her chest, the blood pressure cuff on her arm, and the cups on her fingers.

"Okay," Mary said. "Is your name Gillian Lang?"

"Yes."

"Is your husband Steven Lang?"

"Yes."

"Do you own a dog?"

"No."

"Are you having an affair with Jamison Maddox?"

Gillian paused. "Yes," she said.

"Are you in love with Jamison Maddox?"

"No," Gillian said.

"Well, okay," Mary said. "Everything seems to be working."

Gillian began to remove the polygraph equipment from herself. As she was doing so, she said, "That's good, but I think I should order you a new machine. I'll try to do that today if I get the time."

She left Mary's office a moment later.

She'd answered truthfully when Mary had asked if she was having an affair with Jamison because she knew that Mary knew about their affair.

She'd also answered truthfully when Mary had asked if she was in love with Jamison.

19

Gillian returned to her office and checked the bank account where she'd told Jamison to transfer his savings. There was now a hundred and thirty-seven thousand in the account. Not a lot of money to start a new life, especially when considering that they were going to spend a good chunk of that money escaping. She remembered how much money Jamison had spent on their New York trip. He'd spent money like he was still working on Wall Street; she was going to have to instill in him some fiscal discipline.

She moved the money to another account that she'd already set up then made sure there was no record of the transfer on her machine. She'd thought about removing the hard drive from her computer but had decided not to. For one thing, there was no one else at Drexler Limited that had her skills when it came to computers, so she was confident that no one would be able to reconstruct the money trail. The other reason she didn't remove the hard drive was that she'd left a few small clues in her Internet search history that showed she was interested in Costa Rica. And if everything went as planned, she'd do one other thing to make it appear that she was headed south of the border.

Gillian left her office and returned to her house to pick up the suitcase she'd packed. In addition to the suitcase there was a laptop case containing a new laptop already loaded with all her hacking software. She'd ordered the new laptop for herself a couple of weeks ago, anticipating she might be leaving soon with Jamison. The laptop was the best weapon she had but she decided she also wanted a more conventional weapon as well. She went to the gun cabinet where Steven kept his firearms and removed a Beretta semi-automatic and a box of ammunition. She couldn't help but think that if she was actually forced to use the Beretta it would mean that her plan had gone badly off the rails.

She drove to Jamison's apartment and went inside the building. She knocked on his apartment door and he opened it, grinning, looking like an excited teenager about to take off on a road trip—which made her think that he didn't really understand how perilous their situation was. But maybe that was good; if he had understood he might have decided not to accompany her. Then she thought, no, that wasn't true. He was so in love with her that he'd follow her through the gates of Hell.

"Are you ready to go?" she asked.

"All set," he said, pointing at a suitcase and a laptop case.

"And you didn't tell anyone that you're leaving, did you?"

"No, but I feel bad not telling my landlady. She's a nice old gal, and she'll be forced to deal with all my furniture and the stuff that's going to rot in the refrigerator."

"Yeah, well, that's unavoidable. Let's go."

□ □ □

Jamison tossed his suitcase and his laptop into the trunk of Gillian's car—a five-year-old Mazda sedan—and they took off.

"Where are we going?" he said.

"El Paso, Texas," she said. "But we're going to head east initially, toward Chicago, to blur the trail a bit and pick up a few things."

"El Paso? Are we heading into Mexico?"

"No. But it's going to take us at least twenty-four hours to drive to El Paso and we're going to drive straight through. We'll take turns driving. And like I said, we need to pick up a couple of things. First, we're going to stop in Arlington Heights and buy four pay-as-you-go phones. One for each of us, and two spares."

"Okay," Jamison said.

Gillian said, "Get my purse and take out my cell phone and my wallet."

Jamison grabbed Gillian's purse off the backseat, which was heavy as it was filled with the typical crap women put into a purse. But when he opened the purse, he found something else to explain the weight: a pistol.

He pulled it from the purse and said, "Jesus, Gillian, a gun?"

"Be careful with that, it's loaded. Get my wallet and my phone."

Jamison put the gun back and took her phone and wallet out of the purse.

Gillian said, "Take all the credit cards out of my wallet. We're going to stop at the next rest area or truck stop we see—someplace where people are just passing through on their way to someplace else—and drop the cards on the ground in a couple of different places, like the restrooms. I'm hoping someone will find them and use them as that will give them a false trail to follow. And I'll make a couple of calls from my phone to your phone. They'll be able to see where I called from, then I'll do the same thing you did, and stick my phone on a long-haul rig.

"As soon as we get new phones, you'll get on one and check Craigslist for cars. I want to buy one as soon as possible from someone who'll take cash and won't be inclined to fill out a bunch of paperwork. But we need something reliable, preferably something with four-wheel drive, and one that will last for at least ten thousand miles. After we have a new car, we'll swap out the license plates—we'll swipe the plates off another car—and then we'll dump this car. We'll leave it in some shitty neighborhood with the keys in it and hope someone steals it."

"You've given this a lot of thought," Jamison said.

"I've been thinking about it for years."

"But why are we going to El Paso? I have to tell you that living in Texas doesn't really appeal to me."

"We're not going there to live. We're going there to become new people."

Just as she said this, they passed a sign on the other side of the road that said: *Welcome to Redemption*.

□　□　□

Three hours later they had new cell phones and were headed southwest toward El Paso. While Jamison had been inside purchasing the phones, Gillian found a mailbox and dropped a stamped envelope into it addressed to Claud Drexler. They were now driving a Ford Expedition with ninety thousand miles on the odometer that Jamison had bought for eight thousand dollars in cash. As they were leaving Illinois and crossing over the state line into Missouri, they passed a cornfield and Gillian prayed that that would be the last cornfield she'd ever see.

20

Judy arrived back in Redemption about six a.m. with her brothers. Sam and Matt headed to their homes while Judy stopped at her mom's house to fill her in on how things had gone in Kansas City.

She let herself into Mary's house and found her mother in the kitchen. Mary had just gotten up and was still in her bathrobe, drinking coffee and watching one of the morning shows on the small television on the kitchen counter. When she saw Judy, Mary said, "Hi, honey. Want some breakfast?"

"You bet," Judy said.

While Mary prepared a breakfast of blueberry pancakes and sausages—blueberry pancakes were Judy's favorite—Judy said, "Things went fine in K.C. I decided to wait until the graveyard shift started, you know when the swing-shift nurses would be handing things off to the graveyard ones and they'd all be at the nurses' station. I bought some scrubs, stole an ID badge off the coat of a nurse's aide, and put on a surgical mask and one of those shower caps they wear. I was concerned about the guy's roommate seeing me because the old bastard always seemed to be awake every time I went by the room. I was afraid I might have to deal with him too, but it turned out I didn't. Anyway, I slipped into the room, pretended I was checking his IV line, and injected him with the same drug we used for that little shit Dennis Connor."

"What about the cannery worker?"

"As far as I know, the body still hasn't been discovered. Based on what Sarah told me about the guy, his wife split a couple of years ago because he used to smack her around, and he didn't have any friends because he was such an asshole. It could be days before they find the body. So I think we're good. You got any idea what will happen next?"

Mary shrugged. "That's up to Claud and Sarah, but I imagine what they'll do is bring in another consultant and go to work on the next cannery foreman on the list."

Mary's phone rang as Judy was polishing off a second plate of pancakes. She answered it saying, "Good morning, Steven."

Steven Lang said, "I can't reach Gillian. Do you have any idea where she could be?"

◻   ◻   ◻

Claud got off the train at Union Station, then, as he always did, he walked a few blocks to see if anyone might be tailing him, as unlikely as that was. It was just an old habit, one that was second nature to him, always checking to make sure that he wasn't being watched.

He caught a cab, had the cabbie drop him off at a large department store, wandered through the racks of clothes, using the mirrors in the space to check for a tail, and went out a different door and caught another cab.

The second cab dropped him off at a four-story brick building that had been erected during World War II and was located in a part of Chicago that looked as tired and run-down as the building. The building housed a number of small firms: accountants, commercial real estate agents, graphic artists, website designers, and two law firms. One of the law firms had six employees. The second was a one-man operation.

This lawyer was the client's man.

Claud never communicated directly with the client; all communications went through a middleman to protect both Drexler Limited and the client. Over the years, Claud had dealt with almost a dozen different people as the client's man was periodically replaced. Twice the "client's man" had been a woman.

Claud went to the second floor and rang the bell outside the door of the law office of John D. Cummings—the name used by the client's man. Not readily apparent was a camera above the door frame that showed who was ringing the bell. He was buzzed into the office.

There was an anteroom with a desk for a secretary/receptionist, although there was no secretary and never had been. The client's man was in his office, a small room decorated to look like an attorney's office with a law degree in a frame and a bookshelf filled with dusty, leather-bound legal tomes that had never been read.

The client's man was sitting at his desk. The window behind his desk showed a portion of the L, the elevated rail line for Chicago's rapid transit system. Not visible was a special coating over the window glass that made it impossible for parabolic microphones to pick up what was being said in the office. The room was swept for bugs on a daily basis.

The client's man was small, almost delicate looking; his facial features were unremarkable. He was the last person you'd notice in a crowd and the first one you'd forget. He wore an inexpensive blue suit, fitting for a not particularly successful lawyer. He smiled when he saw Claud. They weren't exactly friends—they'd never gone out to dinner together or socialized in any way—but they'd known each other for about five years and were friendly. Their meetings were usually short and almost entirely devoted to business matters, but Claud had been pleased to discover that, like himself, the client's man was a baseball fan.

"So? You said the matter was urgent."

"Yes. I have some bad news," Claud said, "and I may need your help."

By "your help" Claud meant the *client's* help.

"Okay," the client's man said.

"But before I get to the bad news, some good news. The situation in Kansas City has been resolved. We'll have to bring in another consultant, hopefully one who's better at reading people, but we should be back on track in a month or so."

"Good."

"Now to the reason I'm here. Two of my employees, a man and a woman, have gone missing. They ran off together. The man doesn't know anything, but the woman has worked for me for years."

"Why did they run?"

One thing Claud liked about the client's man was that he wasn't given to unproductive, emotional outbursts.

Claud said, "They were having an affair—the woman's married—and I guess they fell in love and decided to start new lives somewhere else. I was aware of the affair, of course, but I never, in a million years, thought this woman would do something so foolish. She's always been completely reliable. We've started searching for them and I'm certain we'll find them eventually, but, as I said, I may need your help."

"What can I do? Do you need me to bring in some people?"

"No, not yet. But we need to know if they cross a border or catch an international flight. I have copies of their driver's licenses."

"Do you think this woman will expose your operation?"

"I'm almost certain she won't. She'd be incriminating herself if she did. Nonetheless, we obviously can't take the chance and they need to be found as soon as possible. Afterward, of course, I'll deal with them."

21

They arrived in El Paso, tired and hungry from the twenty-four-hour-plus drive. The only food they'd eaten was snack food they'd bought when they stopped for gas. They'd barely talked on the long drive. When Gillian hadn't been sleeping, she'd seemed preoccupied, Jamison assuming she was worrying about the possible consequences of fleeing Redemption.

While sitting in an Applebee's having lunch, Gillian said, "Like I told you, the reason we came here is that we need new identity documents, like driver's licenses and passports."

"And you know a guy in El Paso who can provide us with fake passports?"

Gillian laughed. "No. It's almost impossible to forge a U.S. passport. Today's passports contain invisible RFID chips that are read by scanners. There are holograms and watermarks and words printed in UV ink that aren't visible to the naked eye. The pages contain invisible fluorescent fibers and words printed in distinct fonts that include deliberate errors."

"Okay," Jamison said. "So if we didn't come to see a forger, who did we come to see?"

"A midwife."

"A midwife?"

"Yes. She's going to provide us with birth certificates. If we have valid birth certificates, we can get all the other documents we need, and the documents will be legitimate, not fakes. That's why a birth certificate is called a *breeder* document: it breeds other documents."

Gillian said, "You see, a birth certificate is generated by someone associated with a baby's birth—you know, a doctor, a nurse, a clerk at a hospital—who fills out a form called a 'Record of a Live Birth.' This form is then sent to the vital records department of the state or county where the baby was born, and the department issues a birth certificate to the child's parents. A birth certificate doesn't contain photos or fingerprints or require witnesses to prove that a person's birth certificate really belongs to that person. It's simply a record that a birth occurred and provides the sex of the newborn, the date of the birth, and where the birth took place.

"Well, midwives, just like people in hospitals, can initiate the forms needed for the state to issue a birth certificate, but unlike doctors and nurses who work in hospitals, midwives operate independently. There's no supervisor looking over their shoulders, no legal department concerned about the hospital being indicted for fraud."

"Anyway," Gillian said, "about six years ago I worked with a drunk named Fred Connor—he's dead now. We needed pristine IDs for a couple of people and Fred knew a midwife in El Paso who was in the business of selling birth certificates. The woman's still here and I contacted her before we left Redemption, and once we get the birth certificates, we'll get all the other documents we need."

"It's that easy to get a birth certificate?" Jamison said. "You just find a crooked midwife? I'm surprised there aren't more controls."

"There are more controls today, and a lot of changes were made after 9/11, but this woman has been in business for a long time. She's over seventy now and she stockpiled a bunch of certificates. They're her pension plan, and she sells them mostly to illegal immigrants coming in from Mexico, that is, to the ones who can afford her price. She's not cheap."

"Does anyone else at Drexler know about her?"

Gillian said, "I don't think so, not with Fred Connor being dead. But we do have a problem. This is going to cost us thirty thousand, and since we spent eight thousand on the car, that leaves us only about a hundred grand to live on until we find jobs."

Gillian didn't say it, but she was thinking: *I hope you've been thinking about our finances.*

◻ ◻ ◻

The midwife, as Gillian had said, was a woman in her mid-seventies. Her hair was dyed jet black and she was morbidly obese and needed a walker to move. She had small, cunning dark eyes; Jamison's instinct told him that she wasn't to be trusted. She lived in a small house in a Hispanic section of El Paso and her living room was filled with small statues of saints and pictures of Jesus hanging on the walls. Jesus was being crucified in most of the pictures.

Gillian gave her a bag filled with cash. Before coming to see the woman, she and Jamison had gone to five different banks to get the cash, six thousand from each bank, the money coming from the account Gillian had established before leaving Redemption.

After the woman gave Gillian the birth certificates, Gillian said, "I want one other thing. I want a U.S. passport for somebody about my age that looks sort of like me. The hair color doesn't matter."

The woman nodded. "Let me see what I have." It was a struggle for her to get up from the chair where she'd been sitting, so Jamison helped tug her up. "Gracias," she said. She left the living room, moving slowly and painfully with the walker.

When she was out of the room, Jamison said, "I thought you said we'd get passports based on the birth certificates. Why do you need another one?"

"I'll explain later," Gillian said.

The woman came back five minutes later and handed Gillian two U.S. passports before dropping heavily into her chair. She said, "Those are the only ones I have for a white woman around your age."

Gillian looked at the photos in the passports. The first one was for a woman about five years younger than she was, but the woman was overweight and her face was very plump. The second passport was for a woman ten years older than Gillian who had brown eyes and long, dark hair. She was a beanpole: two inches taller than Gillian and fifteen pounds lighter. She had a small, dark mole on the left side of her face, near the edge of her mouth. She showed the passport to the midwife and said, "How long have you had this one?"

The midwife smiled. "That's the good news. My nephew got it in Juarez only three days ago."

This was good news because the passport may not yet have been reported stolen and entered into a stolen passport database. And what Jamison didn't know was that in addition to providing birth certificates for future American citizens, the woman's relatives were thieves who stole purses and wallets and passed on the identity documents to her.

"Okay, thanks," Gillian said.

"Thanks?" the woman said. "That'll be five thousand."

"I just gave you thirty for two birth certificates, which I'm sure is more than you usually charge. That should cover the passport."

"Five," the woman said.

Gillian stared at the old woman for a long moment and said, "This isn't a good time to fuck with me."

The woman must have seen something in Gillian's pale blue eyes—or maybe she knew something about Gillian that Jamison didn't know—because she said, "All right, fine. You can have the passport."

Back in their car, Jamison looked at his new birth certificate. His new name was David Logan; David was five years older than he was. He supposed it could have been worse. Gillian was now Elizabeth Hall; she'd have to decide if she wanted to be a Liz or a Beth; she'd never be a Betty.

He looked over at Gillian; she was just sitting there, staring straight ahead, and hadn't started the engine. Jamison asked, "Is something wrong?"

Gillian said, "The smart thing would be to go back and kill her. If by some chance Claud can trace us to her, she'll give up what she knows about us. They'd torture her to make her talk, but I doubt they'd have to do that. All they'd have to do is offer her money. She's a greedy cow."

"I thought you said no one knows about her but you," Jamison said.

"I think that's the case, but it's impossible to be sure."

"Well, it doesn't matter," Jamison said. "There's no way in hell we're killing her. I'm not going to be involved with killing anyone."

"Yeah, I know," Gillian said with a sigh. "I don't even know why I said that. We'll just have to hope for the best."

But Jamison was genuinely shocked that she'd even thought about killing the old woman. It had to be the stress of running and her fear of Claud catching them that would make her even consider doing something like that.

22

C laud sat in his office, feeling ancient, feeling betrayed.

As he'd told the client's man, never in million years would he have guessed that Gillian would turn her back on him and the family.

Her affair with Maddox had never concerned him. Maddox wasn't the first affair she'd had, none of the others had lasted long, nor had they ever affected her work in any way. She'd certainly never fallen in love with any of the men she'd slept with in the past, nor had she ever given any indication she was thinking about leaving her husband. She and Steven had always had a distant relationship—not unusual in an arranged marriage—but there'd been no signs that things had gotten so bad between them that Gillian had found her situation intolerable.

Jamison Maddox, for whatever reason, had been the catalyst for her leaving. He was a bright, charming, good-looking young man but there was no *depth* to him. He'd been talked into committing a crime to make money he didn't need, and then testified against his fellow criminals to avoid paying the price. He'd lived a pampered existence; he'd never really suffered or sacrificed. Why would Gillian fall in love with him of all people? Members of the family always assumed that Steven, because of his serious, humorless demeanor, was a man without passion but Claud had always known that Gillian was actually the cold-blooded one. What was it about Maddox that made Gillian willing to risk her life to be with him?.

Mary and her children were all engaged in the hunt. They'd searched Gillian's house and Maddox's apartment. They reviewed cell phone and credit card records looking for clues to their whereabouts. They'd located their cell phones. Gillian's was currently near Philadelphia and moving northeast. Maddox's was near Atlanta and moving southeast. Claud didn't send anyone after the phones, however, because he was positive that Gillian and Maddox were nowhere near their phones. Gillian Lang was arguably the smartest person who had ever worked for him and she would have done everything possible to make sure she couldn't be found. The first thing she would have done was gotten rid of her phone because she knew it could be used to track her.

Claud was certain he'd find them eventually. No matter where they went, nor how long it took, they'd eventually be run to ground, and then Gillian would be forced to tell how much she'd revealed to Maddox and anyone else outside the family. Claud just hoped he had the energy and the stamina for the hunt. Or for that matter, at his age, the time.

◻ ◻ ◻

Claud remembered, like it was only yesterday, when he and his wife and the other four couples arrived in Redemption in 1961. Ten bright, daring young people willing to do whatever was necessary to succeed. And succeed they did. Some of the jobs they pulled off in those early years had been extraordinary.

Now Claud was the only one of the original ten who remained. His wife committed suicide, the others died from natural causes, except for

Aaron Pine, Mary White's father. Claud had killed Aaron—although Aaron's death, too, had been officially declared a suicide. Aaron hadn't done anything wrong. He'd been the unfortunate victim of Alzheimer's and couldn't be trusted not to say things he shouldn't. There'd been tears in his eyes the day Claud placed a gun to his old friend's temple.

The original five couples had all bred children, except for Claud and his wife. His wife, he came to understand, had been clinically, chemically depressed all her life but he often wondered if their infertility had exacerbated her condition.

The children, and then the grandchildren, were groomed to follow in the footsteps of the first generation—and most of them did. There had, unfortunately, been some failures. Some children, when they became teenagers or young adults, became infected by the culture of the outsiders who surrounded them and refused to accept their destiny. In the sixty years of the family's history, two others, in addition to Dennis Connor, had to be dealt with and Claud gave the order. One died in a drowning "accident"; the other supposedly overdosed on drugs. People in the family thought Claud was ruthless and heartless—and he was ruthless—but he wasn't heartless. The deaths of those young people haunted him.

And Gillian Lang would be next.

When they first arrived in Redemption, they'd pretended to be five couples who became close friends. Drexler Limited did not exist at that time. Each of the couples set up a business or pretended to be employees of a business that provided a reason for travel and long absences, and although under Claud's supervision, they'd initially acted somewhat independently.

Things changed in 1989, the year Drexler Limited was formed. The change came about because the world had changed—and so Claud brought most members of the family under the same umbrella except for some who were given outside roles, like Agnes Pine becoming mayor of

Redemption. Before Agnes, Mary White's late husband, Mike, had been a member of and then the chief of the Redemption police department. It was always good to have someone embedded in the city's hierarchy, and particularly in law enforcement.

Advances in technology brought about more changes. In the beginning, to acquire the information the client needed, they bribed and blackmailed people, they tapped into phone lines, they planted bugs that were connected by wires to recording devices that had to be collected. But then along came the miracle of computers and wireless technology and cell phones. A cell phone was essentially a radio—a broadcasting device—and they could listen in on the broadcasts; parabolic mics were used to capture the words of people sitting hundreds of yards away. And a person sitting in a room *thousands* of miles away could hack into computers to acquire much of what the client needed. It was no longer necessary to sneak into a building or break into a safe to get information; all one needed to do was slither through a firewall. To keep up with this constantly changing technology, some family members had to be sent to universities.

Another change came about because attrition took a heavy toll on the second generation. One couple died in a car accident; two were relatively young victims of cancer; Fred Connor drank himself to death, although it wasn't alcohol that killed him. In order to meet the client's needs Claud was forced to bring in outsiders, people like Jamison Maddox, who were experts in certain areas. Making sure these outsiders did their jobs without really understanding what their jobs *were* became another challenge.

Claud was frankly amazed at his success. He'd never believed in God, but it was almost miraculous, that in sixty years of perilous undertakings, that no one in the family had ever been arrested. Or had betrayed him. Now it appeared as if he needed one more miracle to ensure that Gillian Lang didn't cause the family's downfall.

□ □ □

There was a rap on the door frame and Claud looked up from his desk to see David Pine. For reasons Claud had never understood, Gillian wasn't the least bit fond of her father and had nothing to do with him. He didn't know if David had done something to make his daughter dislike him or if Gillian was simply incapable of love.

David was now in his sixties, a couple of years older than his sister, Mary. As is the case in every family, some members are brighter than others—and David wasn't all that bright. He was most often used these days as a courier to carry information to the client's man in Chicago. When he'd been younger, he'd been used on a few jobs but always in simple roles, ones not requiring any initiative, and he'd always been closely supervised. But David was a good man—loyal and trustworthy—unlike his brilliant, beautiful daughter.

"Yes, David," Claud said.

"Sorry to bother you, Claud, but Mary said I should bring this to you." He handed Claud a plain white business envelope that was addressed to him. Drexler Limited got very little mail that wasn't junk mail.

Claud looked at the envelope and saw it was postmarked from Arlington Heights, a suburb of Chicago. There was no sender's name or return address on the envelope. He opened the envelope and removed the single page inside, a handwritten note on a half sheet of copy paper. It said:

Claud, by now I'm sure you know that I've decided to leave the family. I sent you this letter to let you know that as long as you leave me and Jamison alone, I have no intention of telling anyone what the family does. As you well know, it's not in my best interest to discuss the family's business because I've been an accomplice to everything you've done. And I haven't told Jamison anything. He thinks I'm running away from an abusive husband. (My apologies to Steven.) But Claud, if I learn you're hunting for me, I will tell what I know. I don't want to, but I will to protect myself. And in the case of my untimely death, a lawyer who you won't be able to find will send a letter to the U.S. Attorney General. So, Claud, please believe me when I say that I have no desire to reveal your secrets and I'm begging you, for your sake as well as mine, to leave us alone. Best wishes. Sincerely, Gillian.

Claud sat there for a moment, contemplating Gillian's note.

He believed her. He believed that she really didn't want to reveal the secrets of Drexler Limited.

But it didn't matter if she was telling the truth or not. He couldn't take the chance. As for her having a letter prepared to send to the attorney general, he suspected that was a lie, but he'd find out for sure once they found her.

23

Gillian walked from the motel where she and Jamison were staying to the Bridge of the Americas, one of the border crossings between El Paso and Ciudad Juarez. Then she stood for half an hour watching the people crossing into Mexico.

Unlike the American border control agents, who always asked to see a passport and often searched vehicles when people entered the United States, the Mexican border guards took a more casual approach, particularly with people crossing into Juarez on foot. Mexico wanted the dollars that American tourists brought into their country and didn't want to do anything to discourage them from coming. Gillian noticed that some of the border agents didn't always ask the people walking across the border to show a passport while others did—but Gillian couldn't figure out *why* some people were asked and others weren't. Finally, she noticed something and smiled.

Three young, college-age women were stopped by a handsome, young Mexican border guard and asked to show their IDs. A few minutes later, two young, attractive women crossing together were stopped by the same guard. It appeared as if he was stopping the good-looking, young women to break up the monotony of his job, and after checking their IDs would spend a few minutes flirting with them. Gillian approached the same guard. She wasn't as young as the women he'd stopped but she was confident she was attractive enough that he'd notice her. She *wanted* him to notice her; she wanted him to check her ID. She wanted her entry into Mexico to be recorded.

Sure enough, the guard stopped her, smiled at her, and asked, almost apologetically, to see her passport. She handed him her passport—the one identifying her as Gillian Lang. He ran the passport through a scanner, then asked what she planned to do in Mexico. She said, "Oh, just a little shopping." He smiled—his teeth brilliantly white in contrast to his dark skin—and said that if she was still in Juarez at five, there was a wonderful cantina only a couple of blocks from the border crossing called Dante's and he would love to buy her a margarita. She wondered how many women he'd said the same thing to, but all she did was smile and say that she'd keep his offer in mind. As she walked into Mexico, a camera captured her image.

Within walking distance of the border crossing was a shop she'd found on the Internet that sold wigs made from real human hair. She bought a shoulder-length wig with black hair to cover her short blonde hair; the style of the wig matched the photo in the stolen passport she'd obtained from the midwife. She bought shoes to add two inches to her height. From an optometrist, she purchased non-prescription contact lenses tinted to make her blue eyes brown and a pair of glasses with plain lenses and over-sized black frames. At a third shop, she bought a sun hat and a shapeless dress that reached her ankles; the dress would hide her figure and she was hoping it would make her appear thinner than she was and closer to the weight of the woman in the stolen passport. Lastly, she went into a restroom, and using a cosmetic pencil, she spent ten minutes creating a mole on the left side of her face, next to her mouth. She looked into the restroom mirror and studied herself. Close enough—she hoped.

Three hours after arriving in Juarez, she crossed back into the United States without a problem using the passport she'd obtained from the midwife.

Gillian had wanted to create a false trail for Claud to follow. She knew the client had contacts in Mexico and would be able to see if she crossed the border, which is what she wanted. Whether or not Claud would chase her into Mexico she didn't know. She was hoping that he'd believe the note she'd written to him, the one begging him to leave her alone—but she doubted that he would.

□　□　□

While Gillian had been in Mexico, Jamison had packed their suitcases, put them into the car, and filled up the gas tank. They were now sitting in a restaurant, eating lunch before departing El Paso.

"Okay," Jamison said while they waited for their order. "Now where are we going?"

Until now, he'd pretty much allowed himself to be dragged along in Gillian's wake as she'd thought through all the details of their escape—but he was tired of being kept in the dark and wanted to be involved in planning whatever came next.

Gillian said, "I want to go somewhere where I can see the ocean. I've spent my whole life in the Midwest, and I want a change of scenery. But we need to go someplace where the cost of living isn't exorbitant, which means if we stay on the West Coast that eliminates nice places like San Francisco and Portland and Seattle. Plus, I think we should avoid big cities even though there are some advantages to being in one. You can get lost in the population of a big city and it would be easier to find jobs, at least low-paying ones. The problem with a big city is that there are cameras everywhere and large law enforcement agencies that might look for us."

"Why would the cops look for us? We haven't done anything to make them look."

"They'll look because Claud Drexler and the syndicate will create a reason for them to look. I don't know what the reason will be, but they'll invent one. I wasn't exaggerating when I told you that they have powerful connections."

Before Jamison could speak, she said, "There's a town on the Oregon coast called Dolphin Cove. It's a beach town, one of those places that thrives in the summer thanks to the tourists, but come October the tourists leave, the population shrinks by half, and the cost of living drops. I was thinking we might rent something there, but not in the town itself. We'd be too noticeable as strangers in a small town. I found a little farmhouse online that's available. It's isolated, no close neighbors, four or five miles from the town and the beaches. It's kind of a dump but it's affordable. I was thinking that for a few months we'd just lay low and avoid people as much as we can. If anyone asks who we are, we'll tell them we're a couple of city dwellers from some big, ugly place like LA and that we got sick of our jobs and our lives there and decided to take a break. You know, like a sabbatical. Or maybe we'll say that you're a writer and you decided to spend a year communing with nature while you write the great American novel."

Jamison laughed.

Gillian's face became more animated. She said, "We'll go on hikes. Go kayaking in the ocean. We'll read a lot of books. We'll take up some hobby, like, hell, I don't know, painting or woodcarving."

"Woodcarving?"

"Okay, not woodcarving," Gillian said. "But I'd like to remain pretty much invisible for the next six months if we can. I'm hoping that after six months, Claud will stop actively searching and just sit back and wait for us to do something stupid to expose ourselves."

She took Jamison's hand. "I'm not saying we should spend the rest of our lives in this place. All I want to do is take a break for a few months. I want to relax. I want to enjoy the ocean. I want to enjoy *you*. After a few months, we'll evaluate things and decide what comes next. Maybe we'll decide we like living there and stay. The problem is, at some point, we're going to have to find jobs. This farmhouse I was looking at is cheap enough that we can get by for several months on the money we have, but when the money runs out . . . Well, then we'll need to find some way to support ourselves."

Jamison could see that she really did need a break. She was stressed out from doing what she'd done at Drexler Limited and escaping from Redemption had only increased the stress. And the idea of spending a couple of months just taking it easy was appealing, but after a while he imagined they'd get bored. Or at least he would. As for getting jobs, what kind of job could you get in a small beach town? A clerk in some retail store that sold crap to tourists? Manual labor working for a small company? Yeah, he could just see himself hiring on as a helper to some guy who pumps out septic tanks.

He said, "What would you want to do if we didn't have to worry about money?"

"I don't understand what you mean," Gillian said. "We *have* to worry about money. We've only got about a hundred thousand, and after it's gone, we'll have to find work."

"But what if we had more than a hundred thousand? A lot more. How would that change things?"

Looking irritated, Gillian said, "But we don't have more. So what difference does it make?"

"Just humor me. What would you do if money wasn't a concern?"

Gillian shrugged. "I suppose I'd still want to do the same thing. Find a place to live near the ocean and just lay low for a few months, although we could find someplace decent to rent. After that, if money really wasn't a concern, we could do something like start a small business. A coffee shop, a boutique. I don't know. Some business where we'd fit in with the community. But what's the point of playing what-if games? We have to deal with reality."

Jamison said, "My mother has a lot of money. She's worth over a hundred million, and that's not counting all the real estate she owns. I'm not sure exactly how much she has—I can find out—but I know she has a lot. I've been thinking about asking her for some, like about five million."

"Five million?"

"Yeah. That would be a lot for us but practically a drop in the bucket for her. I don't know if she'll do it—my mother's incredibly self-centered—but maybe I can convince her to help her only son."

Gillian shook her head. "Claud will be watching her and monitoring her communications. If you call her, he might be able to trace the call to where we are. And if you go see her, we're dead."

"I wasn't thinking about calling her. But I was planning to see her. This is something I'd have to do in person. So we're going to have to come up with a safe way to do it."

Jamison held up a finger to silence Gillian.

"My mother owns a ranch in New Mexico, near Santa Fe. She likes to go there in September. I don't know if she's there now, but she probably is. If she is, and if I can find a way to sneak onto the ranch without being seen, I'll talk to her. I can't promise that she'll help and if it's too dangerous, then we won't do it and we'll just have to get by with the money we have."

□ □ □

This is what Gillian had been praying for.

This was why she'd chosen Jamison.

Her dream had always been to flee Redemption yet have enough money to live a comfortable life. Her plan had been that at some point, not right away, but after a couple of months, to nag Jamison into asking his uncle Jed for some financial help, knowing how close he and his uncle were. She had already given some thought about ways for Jamison to approach Jed and not get caught by Claud's minions. She never would have guessed, however, that he'd ask his mother for money, considering their relationship

The other thought that had occurred to Gillian more than once was that when Vera Maddox died, Jamison would most likely inherit her money. As Vera was only fifty-seven, they might have to wait a long time before that happened—unless Gillian did something to expedite Vera's passing, which she'd also thought about. But there was no reason to go down that path if Jamison could convince her to help. Five million was enough that they could have a comfortable life for some time to come. And further down the road, a lot further—after both Claud and Vera were gone—and Vera not necessarily of natural causes—Jamison would become the heir to her estate and their lives would become a whole lot more than *comfortable*.

But first things first. They had to figure out a way for Jamison to meet with Vera without being seen and then Jamison would have to convince his heartless mother to share a bit of her fortune with her son. Neither of those things was going to be easy.

24

Claud sat in his office with his eyes closed, his large, gnarled hands steepled beneath his chin, wondering if there was anything more he could do to find Gillian.

He suspected that she and Maddox were still in the United States. The country was huge and they could have easily disappeared into a large city or even be hiding in a sparsely populated rural area if they maintained a low profile. They could also drive to wherever they wished to go in the continental United States. International travel, on the other hand, would be risky for them, particularly if they had to fly. Passenger manifests could be checked. They'd have to show passports; they'd be photographed in airports. Gillian had to know that he would be able to track them if they traveled under their real names and even if they had false IDs, international travel was more dangerous than domestic travel thanks to passport controls, airport surveillance cameras, and border crossings protocols. So although he couldn't be sure, Claud suspected that they were in the United States in spite of some things he'd found to indicate otherwise.

They had discovered information in Gillian's computer indicating that she had spent some time online researching Costa Rica. Costa Rica was one of the safest countries in Central America and would be a decent place for a couple of American expats to settle. But Claud suspected that Costa Rica was a red herring and that Gillian had wanted the information in her computer to be found. Nonetheless, he was forced to see if she'd fled there.

Through the client's contacts in Mexico and U.S. Homeland Security, they looked to see if she and Maddox had boarded a plane and flown to Costa Rica. They hadn't, at least not using their real names. Next, they checked to see if they'd crossed a U.S. border into Mexico. It was a long drive, but you could drive through Mexico, Guatemala, Honduras, and Nicaragua to reach Costa Rica.

Claud was surprised to learn that Gillian had indeed crossed the Mexican border at El Paso less than forty-eight hours after leaving Redemption. She'd used her U.S. passport and there was even a photo of her lovely face looking into a camera. Claud, however, thought this was another ruse. Gillian would have known that by using her passport at a border crossing she would leave a trail for him to follow. And where was Maddox? There was no record of him crossing into Mexico. So he suspected that her crossing into Mexico was another red herring—but he was forced to chase it anyway.

Even though he was almost certain it would be futile, he hired a detective agency in Costa Rica to hunt for them. The detectives didn't know why they were hunting; they'd only been told to report back to Claud if they found them. So Costa Rican detectives were checking hotels and rental car agencies and rental properties, passing the fugitives' photos out to merchants and concierges and beat cops. So far, and not surprisingly, they hadn't found them—and Claud doubted that they would.

While the detectives were looking for them in Costa Rica, Mary's children were watching Maddox's relatives. It had finally occurred to Claud *why* Gillian had found Maddox so appealing. It wasn't just his charm and his good looks. Claud suspected that the real reason she'd been attracted to him was that he came from an extraordinarily wealthy family. If Vera Maddox were to die—although the woman was only fifty-seven—Jamison Maddox would inherit over a hundred million dollars, assuming his mother's estate would pass to her son. His uncle Jed was worth about the same amount, and Claud suspected that Gillian was probably counting on Maddox to get either his mother or his uncle to help them financially.

So Matt White was watching Jed Maddox in New York, Sam White was watching Vera Maddox in New Mexico, and Judy White was watching Maddox's only other relative, his cousin, Naomi. And not only were they watching them, they were also monitoring their cell phones in the event that Maddox called them. Claud suspected that if he contacted anyone it would be his uncle. He was close to his uncle and barely had anything to do with his mother. As for his cousin, although Naomi Maddox was Jed Maddox's daughter, she didn't appear to have much money. She lived in a small apartment in Tribeca and had a low-paying job working for a polling company. Also Naomi, based on Judy's observations, was somewhat odd; Judy suspected she might have some sort of mental disability. So although Claud doubted that Maddox would risk approaching his cousin or his mother, they needed to be watched nonetheless.

The problem, however, was that Claud thought it extremely unlikely that Maddox would either call or visit his relations any time soon because Gillian would know that Claud would have people watching them. So he had decided, as much as he hated to do it, to get law enforcement involved in finding them. He didn't want to involve the law because that was going to really complicate things, but he didn't see that he had a choice.

He told Agnes Pine, Redemption's mayor, to have the Redemption police department issue a bulletin saying that Gillian and Maddox had embezzled from Drexler Limited. The bulletin would include their photos and be distributed to every police department in the country, and Claud was hoping that with someone as attractive as Gillian the cops might actually notice the bulletin. The problem was that it was going to take a lot of time to issue the bulletin, and some police departments might be missed and others might ignore it. A wanted bulletin issued by the FBI would have been much more effective, but Claud had no control over the FBI and the last thing he wanted was for the FBI to be involved.

He realized that the likelihood of the wanted bulletin succeeding was small, but if some sharp-eyed cop did spot them and arrest them, then that posed another problem: Mary's kids would have to find a way to get them out of police custody or deal with them while they were in custody. So issuing the bulletin was a problematic long shot but it was something that had to be done in an attempt to find them.

And they had to be found. Even though Claud still believed that Gillian wouldn't expose him—it wasn't in her own self-interest to do so—the client wasn't entirely convinced.

It wouldn't do to make the client unhappy—not if Claud, himself, wanted to survive.

25

Vera Maddox's hundred-acre ranch was located about fifty miles north of Santa Fe and had a striking view of the Sangre de Cristo Mountains.

They drove by the main road that passed in front of the ranch, both of them wearing sunglasses and baseball caps that partially obscured their faces. Gillian had told Jamison to drive at the speed limit and not to slow down as they passed the ranch. While he was driving, she scanned the area looking for anyone watching the place. She didn't see anyone, not that she'd expected to. If Mary's well-trained kids were the ones doing the watching, they'd make themselves invisible.

As might be expected of Vera Maddox, her ranch house was not some little house on the prairie. Gillian had looked it up on Zillow: three thousand square feet, two stories, three bedrooms, four bathrooms, an attached two-car garage. On the main floor was a large, modern kitchen with marble countertops, a library/den, and a great room with a fireplace and mountain-facing picture windows. The master bedroom had an enormous walk-in closet and a bathtub that would hold two people comfortably. In the backyard was a swimming pool and a flagstone patio, and in front of the place was a manicured lawn with a couple of shade trees. Near the house was a large red-painted structure—a barn or a stable—and a corral holding two sleek horses. But there were no cars parked outside the house and Gillian was too far away to see anyone inside the house through the windows.

Gillian said, "Shit. How can we find out if she's there without you calling her?"

"I could call one of her friends and say I need to reach her and haven't been able to. The friend I have in mind would know if she was here."

"The problem with doing that is that if her friend calls her, Claud's people may intercept the call and hear that you're trying to contact her."

They drove in silence for a couple of miles before Jamison said, "The simplest thing to do is just go knock on the door and see if she's there."

"You can't do that," Gillian said, sounding exasperated. "If someone's watching they'll see you and follow you when you leave. And then they'll kill us."

"Not necessarily," Jamison said. "I've got an idea."

Gillian noticed that he was smiling slightly and he had that amused look in his eyes. He was obviously enjoying himself, as if what they were doing was some kind of game. Well, at least he wasn't a coward and for that she was grateful.

❑ ❑ ❑

They drove around a high-end residential area in Santa Fe until Jamison found what he was looking for: an old pickup truck filled with yard maintenance equipment. The bed of the pickup contained a lawn mower, a leaf blower, hedge trimmers, rakes, shovels, and brooms. The rakes, shovels, and brooms were standing upright in a rack in the bed. The owner of the truck—a short Hispanic man in his sixties wearing a soiled, sweat-stained straw hat—was trimming a low hedge by hand with garden shears. It appeared that he was a one-man operation as they didn't see anyone helping him.

They waited until the man finished his work and collected his money from an elderly lady wearing a bathrobe at eleven in the morning, then followed him to a food truck that served tacos and tamales. The gardener ordered his lunch and sat down at a picnic table by himself. Jamison thought the guy looked bone-tired and figured that at his age the manual labor he performed on a daily basis, often under a scorching sun, had to be killing him.

Jamison approached the man alone; Gillian remained in their car.

The man looked surprised when Jamison sat down at the picnic table, but didn't say anything.

Jamison said, "Do you speak English?"

"Yes," the man said.

"What's your name?"

"Rafael. Why are you asking?"

"Rafael, I want to borrow your truck tomorrow morning."

"My truck?"

"Yes. I want to borrow it for three or four hours. I know you need your truck for your work so I'll give you five hundred dollars. In cash."

"Is this some sort of joke?"

"No, it's not a joke. I work for a bigshot lawyer and I'm trying to serve a subpoena on a guy who's dodging me. He lives in a gated community. If I drive up to the gate in my car, the guard will ask who I'm coming to see and then he'll call the guy and tell him, and he'll tell the guard not to let me in. But people in this community use a bunch of different guys who drive trucks like yours to take care of their yards, and they're not always home when the gardeners are working. So if I drive up in your truck, the guard will see the lawn mowers and stuff in the back, and I'll give him the address of a couple that I know are working and I'll be able to get in."

"No offense," Rafael said, "but you don't look like a guy who does what I do."

Jamison smiled. "I'll also need to borrow your hat."

"I don't know," Rafael said. "This sounds kind of, I don't know . . ."

Jamison suspected the word Rafael was looking for was *fishy*. Jamison said, "I'm not going to use your truck to do anything illegal. I'm not going to rob a bank. I only want to borrow it to get through a gate." Jamison pointed at the SUV where Gillian was sitting. "And you see that Ford Expedition? I paid eight thousand for it, which I'm sure is worth more than your pickup. When you give me the keys to your truck tomorrow morning, I'll not only give you five hundred bucks, I'll also give you the keys to the Ford. So if I don't come back with your truck, you'll be able to sell it for enough to buy another one and all new equipment. And in case you're wondering why I'm willing to pay you so much, it's because if I serve the subpoena on this asshole, I'll make two grand and I'll be able to expense the money I give you. So what do you say?"

Rafael stared at him for a moment then finally nodded. "Okay, but you give me half the money now. That's just in case you don't show up tomorrow after I cancel my morning appointments."

"Deal," Jamison said and took out his wallet and counted out two hundred and fifty dollars. "I'll see you here at seven tomorrow. And make sure you bring your hat."

26

At seven the next morning, Jamison drove to the taco stand where Rafael had eaten the day before, handed Rafael the keys to the Expedition, another two hundred and fifty dollars in cash, then plucked Rafael's sweat-stained straw cowboy hat off his head and put it on. In addition to the cowboy hat, Jamison was wearing a long-sleeved work shirt unbuttoned over a white T-shirt, faded jeans, and worn work boots that he'd bought at a Goodwill store the night before.

From the taco stand he drove to a feedstore on the outskirts of Santa Fe and bought two bales of hay and tossed them into the back of Rafael's pickup. A little before nine a.m., he turned down the road leading to his mother's ranch house and drove through the unlocked gate.

Jamison thought it unlikely that his mother would be out riding one of her horses at nine in the morning. She wasn't an early riser and might still be in bed. What he didn't know was if she'd be in bed by herself or with one of her boyfriends. If she was with someone, there was nothing he could do about that. He'd just have to convince her to talk to him alone.

He drove the pickup over to the horse corral. He figured that if anyone was watching Vera's place that person would have to be hidden on the property across the road, a large unoccupied area that looked as if it might be used for grazing cattle.

He got out of the pickup moving slowly, his back bent and limping as if his right knee was bothering him. He also made it appear as if it was hard for him to move the bales of hay out of the pickup and carry them over to the fence surrounding the corral. He'd turned up the collar on the shirt he was wearing and the brim of Rafael's cowboy hat was tilted downward to obscure his face. The whole time he was moving the bales, he kept his head faced away from the property across the road.

The hay unloaded, he limped back to the pickup and drove over and parked near the front door of the ranch house and rang the doorbell.

❑ ❑ ❑

Sam White had drawn the shit assignment.

His brother and sister were probably sitting in comfortable coffee shops in Manhattan, within sight of Jed and Naomi Maddox's apartments. They sure as hell weren't lying on the ground with the sun beating down on them, sweating in desert camo clothes. The only good luck that Sam had had was that he hadn't been bitten by a rattlesnake.

He was watching Vera Maddox's place from a gully surrounded by clumps of sagebrush that provided cover. The gully was on public land, about five hundred yards from Vera's ranch house, and because of the distance he had to use binoculars to see what she was doing. He'd driven his rented Jeep into the gully at night and it wasn't visible from Vera's house or to cars driving on the road that passed in front of the ranch. He had a sleeping bag, a propane-fueled camp stove to cook on, and enough canned food and containers of water to sustain him for a week. He was going out of his mind with boredom and stunk to high heaven because he hadn't bathed since he'd been there.

If Vera kept to her morning routine, about ten or so she'd come out of the house and saddle up one of her horses. She'd be dressed in designer jeans, a fancy western cowgirl shirt, expensive cowboy boots, and a cowboy hat. After she saddled the horse—she seemed to know what she was doing—she would ride around her ranch for about an hour, taking in the mountain view, the horse moving slower than a man could walk. Not once did she kick the animal into a trot, much less a gallop.

While she was out riding, a heavyset Hispanic woman would show up in a battered Toyota. She appeared to be Vera's cook and housekeeper. When Vera returned from her morning ride, she'd put her horse in the corral and then go sit on the patio near the swimming pool and the Hispanic maid would bring her lunch. (Later the Hispanic woman would go to the corral and unsaddle Vera's horse and wipe it down; she was apparently a jack-of-all-trades.)

After lunch Vera would put on a swimsuit—she had a good figure for a gal her age—take a few laps in the swimming pool, then sit in the sun and start making phone calls. Or sometimes, after her swim, she'd go in the house—and start making phone calls. Basically, all the woman did all day, until she went to bed, and unless she had guests, was talk on the phone.

A couple of people had visited her while Sam had been watching. One was a woman about Vera's age, who, like Vera, appeared to have money based on her clothes and the car she drove, and they went horseback riding together. Another time a handsome gray-haired couple, who just *looked* rich, came over and they sat by the pool with Vera and the maid brought them round after round of drinks and appetizers and eventually dinner. So far those were the only people Sam had seen with her.

As for the phone calls, which he was able to listen in on because she used a cell phone, Vera talked to a gaggle of people about every topic under the sun. She called investment guys and talked about her money; she talked to a lawyer about someone she was suing in her apartment building in Manhattan because this person was having some remodeling done that annoyed her. She talked to one guy who sounded as gay as Liberace about a play he was producing and hassled him about what the play was costing. A lot of the calls were just gossip calls, where Vera and whoever she was talking to made snide comments about friends they had in common.

But the woman wasn't all bad; she had a soft spot for animals, particularly horses. She belonged to one group that found homes for thoroughbreds after their racing days were over and he learned that Vera's two horses were racehorses that she'd rescued. She also gave money to a group in South Dakota that was committed to saving the wild mustangs that roamed the West.

The one person she didn't call or discuss was her son. Maybe if he'd been a pony she would have felt differently. On one phone call, a friend of hers asked what her son was up to and Vera's response was: "I have no idea. The last time I talked to him he was living in some god-awful place in Illinois, but as to what he's doing, I don't have a clue."

Most important, when it came to Sam's mission, her son never called her—and after listening to Vera Maddox as much as he had, Sam could understand why. The woman was a self-centered bitch. He was so grateful that his mother, Mary, wasn't that way.

Sam figured that he was wasting his time watching Vera. It was pretty apparent based on Jamison's history with the woman and her attitude toward him that he probably wouldn't contact her. If he was going to contact anyone, it would be his uncle Jed. He needed to talk to Claud and convince him that he was wasting his time in New Mexico.

Just as he'd had this thought, he saw an old pickup drive through Vera's gate. The pickup stopped near the corral and a guy unloaded two bales of hay. He trained his binoculars on the man but all he could see was his back as he removed the bales from the pickup; he was wearing a beat-to-shit old straw cowboy hat on his head, and Sam couldn't see his face.

The way the guy moved—slow, limping—he appeared to be elderly; he didn't move like a young man. He noticed that there were a bunch of rakes and shovels and brooms in the bed of the pickup and wondered if the poor bastard was going to muck out the stable next. But he didn't. Instead, he drove over and parked the pickup near the front door and rang the doorbell, probably so Vera could pay him for the hay.

Sam saw Vera open the door.

□ □ □

"My God," Vera said. "What on earth are you doing here? And why are you wearing that disgusting hat?"

Jamison wondered what a normal mother would have said to a son she hadn't seen in over a year. A normal mother would have been delighted to see him; a normal mother would have hugged him. He couldn't remember the last time Vera had hugged him. And a normal mother's first questions probably would have been: *Is everything all right? Are you okay?* Those questions apparently never crossed Vera's mind.

"Mom, I need to talk to you. It's important. Let me in. Please."

Vera hesitated then said, "Well, all right, but I'm going for my ride in an hour. So I hope this won't take long."

"It won't," Jamison said, thinking: *Unbelievable.*

Vera was wearing a fluffy pink bathrobe, but her hair was combed and her makeup was on. And he had to admit that she looked great. Thanks to a personal trainer and one of the best cosmetic surgeons in New York, she looked ten years younger than her fifty-seven years. She reminded him of Zsa Zsa Gabor—the movie star who never seemed to age until one day she finally died of old age. In fact, with her blonde hair and her flawless, unlined complexion, Vera actually looked a lot like Zsa Zsa—but then maybe all white women in their fifties with blonde hair and good plastic surgeons looked like Zsa Zsa.

Vera motioned for him to come in, shut the door, then turned and walked to the kitchen with Jamison following. She sat down at the kitchen table, picked up a coffee cup, then said, "Oh, uh, do you want coffee?"

"No," Jamison said.

"So why are you here? And why didn't you tell me you were coming?"

Jamison took a breath and launched into the story that he and Gillian had agreed upon.

Jamison said, "I'm in trouble and I need money. A lot of money."

"Oh, my God, what have you done now? Did you commit another crime?"

"No. I didn't commit a crime. But I'm running from some people who will kill me if they catch me."

"What on earth are you talking about?"

"I told you, although you probably don't remember, that I went to work for a company in Illinois. Well, I found out this company was committing fraud on a massive scale, mostly Medicare fraud. Once I learned what they were doing, I said I was quitting. I wasn't about to get involved with a bunch of crooks, not after what happened in New York. When I said I was leaving, they said fine, like they didn't care, but then they sent a guy to my apartment and he tried to kill me. Apparently, they decided they couldn't take the chance that I might go to the cops."

"You're making this up," Vera said.

"No, I'm not. Why would I make something like this up? I'm telling you they sent a guy to *kill* me, a guy with a gun that had a silencer. He was a professional hit man. It was just luck I was able to get away and I've been on the run ever since."

"But why did you come to me? Go to the police."

"I *can't* go to the police. The police will consider me an accomplice, and technically, I am an accomplice because even though I didn't know what they were doing at first, I helped them. But that's not the main thing. This group, this company, it's like the fucking mafia. If I go to the cops, they'll try to kill me again before I can testify and next time, I won't get lucky. I'm serious, Mother. These guys will kill me if they catch me."

"But what does this have to do with me?" Vera asked.

Even though the story was false, he was genuinely shocked by her attitude. "Jesus," he said. "Don't you care that people are trying to kill me?"

"Well of course I care, but what do you expect me to do. Let you hide out here?"

"No. If they found me here, they'd kill you too."

"My God. So what do you want from me?"

"I told you. Money. I have to get out of the country and disappear to someplace where they won't be able to find me. South America, Asia, I don't know where, but far away from the United States. These people have connections all over the country. Like I said, they're like the mafia. But I need enough money to stay out of sight for a long time and maybe forever. It might not ever be safe for me to come back to the U.S. And I can't apply for a job to support myself. They'll be able to trace me because everything is done on computers these days. So I need enough money to live on, enough to last a long time."

"How much?" Vera said.

"I was thinking, five million. That's all."

"That's all!" she shrieked.

"Mother, you're worth over a hundred million dollars."

"How do you know how much I'm worth?"

"Because I do. Five million isn't even five percent of what you have if you count your real estate holdings. You won't even miss the money."

"I don't know," Vera said.

"For Christ's sake! I'm your son. Your only son. And when you die—and one of these days you will die, whether you believe it or not—I'll inherit your estate. I just want a little of the money I'll inherit one of these days because you can't possibly spend everything you have before you die."

"What makes you think I'm leaving you anything in my will? There are a lot of causes I support, and I've always felt that you should be able to make your own way in the world."

"Fine. Write me out of your will. I don't care. All I want is five million so I can survive and not get killed. And if you give me the money, I promise I won't ever bother you again."

"I need to think about this."

"There's no time for you to think about it. I have to get out of here as soon as possible, for your sake as well as mine. If they find me here, they might kill you, too. I'm meeting a guy in El Paso tonight who can get me across the border into Mexico without going through a checkpoint. I haven't figured out where I'm going after that. All I know is that I have to get out of the U.S. as soon as possible and there's no time for you to spend thinking about it."

Vera sat there, stone-faced. She may have been scowling but with the Botox injections it was hard to tell.

"For Christ's sake. I'm your only child and I'm going to get killed if you don't help me. For once in your life, act like a mother."

"All right, fine," she said. "But I'll only give you three, not five. And only if you promise you won't come back for more."

"I promise."

"Now what am I supposed to do? Write you a check? I don't keep three million in a checking account."

Jamison decided not to haggle with her over the amount, thinking he was lucky she was giving him anything at all. He also wondered if she'd decided to give him the money so she wouldn't ever have to have any-thing to do with him again, yet her conscience would be clear because she'd helped him. But that assumed she had a conscience.

"No, you don't write me a check," Jamison said. "Where would I cash a three-million-dollar check? You need to transfer the money online from your Chase account to an account number that I'll give you."

"How do you know about the Chase account and how much I have in it?"

"Because I do. Remember what I used to do for a living."

"And you promise you won't come back and ask for more? No, wait a minute. It doesn't matter if you promise. I won't give you any more no matter what kind of trouble you're in."

"I won't need more. Now would you please get your laptop and make the transfer."

But Vera didn't move, and Jamison couldn't think of what else he could say to persuade her—but then she finally left the table and he let out a sigh of relief. She came back with her laptop and he helped her navigate her way through the transaction, placing the money into an account that Gillian had set up yesterday. As soon as the transaction was complete, Gillian would move the money so the transaction couldn't be traced to them.

As he was leaving, Jamison said, "You can't tell anyone that I was here. And if you call someone, these people might find out. They have the ability to monitor phone calls. So for your own safety, don't tell anyone."

Vera studied his face for a long moment. He wondered if she was thinking that this might be the last time she ever saw her son.

She wasn't.

She said: "You've always been such a burden."

27

The hay guy finally came out of the house and Sam wondered what he'd been doing inside for so long. He'd been in the house for almost twenty minutes. He supposed it was possible that Vera had had a cup of coffee and chatted with him, but she didn't seem like the type who would have coffee with the hired help. More likely she'd given him a list of things to do or maybe she had him come into the house to do something she needed done. Like fix something or move something heavy.

He trained the binoculars on the guy's face as he limped back to his pickup but couldn't see it because the straw cowboy hat was tilted downward, but he was about ninety percent sure it wasn't Jamison Maddox. Maddox was young and this guy wasn't. And where would Maddox get a beat-up old truck with a bunch of tools in the back? On the other hand, Maddox was a smart son of a bitch. Sam mulled that over for a moment then decided that he'd follow the hay guy. Watching and listening to Vera wasn't producing anything and the hay guy being inside the house with her for so long bugged him.

He waited until the guy had driven half a mile—he was headed in the direction of Santa Fe—then hopped into the Jeep, drove it out of the gully, and took off after him. The pickup was easy to follow as the road was straight and flat. Once he got near Santa Fe, where there was a lot of traffic and four-lane roads, he'd pull up alongside him or pass him. All he needed to do was get a look at his face.

Then he thought: *No, better not do that.* Although it was unlikely the hay guy was Maddox, if he was, he couldn't let Maddox see *his* face. Maddox knew what he looked like because they'd met at the company's Fourth of July picnic. He'd have to wait until the guy got out of the truck to get a look at him.

◻ ◻ ◻

Jamison called Gillian. "I got the money."

"I know," she said. "I'm already moving it."

"I should be back at the motel in an hour. I just have to drop off Rafael's truck and get our car back."

"I'll have us all packed and ready to go by the time you get here. Oh, Jamison, I'm so happy. I love you."

"Love you, too," he said.

He drove along, feeling good, feeling relieved. He and Gillian should be all right for a long time to come provided Claud Drexler didn't find them. He didn't know what the future held but now he was looking forward to it more than ever.

He glanced in the rearview mirror and noticed a car behind him. He wondered where it had come from. One moment the road behind him had been empty of vehicles then suddenly a car had appeared. There wasn't anything out near his mother's ranch, just a couple of other big ranches and a lot of public land. Whoever was driving the other car, he or she had probably come from one of the other ranches.

Then a thought occurred to him. *What if the driver behind him hadn't come from one of the other ranches?* What if he was one of Drexler's men who'd been watching his mother's place, saw Jamison visit her, and recognized Jamison despite the precautions he'd taken? And what if he was now following him to see if he'd lead him to Gillian? Most likely the driver had come from one of the other ranches and was just heading into Santa Fe for something, but Jamison decided he couldn't take the chance that he might be wrong. The first thing he needed to do was see if the guy was following him.

He was on I-84, headed south toward Santa Fe. He took the exit for Camino Encantado, a street that headed southeast. When he took the exit, so did the black Jeep that was behind him. The Jeep was too far back for him to see the driver's face.

He drove a couple of blocks, still going southeast, and the Jeep stayed behind him. A block ahead, on the left-hand side of the street, he could see the golden arches of a McDonald's. When he reached it, he made an abrupt left turn into the parking lot, not signaling before he did.

◻ ◻ ◻

Goddamnit, Sam thought. He hadn't been expecting the guy to go to McDonald's, and was caught by surprise when he did, although it was a perfectly normal thing for him to do, stop for breakfast after delivering the hay. He thought for a moment about going into the McDonald's after him but decided not to. Although he still didn't think the guy was Maddox, he couldn't let him see his face.

Across the street from the McDonald's was a gas station and he pulled into it and up next to a pump. When the hay guy parked in the McDonald's parking lot, he figured he should be able to get a clear look at him when he went in to order or when he came back out of the restaurant after he'd eaten.

But then, goddamnit, the guy didn't park in the parking lot. He drove into the drive-through lane.

◻ ◻ ◻

Jamison watched as the Jeep pulled into the gas station across the street from the McDonald's. Coincidence? Possibly. Maybe the driver was just low on gas. But now he had a way to find out if he was really being followed.

He ordered a cup of coffee and an Egg McMuffin; he actually was hungry as he hadn't eaten breakfast. After he was given the paper bag containing his sandwich, he exited the McDonald's parking lot, lowering the sun visor and keeping the brim of his cowboy hat tilted down over his face. He turned right out of the parking lot, going northwest, back the way he'd come from. Now if the Jeep came after him, he'd know he was being tailed.

◻ ◻ ◻

When Sam saw the hay guy's pickup make a right-hand turn after leaving the McDonald's, he slammed his fist on the steering wheel. Did the guy backtrack because he knew he was being followed? No, not necessarily. He may have just taken a detour to the McDonald's because he was hungry and now was back on the route to wherever he'd been headed.

Son of a bitch! All he needed to do was see the damn guy's face.

Having no choice, Sam took off after the pickup.

◻ ◻ ◻

Jamison looked into the rearview mirror. The black Jeep was behind him. Now he knew. The Jeep driver deciding to get gas when Jamison pulled into the McDonald's may have been a coincidence, but now there was no doubt that he was being followed.

Jamison had to lose whoever was tailing him before he returned the pickup truck to Rafael. He couldn't allow the guy in the Jeep to see him do that, and he couldn't allow him to follow him back to the motel where Gillian was waiting. He drove for a mile, still heading northwest. When he came to I-84, he didn't get back on the freeway. He continued northwest on Camino Encantado, still trying to decide what to do, and that's when he saw a road construction sign and noticed a long line of stopped cars ahead of him. The construction people had turned Camino Encantado into a one-lane road. They would let a bunch of cars heading northwest go through, then they'd stop the northwest traffic and let a bunch of the southeast ones go.

Jamison reached the tail end of the stopped line of cars. The black Jeep was six cars behind his. After five minutes, the traffic started moving and Jamison passed a woman wearing a yellow hard hat and an orange vest; she was holding a sign that said SLOW on one side and STOP on the other. Just after he went past her, a large backhoe backed out of the construction site and she flipped the sign to STOP—and Jamison smiled.

As soon as he cleared the construction area, he stomped on the gas, made a couple of turns, and headed toward the taco stand where Rafael was waiting. As he was driving he ate his Egg McMuffin.

◻ ◻ ◻

"You bitch!" Sam screamed when the construction gal swung her sign around and stopped the traffic. He knew that by the time the backhoe got out of the way and he'd be allowed to move again, the hay guy would be long gone. Finally, the woman turned the sign and he took off. He drove as fast as he could, assuming the guy was still heading northwest on Camino Encantado, but didn't see him. He'd lost him.

So. Was the hay guy Maddox or not? He didn't know. He still thought it unlikely that Maddox had come to see his mother. Why would he do that? About the only thing he could think to do was go back and listen in on her cell phone calls and see if she talked about him visiting her.

Well, there was one other thing he could do. He could go torture the shit of Vera Maddox and see if she'd admit that the hay guy had been her son. He'd have to talk that over with his mom.

◻ ◻ ◻

Jamison returned the pickup to Rafael, gave him back his straw hat, and because he was now three million dollars richer, he handed him another two hundred bucks and said, "Buy yourself a new hat."

Fifteen minutes later he was back at the motel where Gillian was wait-ing. After they tossed their luggage into the car and took off, he said, "We might have a problem. I was followed after I left my mother's place. Someone must have been watching her."

"Oh, shit! Why didn't you call and tell me?"

"Calm down. I lost the guy, whoever he was. And I don't think he identified me."

"But he might have?"

"Yeah, maybe, but I doubt—"

"Did you tell your mother where we're going?"

"No, of course not. What I told her was that I was crossing into Mexico tonight."

"Don't say anything for a minute," Gillian said. "I have to think."

If whoever followed Jamison had identified him, then Claud would know that they hadn't gone into Mexico and weren't headed for Costa Rica. But then Gillian had always known that Claud might not fall for that trick. But if Claud knew they were near Santa Fe, he'd flood the area with people to try to find them. But so what? He didn't know the kind of vehicle they were driving and he didn't know the names they were using. But if Claud thought—or even suspected—that Jamison had visited his mother, what he might do was *make* Vera tell him what she and Jamison had discussed. But again, so what? Jamison hadn't told Vera where they were really going and Claud might even believe the lie that Jamison had told his mother, that he was headed into Mexico. All Claud would learn if he interrogated Vera was that Jamison was three million dollars richer, but who cared since Claud had no way to trace the money that Vera had given her son. And once they left Santa Fe, unless by some fluke Claud's people just happened to see them as they were driving, Claud would have no way to know where they were going.

"I think we're good," she said to Jamison. "We'll stick to the plan and go to Oregon."

"If I was identified, do you think Claud might harm my mother? You know, torture her or something to make her talk?"

"No, absolutely not. Harming your mother would pose a risk as that would get the cops involved. And what would be the point? Claud knows you're not stupid and knows that you wouldn't have told Vera anything that would give her a clue as to where we're headed."

She patted his hand and said, "Honey, you did great today."

28

"But you don't know for sure that it wasn't him?" Claud said.

"No, for the second time," Sam said. "I don't think it was him because of the way he moved and the truck he was driving, but I never got a clear look at his face. And I'm sure he didn't intentionally ditch me when I was following him. He just lucked out because he drove into a construction area and I lost him."

Sam was on a conference call with Claud and his mother and he was starting to wonder if the old guy was losing it. He kept asking the same questions over and over again.

"But why would that woman spend twenty minutes talking to a man delivering hay?" Claud said.

"I don't know," Sam said. "Maybe she was lonely and wanted someone to talk to. Maybe she was giving him a list of other shit she wanted delivered for her horses, fuckin' oats or something. Maybe she had some problem in the house she needed help with. I don't know."

No one spoke for a few seconds and Sam was about to ask—also for the second time—*What do you want me to do?* when Claud finally spoke.

"I don't see that we have any choice but to question Vera Maddox. Jamison hasn't contacted his uncle or his cousin, he hasn't made any phone calls to his mother, the detectives I hired in Costa Rica haven't found Gillian, and neither of them has flown on a plane. I still think they're in the United States and they're together, and right now, this man, this hay person, spending twenty minutes with a snob like Vera Maddox is an anomaly and we have to follow up on it."

Now that a decision had been made it was time to talk tactics.

"What kind of security does she have at her ranch?" Mary asked.

"None that I can see," Sam said. "But I would think that she'd have some kind of alarm system as she's hardly ever at this ranch, but I didn't see any security company signs."

"Is she alone at night?" Mary asked.

"Yeah. She might have company, like the other day she had some couple over for dinner and they stayed until nine or so, but she doesn't have live-in help."

Sam paused then said, "She turns off the lights around eleven when she goes to bed. If she has a security system and is afraid because she's alone, I would think that's when she'd turn it on. She wouldn't turn it on earlier because she might accidently set it off if she opened one of the outside doors. It gets dark around eight here, so I could wait until it's dark and go into the house before she goes to bed. You know, break a window or jimmy open a door. I can't pick locks the way Judy can. Anyway, if I go in fast and hard, I can grab her before she has a chance to call the cops. And as far out as she lives, I imagine even if she called the cops, it would take them forever to get there."

Mary said, "Do you want me to send Matt or Judy to help you?"

Claud and Sam both said no at the same time. Sam said, "I won't need any help," and Claud said, "We don't have time to wait for Matt or Judy to fly out there. We need to know what Vera knows as soon as possible."

"Okay," Mary said. Then added, "You be careful, honey."

"I always am," Sam said.

❑ ❑ ❑

Sam waited until nine p.m.

The Hispanic housekeeper/cook had left at eight after fixing Vera's dinner and cleaning up the dishes. Vera was now sitting in the house alone and, as usual, talking on her phone. When he left the gully to sneak down to the house, she'd been talking to some guy in Maui about the place where she planned to stay at Christmas, bitching that the last time she'd been there the Internet connection had been too slow and no one had cleaned the swimming pool.

He parked his Jeep near the ranch's main gate; he wanted his vehicle close by so he could get away quickly but he didn't drive up to the house because he was worried she might hear him. There was enough moon and starlight that he could see well enough walking down the road to her house. It was a two-story house, and lights were burning on both floors. Like Gillian had, he'd checked out the house on Zillow and he imagined she was downstairs in the common areas—the living room, the den, or the kitchen. The master bedroom was upstairs.

When he was a hundred yards away, he started low-crawling so she wouldn't see him in case she looked out a window. He was dressed completely in black: a black watch cap on his head, a black long-sleeved T-shirt, black jeans, black tennis shoes, and thin black leather gloves on his hands.

He was carrying a one-foot-long crowbar that he'd use if he needed to pry open a door or a window. He had a Glock tucked into the back of his pants and a silencer in the front right-hand pocket of his jeans. Since Vera didn't have any nearby neighbors, he doubted he'd bother with the silencer. In his right-hand back pocket he had a bunch of zip ties he could use to restrain her.

The plan, as he'd told his mom, was to get into the house quickly, locate Vera, scare the shit out of her by pointing the Glock at her face, and then ask her about the hay guy. If she hesitated or didn't act intimidated or if he suspected she was lying, then he'd tie her to a chair and lop off one of her fingers with a kitchen knife. He figured he'd only have to lop off one to get her to talk. Once he was satisfied that she'd told him the truth, well, either the knife or the gun would do. After she was dead, he'd ransack the place and take a few small things that were easy to carry, like cash or jewelry, and be on his way.

He crept around the back of the house to the pool area where there were French doors leading into the kitchen. He tried the handle on one of the doors but it was locked. Too bad. The double doors had small glass panels, and he pressed the tip of the crowbar against one of the panels close to the door handle. The panel cracked—the sound much louder than he'd expected—but if she was somewhere deep in the house or upstairs in her bedroom, she might not have heard it. He pushed his gloved hand through the broken panel, flipped the lock, and entered the house. He pulled the Glock from the back of his pants and started moving quickly, not running, but walking fast to find her.

Although there were lights on in the living room she wasn't there. He saw her cell phone sitting on a coffee table next to a glass of brandy. Huh. Why would she have left her phone there? He checked the kitchen and the downstairs bathroom to make sure she wasn't hiding in the bathroom. She wasn't on the first floor. Maybe she'd heard him when he broke the window and had run upstairs. Or maybe she was upstairs taking a shower, getting ready for bed. It didn't matter, upstairs was the only place she could be. He crept quietly up the staircase, came to the first closed door, and pushed it open.

Three slugs hit him in the chest, the .357 magnum revolver that Vera was holding sounding like a cannon. He was dead before he hit the floor.

29

It took the sheriff's deputies half an hour to respond to Vera's 911 call. The dispatcher told them that a woman had called and said she'd just killed an intruder.

"Is she okay?" one of the deputies asked.

"She said she was," the dispatcher said. "In fact, she sounded completely calm as if killing the guy didn't bother her a bit. She's probably in shock."

The deputies, both male, arrived in separate cars to find Vera Maddox waiting for them on the front porch. She wasn't holding a weapon; she was holding a snifter filled with very expensive cognac.

She said, "He's upstairs. I'll show you."

"No," one of the deputies said. "You stay right here. I'll go take a look and my partner will stay with you. Where's the gun you used?"

"Oh, it's on the dining room table."

The deputy went upstairs to look at the corpse and came back down a couple of minutes later. Vera, ignoring his order to stay on the porch, was now sitting on a couch in the great room, still sipping her cognac. The second deputy was standing a few feet from her. On an end table near him was a .357 revolver in a plastic evidence bag. The deputy who'd viewed the body said to his partner, "Well, he's dead. Three shots right in the heart." To Vera he said, "Ma'am, my partner's going to stay here with you while I walk through the house and around outside to make sure no one else is here."

"That's fine," Vera said.

The deputy couldn't tell if she was in shock or not. She didn't seem to be.

Ten minutes later he came back to the living room and sat down in a chair across from her. He said, "Ma'am, can you tell me what happened?"

Vera said, "I was sitting where I am right now, just having a drink, when I heard a sound. It sounded like glass breaking and it came from the kitchen. As soon as I heard it, I ran up the stairs to my bedroom where I keep a gun in the nightstand next to the bed. A couple minutes later, a man pushed open the bedroom door and I shot him when I saw he was holding a gun in his hand. And that's it. That's what happened. Do you have any idea who he is?"

"No, ma'am. He didn't have any ID on him."

□ □ □

For the next four hours, Vera's ranch house was filled with people: a sheriff's detective; four deputies, including the two who had answered the 911 call; some technicians who photographed the dead man and the window he'd broken to enter the house; and a couple of guys who came in an ambulance and loaded the body into a black bag and hauled it away.

While this was going on, Vera packed two suitcases and a carry-on bag and made a reservation at a hotel in Santa Fe. She told the deputy that she couldn't stay in the house after what had happened and he said he could understand that. After she was packed, she called three people. First, she called the man who took care of the ranch and her horses when she wasn't there and told him she was leaving and to make sure the window in the back door was fixed and to replace the bloodstained rug in her bedroom. Next, she called her lawyer. She woke him up because it was about four in the morning in New York when she called. She told him she wanted his ass on the next plane to Santa Fe. Finally, she called a woman in Greece.

The next afternoon, with her lawyer present, she told the detective assigned to the case that she was leaving New Mexico because she no longer felt safe. The reason she'd told her lawyer to fly out was to make sure the cops didn't try to stop her from leaving. They didn't. It was a clear-cut case of self-defense.

She asked the detective, "Did you identify the man I killed?"

He said, "We're not sure. The guy's fingerprints aren't in any national or state database. We found a Jeep parked near your place and it was packed with a bunch of camping equipment, you know a sleeping bag, a camp stove, bottles of water, stuff like that. The Jeep was rented to an Eric Brinker and in the glove compartment where we found the rental car papers, we found a wallet with a driver's license belonging to Eric Brinker and the photo on the license matches the dead man.

"The problem is, the license is a fake. So we're not really sure who the guy is, but he must have been some kind of pro considering that he had a silencer on him and didn't take his ID with him when he broke into your house. Pros do that. They don't take their wallets because they don't want to take the chance of them falling out of a pocket. The fact that he had a fake ID also makes us think he wasn't just some drug addict who needed cash for his next fix. All we can figure is that he decided to rob your place because it's isolated and because it looks like a place where someone with a lot of money might live. Are you sure you can't think of any other reason why someone would break into your house?"

"No, I have no idea," Vera said.

She'd decided not to tell the cops about the visit from her son and about Jamison telling her that he was being chased by dangerous criminals. All that would do was cause a lot of unnecessary complications as she had no idea where Jamison was or who these criminals were. It appeared, however, that Jamison had told her the truth and that he really was being pursued by people who not only wanted to kill him but would also be willing to kill her because she'd met with him. Right now, the only thing Vera wanted to do was get out of New Mexico and go somewhere that she'd be safe.

The woman she'd called in Greece was married to a charming rogue named Andreas Kapodistrias. Andreas was a retired arms dealer—and he'd probably dealt in other things, like drugs. Vera had met Andreas years ago and she got along *fabulously* with his wife, a former Italian opera singer, and she stayed with the couple every time she went to Greece. The thing about Andreas Kapodistrias—probably because of his former occupation—was that he had more security people around him than the president of the United States. He lived on an island, in a walled compound, with guards and cameras everywhere. She couldn't think of any place where she'd be better protected.

She still couldn't believe that Jamison had led a killer to her house. It made her just *furious* that he'd been so irresponsible. He shouldn't have come to her at all or he should have taken precautions to protect her. She was his mother after all.

She was definitely cutting him out of her will.

30

When Mary didn't hear from Sam the morning after he was supposed to have questioned Vera Maddox, she wasn't too worried. She figured that maybe he'd decided to delay the job for some reason. But on the second day, when he still hadn't called, she did become concerned and she called him. Her call went to voice mail. That's when she Googled Vera Maddox, Santa Fe, and learned that Vera Maddox had killed her son.

When Judy got the call from her sobbing mother, telling her that Sam had been killed, she and her brother Matt immediately left New York and returned to Redemption.

◻ ◻ ◻

Matt, Judy, and Mary all met in Claud's office, Mary almost catatonic with grief.

Judy said, "We found out that bitch flew to Greece. I'm going after her and I'm going to kill her."

"No, you're not," Claud said. "Our priority is finding Gillian, not avenging your brother."

Before Judy could object, Claud said, "Can they trace Sam to us?"

Seeing Mary was too grief-stricken to answer, and that Judy was too angry to answer, Matt said, "No way. He was carrying a fake ID, of course, and his fingerprints aren't in any database. The phone he was using was a burner and the phones we used to talk to him were burners, too, and we've already ditched them. So I don't see how they can connect the family to him."

Mary mumbled, barely audible, "We have to bring his body home."

"No, Mary, I'm sorry, but we can't do that," Claud said.

"Are you telling me my brother's going to be buried in a fucking potter's field?" Judy shrieked.

"I'm sorry," Claud said, "but yes. And there's something else we're going to have to do that's going to be very painful for all of you and Sam's wife and children. People outside the family here in Redemption knew Sam and we have to come up with a story to explain his absence."

Sarah White, Sam's wife, didn't yet know that Sam was dead.

Claud said, "We're going to have to tell anyone who asks that Sam decided to leave his wife. I know you don't want to see his reputation tarnished, but that's the way it will have to be."

Claud waited for Judy to explode and when she didn't, he said, "Where do we stand on finding Gillian?"

Matt answered. "We stand nowhere. The only lead we had was Jamison maybe visiting his mother, and like Judy said, his mother's now in Greece so we can't even confirm that he saw her. She's on some island belonging to a guy who used to be an arms dealer, and based on what it says on the Internet, he's got a lot of security around him. So it'll be tough to get to her until she leaves the place."

Claud merely nodded as he absorbed this information.

Matt continued. "Maddox hasn't called his uncle or his cousin, and I doubt that he will. Gillian's too smart to let him do that. About the only thing that's happening right now is that bulletin the Redemption cops sent out saying they're wanted for embezzling. So far we haven't heard back from anyone and I think it's pretty unlikely that we will."

Judy said, "What if we snatched his uncle? He's enough of a big shot that his disappearance would make the national news. The cops wouldn't be able to figure out who took him, but Maddox would know, and he'd contact us to get his uncle back."

"Gillian wouldn't let him," Claud said.

"Well maybe Gillian wouldn't be able to stop him," Judy said.

"It's an idea. I'll think about it," Claud said. "Now I have to meet with Sam's wife and tell her what's happened and what's going to be expected of her."

Mary started sobbing.

Judy just sat there looking mad enough to kill—mad enough to kill Claud. Doing nothing when it came to catching Gillian—the person really responsible for Sam's death—was unacceptable and she wasn't going to stand for it.

31

They walked hand-in-hand, barefoot on the beach. Noisy seagulls swirled overhead, screeching down at them. The day was clear, but brisk, and the waves were tipped with frothy whitecaps. About a half mile offshore was a striking rock formation. Photographs of the rocks, sometimes covered with sea lions, were on almost every brochure that was used to attract tourists to the little town of Dolphin Cove.

They'd been in Oregon now for two weeks. They'd rented a log cabin—an *exquisite* log cabin. It belonged to a former Microsoft executive who had died and his widow never used it and rented it out. The place was only a few years old and equipped with large-screen TVs and modern appliances that were voice controlled. There was a huge, stone fireplace and a library filled with books that looked as if they'd never been read. Magnificent Persian rugs sat on glossy hardwood floors and oil paintings depicting the Oregon coast adorned the walls. The property was mostly surrounded by an old-growth forest with towering, ancient evergreens and there was a nearby stream where salmon spawned. Thanks to the forest, the cabin was also invisible to nearby neighbors, the closest one being a mile away.

The place was perfect—and affordable thanks to the reluctant generosity of Vera Maddox.

For the first time in her life, Gillian felt as if she could *breathe*, really breathe. The weight of Claud Drexler was no longer bearing down on her. She no longer had to take part in undertakings that could lead to a life behind bars but provided her no personal reward. She no longer had to suffer the fanatics like her husband or think about Mary White and her children watching every move she made.

She was finally free.

She'd told Jamison that they didn't have to stay in Dolphin Cove forever, that after a few months they could move on, but right now she had no desire to leave. And maybe she never would. Mostly all she and Jamison had done since they'd been in Oregon was go on long hikes and sit around the cabin reading in front of the fireplace. Tomorrow, however, they were planning to go to Corvallis, which was about an hour away, and buy a couple of kayaks. She'd seen people kayaking along the coast and she wanted to do the same. There were also three decent golf courses in the area, and she'd told Jamison that she was going to teach him to play and he'd said he would enjoy that. She might even try her hand at painting, or maybe take up a hobby like baking; she never really learned how to cook as Steven had done most of the cooking, but now maybe she would.

At some point, she wanted to travel. She wanted to see every castle and cathedral in Europe and the Great Wall of China and Mount Kilimanjaro and the great savannas of Africa. But she had no intention of traveling internationally until Claud was dead. The old bastard was eighty-one and he couldn't possibly live too much longer. And once he was gone—and by then the client would have accepted that she had no intention of telling what she knew—then maybe she'd take the risk. But for now, she was completely content in Oregon.

She was, however, worried about Jamison; she was worried about him becoming bored. He was enjoying himself now, but it had been only a couple of weeks and she wasn't certain how long it would be before he became restless. One day when he made a comment about the need to do more than commune with nature and lay about, she'd said to him, "Jamison, this is what most people work all their lives for, to be able to retire to a place like this and just play. You're one of the lucky ones, being able to retire before you're even thirty." She could tell that he hadn't been entirely convinced.

To occupy himself, he'd started day trading online in the morning, which she'd actually encouraged as it gave him something to do that he enjoyed. She made sure that he didn't risk much—she wasn't going to allow him to blow their nest egg speculating—and so far, he'd made them a couple of thousand dollars. But she had to find other ways to occupy him. Maybe they could buy a couple of motorcycles and tour up and down the coast. She'd always thought that motorcycles were dangerous but maybe driving a big Harley on winding coastal roads would give Jamison the adrenaline rush he seemed to crave.

She was worried about him and had to make sure he stayed as content as she was, and she'd do whatever was necessary to make that happen. The good news was that he loved her, and she knew he wouldn't ever leave her. And she didn't want to leave him. She just wanted things to go on as they were.

32

Judy was done with sitting around waiting for something to happen when it came to Gillian and Jamison. The bulletin sent to police departments hadn't produced anything and she was certain it never would. What was the chance of a) some cop even looking at the damn bulletin, which was probably one of a couple hundred they got every day and b) that same cop looking at it, and then actually spotting them? Plus, by now, Gillian had most likely changed her hair color and Jamison had shaved his head or grown a beard.

Claud had refused to green-light her plan to kidnap Jed Maddox, even though Judy was convinced it was the best way to draw Jamison out of hiding. It appeared as if Claud was willing to wait until either the bulletin produced a result or Gillian did something reckless to expose herself, like cross a border or catch a plane.

And her mother, who might have been able to convince Claud to let her kidnap Jed Maddox, was no help. She was practically a basket case, unable to get over the loss of her firstborn son. Sam's wife was holding it together, but just barely, although Sam's boys were adjusting to their father being gone. But Judy was absolutely sick of having to perpetuate the lie that Sam had abandoned his wife and kids.

As for Claud, Sam's death didn't seem to have affected the stone-faced old son of a bitch at all. He was back to business as usual, focused on the client's work. The plan to compromise Congressman John Corcoran had succeeded. The congressman had fallen for the hooker Heather Fine, they had videos of him screwing her, and now the client had a powerful politician in his pocket. The project related to the vial-filling-machine company in Virginia Beach was rolling along, and as for the cannery project, although there'd been an initial setback, another operative had been brought in and a foreman had been found who would do what the client wanted.

So with the exception of Gillian being in the wind, things were going well in Claud's world and his interest in locating her was, if not gone, certainly less intense. Judy needed to turn up the heat, she needed to force Claud's hand, and one course of action had occurred to her, although she didn't know if it would pan out. But doing anything was better than doing nothing.

▢ ▢ ▢

Judy rapped on the door frame of Claud's office and he glanced up at her over the top of his reading glasses. She saw that he'd been studying the baseball box scores in the *Chicago Tribune*—which pissed her off.

She said, "I've been thinking about something."

"What's that?" Claud said.

"When Maddox went to New York that one weekend with Gillian, he visited his uncle and his cousin, Naomi. We know that from tracking his movements on his phone. Anyway, he spent about half an hour with Naomi."

"So?" Claud said.

"Three weeks after he met with her, Naomi sent him a letter. Or something. When we searched his apartment after he split, I found a business envelope in a wastebasket and the return address was his cousin's, but I have no idea what was in the envelope. Well, the thing that just occurred to me is who sends letters these days? No one does. They send emails and emails with attachments. They send text messages. They Facetime, they Zoom, they Skype. No one sends fucking letters."

Claud said, "That's a rather sweeping generality."

"Yeah, but it's true. I mean, and no offense, the only people who send letters these days are people your age. No one my age does. So maybe she didn't send him a letter. Maybe there was something else in the envelope, photos, a flash drive, I don't know what."

"Assuming you're correct, what do you want to do?"

"This Naomi chick is weird. I spent a lot of time following her in New York and I think she might be autistic. I mean, the way she interacts with people is odd. She always looks down at the ground when she talks to someone and doesn't look 'em in the eye. And one time this guy touched her when she was standing on the street—he was just trying to get by her and kind of moving her out of the way—and she freaked out. I mean, she had a *fit*. At first, I thought maybe she was retarded but she has a job doing statistical analysis for a polling company, which isn't something a retard could do. In fact, I've read that a lot of autistic people are actually brilliant. You know, like Rain Man."

"Who's rain man?"

"Never mind. I'm just saying this girl probably isn't stupid."

"Judy, would you please get to the point. What do you want to do?"

"I want to break into her apartment and see if there's anything in it related to Jamison that might help us find him and anything that would explain why she would have sent him a letter, or if not a letter, what she sent."

Claud mulled that over for a couple of seconds. "All right. But don't do anything else unless you clear it with me."

"Of course not," Judy said.

Lying to Claud was dangerous, but he wasn't giving her a choice.

□ □ □

Judy did plan to search Naomi's apartment as she'd told Claud. She'd do that before she did anything else. And maybe she'd actually find something there that would lead her to Jamison and that treacherous cunt Gillian. The envelope she'd found in Jamison's apartment really did bother her. But what she was really planning to do was kidnap the little weirdo.

It had occurred to her that kidnapping Naomi, who lived in a crummy brownstone in Tribeca, would be easier than kidnapping Jed Maddox who lived on the seventeenth floor of a building with a doorman and who traveled around in a car with a driver who might be armed.

She'd tell Claud that while she was searching the apartment Naomi came home unexpectedly and she'd had the choice of killing her or snatching her, and she'd elected to snatch her. And then she'd get what she wanted: Jamison would learn that his little oddball cousin had disappeared and he'd contact Claud to negotiate her release.

Fuck all this sitting around doing nothing when it came to getting the people responsible for killing Sam.

□ □ □

Judy sat with her brother Matt in a rented van—one with a windowless cargo box—across the street from Naomi's apartment building waiting for her to go to dinner.

She learned from watching Naomi previously that the woman stuck to a rigid schedule. In the morning, at seven a.m., she'd walk to a coffee shop and get a cup of coffee and a bagel. At noon—*precisely* at noon—she'd get her lunch from places that sold falafels or soup or sandwiches and sit at a table alone outside the restaurant and watch people walk by. (Judy wondered where she sat and ate when the weather was shitty but right now New York was experiencing a fabulous October.) For dinner, she'd get fish and chips—she had fish and chips *every* night—and again would find someplace outdoors to sit and watch the passersby, then go for a short walk afterward. She was usually gone from her apartment for about forty minutes when she had dinner and that would give Judy the most time to conduct a search. If the search produced nothing, then they'd come back tomorrow and kidnap her.

The door to the apartment building opened and Naomi stepped outside at six p.m. on the dot, Judy again thinking that she could have set her watch by her. She had on baggy, highwater jeans that stopped about three inches above her running shoes and a New York Yankees baseball cap that looked brand new. She came down the steps and *marched* toward the fish and chips place; the way she walked it always looked like she was marching, not strolling. Judy was glad to see that there was a line of customers in the restaurant and it would be a while before she got her order.

Judy quickly left the van, walked across the street, and up the stairs leading to the building's main door. She was wearing a hooded sweatshirt to help hide her features from any nearby surveillance cameras. In

New York, thanks to fucking terrorists, there were surveillance cameras everywhere.

The last time she'd been there, when she'd been watching Naomi, she'd noticed that you had to buzz a tenant to get into the apartment building—and that's what she'd been planning to do: hit all the tenants' doorbells until one of them buzzed her in. But then she noticed that the door wasn't locked; it swung open when she tugged on it. There must have been something wrong with the magnetic switch that kept it closed. Thank God for small blessings.

Judy took the stairs to the fourth floor, walked down the hall to Naomi's apartment, looked around to make sure she was alone, and picked the lock. She could have picked the lock with a hairpin or a paperclip; with her lock picks, it was a piece of cake.

Which almost made her cry. She remembered trying to teach Sam how to pick locks but his fat fingers just couldn't get the hang of it.

Inside the apartment, she stood for a while looking at the small, cheaply furnished living space and wondered why someone as rich as Jed Maddox hadn't rented a nicer place for his daughter. Maybe he was a selfish prick like Vera Maddox.

The first place she decided to look was the kitchen table. On the table was a laptop, an inkjet printer, and stacks of manila file folders filled with paper. No wonder the woman never ate at home. Underneath the table was a small two-drawer file cabinet that most likely held more files.

Judy quickly looked at the stack of file folders on the table. The folders were either blue or red and each folder had a white stick-on label and the labels said things like: 1st district Alabama House Campaign; Iowa Senate Campaign; Nebraska Governor's Campaign. It was apparent that all the folders had to do with Naomi's job working for a pollster. Then she noticed one folder at the bottom of the stack that was buff colored. The label said: Jamison Research Project.

WTF?

She opened the folder and saw it was a copy of a letter to Jamison and there was a chart attached. She read the letter quickly, scanned the chart, and said out loud: "Oh, fuck me."

Naomi's inkjet printer was also a copy machine. She made a copy of the letter and the chart, then put the originals back in the file folder and put the folder at the bottom of the stack where she'd found it.

She decided she wouldn't kidnap Naomi until she showed Claud the file. After he saw it, she was positive he'd let her do what she wanted.

Claud was going to shit a brick when he saw the file.

33

Judy sat silently in Claud's office, gnawing on a fingernail, as Claud read Naomi's letter to Jamison and studied the genealogy chart.

She'd expected *some* reaction from him as he read Naomi's report: a curse, a sharp inhalation, a groan. Something. She should have known better. The old bastard was unshakable and the coolest person she'd ever met when presented with bad news.

When he finished reading—it took him *forever*—he ran the report through a shredder that was near his desk. He said, "This young woman . . . What's her name again?"

"Naomi," Judy said. "She's a goofy, little weirdo."

"That may be, but she's certainly thorough."

Claud closed his eyes and just sat there, ignoring her, apparently thinking everything over, while Judy waited impatiently. It was *obvious* what had to be done.

He opened his eyes at last and said, "There's actually only one thing she learned that's damaging."

Judy said, "You mean the part about you and the others all arriving in '61 and her not being able to trace you back any farther."

"Yes," Claud said. "The fact that members of the family married other members isn't a secret. It's a matter of public record should anyone else decide to look at the records. And we've lived here in Redemption long enough that people in this town know who's married to who and that we're a close-knit group. But that one piece of information could lead to the authorities taking a deep dive into the past, which I can't allow."

Judy said, "So we need to find out who Jamison and this Naomi chick have shared this information with and then kill them and everyone they've told."

There was no point in beating around the goddamn bush.

"Yes," Claud said.

Now that Claud had come to the conclusion that had been apparent to her from the onset, Judy said, "I've already worked out a plan for how to snatch her and question her. Matt will be helping me."

Claud merely nodded.

Judy got up to leave—she needed to get back to New York and there were things she needed to do before she left Redemption—but before she reached the door, Claud said, "How's your mother doing?"

Judy shook her head. "Not good. She can't sleep and she looks like she's aged twenty years since Sam was killed. The only thing that's going to make her feel better is when I kill that bitch Gillian and her fucking boyfriend."

Claud said, "You shouldn't swear so much, Judy. It's not ladylike or professional."

Judy didn't know how to respond to that dumb fucking remark. He'd just ordered her to torture and kill a woman and he was worried about her being *ladylike*?

◻ ◻ ◻

Claud sat there after Judy left, wondering if it was time for all of them to leave Redemption. If the authorities learned about Naomi's research, there'd be no choice but to leave. For him leaving wouldn't be a problem. For the others, however, it was going to be hard, and particularly for those with kids, like Matt and Sam's wives. It was going to be hard for Alice Connor, still not recovered from losing her son. Redemption was the only place any of them had ever lived except for him. They had roots here; they had friends and homes and memories here. Although Steven Lang was one of his most dedicated employees, he imagined it would even be hard for Steven to walk away from the house he'd spent so much time renovating. Yes, Steven would miss his house but not his wife. Steven wanted to see her dead for the humiliation she'd caused him.

But where would they all go? And would it even be possible for them to stay together and set up another operation like Drexler Limited. Probably not, at least not for quite a while. Initially they'd have to scatter, running in different directions to minimize the chances of them being caught, but maybe eventually they could all come together again.

The logistics of uprooting the entire family were staggering: obtaining new identities for every member, deciding on the securest ways to travel, locating new places to live. And it might be necessary, depending on who Naomi and Jamison had talked to, to leave quickly and there'd be no time to develop a well-thought-out plan.

But he was getting ahead of himself. If the only person who knew what Naomi had learned was Jamison, then eliminating him eliminated the problem. Still, he needed to get someone working on an escape plan and figuring out all the details in case they did have to run. He'd get Steven started on that right away.

He picked up the Sammy Sosa baseball off his desk and rolled it in his big hands.

Sixty years. What a run he'd had. He doubted that anyone else could have accomplished as much as he and his family had. And now everything he'd ever done was in danger of being exposed because of . . . What had Judy called her? Some goofy, little weirdo.

34

At noon, the day after talking to Claud, Judy and her brother Matt were sitting in the white van parked in a no parking zone within sight of Naomi Maddox's apartment building.

At twelve p.m.—on the dot—Naomi walked out of the building and headed toward a deli where she would order a sandwich, then find a place to sit outside and watch the people strolling by. Judy figured Naomi would be gone from her apartment for at least half an hour.

Judy said to her brother, "Go."

Matt pulled the van into the loading zone in front of Naomi's building.

If the woman had been normal, Judy would have stuck a gun in her back, threatened to kill her, and walked her into a waiting car. She was afraid with Naomi, however, she might freak out and start screaming so she'd had to come up with a more elaborate plan.

Judy took a steamer trunk out of the van's cargo box—one that had wheels on it and could be rolled—and lugged it up the steps and into the building. (The door lock still hadn't been fixed.) She took the elevator to the fourth floor, rolled the trunk down the hall, looked around, picked the lock on Naomi's door, rolled the trunk into Naomi's apartment, and relocked the door from the inside.

She went over to the stack of file folders sitting on Naomi's kitchen table and removed the folder containing the report she'd sent to Jamison. She also removed Naomi's laptop from the table and then placed the computer and the file folder in the steamer trunk. She didn't know if copies of the report had been sent to anyone other than Jamison or if the electronic file was stored someplace other than Naomi's computer, like the cloud, but she'd get the answers to those questions once she had Naomi.

Forty minutes later, Judy heard Naomi insert her key into the apartment door and stepped behind the door so she wouldn't be visible when Naomi opened it.

The first thing Naomi saw when she walked in was the steamer trunk sitting in her living room. As Naomi was standing there, baffled by the steamer trunk, Judy swung the sap in her hand, hitting the little woman hard enough to stun her and make her fall to the ground, then injected her in the neck with the sedative.

Judy was worried about the sedative. After doing a little research online—the fucking Internet was marvelous—she'd obtained it by breaking into a vet's office in Redemption, as she didn't have time to find another source. The drug was something called *acepromazine*, one they used to sedate dogs, and as best she could tell, it wouldn't kill a human. The problem was that she had to guess how much to give Naomi. She figured the woman weighed about a hundred pounds, and she needed to keep her unconscious for at least two hours, so she used a bit more than the amount specified for a seventy-pound canine, one about the size of a big German shepherd. But it would really fuck things up if Naomi had an allergic reaction or overdosed.

She watched anxiously for a couple of minutes after she'd injected the drug to see if Naomi started twitching or foaming at the mouth, and when she didn't, she lifted her up and placed her in the steamer trunk, folding her short legs to make her fit. It was a good thing the woman was so small.

She rolled the trunk to the elevator, took the elevator to the first floor, opened the door, and waved at her brother, who was sitting in the idling van. He helped her carry the trunk down the stairs and place it in the van.

Two and a half hours later—the traffic leaving New York had been a nightmare because of an accident on the George Washington Bridge—they arrived at the small house that Judy had rented from Airbnb using a fake name and credit card. The house was on the Jersey shore, situated on the edge of a marsh, and the beach was more than a mile away. It had only two bedrooms and a single bathroom, the furniture was old, and the appliances outdated. As a vacation place, other than being cheap, it left a lot to be desired—but as a place to stash a kidnapped woman and torture her and kill her and then dispose of her body, it was ideal.

The key to the house was in a lock box attached to the front door and Judy entered the combination provided by the home's owner. Matt rolled the steamer trunk into the house, opened it, lifted Naomi from it, and placed her on her back on the living room floor. She appeared to be breathing normally, like a sleeping person would. Judy checked her pulse—it was strong although her heart was beating only about fifty times per minute. Judy didn't know if that was good or bad.

"How long is she going to be out?" Matt asked.

"How the fuck would I know?" Judy said.

Naomi slept through the night, even though Judy had pinched her, tossed water on her face, and slapped her lightly a couple of times to wake her up.

In the morning, Matt said, "I hope she's not in a coma."

"Would you please, please just shut the hell up," Judy said.

35

Sandy Moran drove her cruiser along the beach-access road as she did every morning. Being the youngest and newest officer on the four-man Dolphin Cove police force meant she got stuck with the graveyard shift, midnight to eight a.m. Most of the action on her shift happened between midnight and two a.m. when the bars closed, and she'd be called to break up a fight or when a bartender thought someone was too drunk to drive. Or she'd pull over some moron weaving all over the road. After two, about all she did was cruise around town looking for "suspicious activity" unless someone called 911 to report something. About the only one who ever did was old Mrs. Walton, who called at least once a week because she thought she heard someone breaking into her house.

Toward the end of her shift, as the sun was coming up, she'd cruise the beach where she might find someone camping illegally or some kid lying in his own puke near a dead campfire where he'd passed out after a party. But the main reason she cruised the beach at dawn was because she enjoyed it when it was mostly empty of people and the offshore rock formation was just poking through the morning fog.

Sandy stopped the cruiser near the beach, poured a cup of coffee from her thermos, and just took in the view for a moment before scanning the beach through her binoculars, looking for anything abnormal. The only things she saw were four early birds strolling alone or walking their dogs and one nut with a metal detector sweeping the beach in front of him, looking for God knows what.

As she was sitting there, an SUV with two kayaks mounted on the roof stopped a couple of hundred yards from her and a man and woman wearing black wetsuits got out and began to remove the kayaks from the roof. She glanced over at them briefly, then went back to staring at the ocean, then whiplashed her head back to look at the couple again. My God, it looked like them. She trained her binoculars on them, looking first at the man, then at the woman. Yes, no doubt about it. It was them.

The guys she worked with—she was the only woman on the force— always gave her a hard time for the way she pored over all the bulletins they'd get from the FBI and the Oregon State police and other law enforcement organizations. They were all supposed to look at them but she was the only who really *studied* them. Two days ago, she'd seen a bulletin from a police force someplace in Illinois with the odd name of Redemption. The bulletin showed a photo of two people, a man and a woman, who'd embezzled a bunch of money. The thing that got Sandy's attention was that the couple was so good looking. The guy kind of reminded her of a younger version of that movie star James Franco. And the woman . . . she could have been a model she was so beautiful, and she had the cutest haircut. She'd thought at the time she saw the bulletin that it had to be disadvantageous for two criminals on the lam to be so attractive because people couldn't help but stare at them.

Sandy remembered the bulletin saying that if the couple was spotted to call the Redemption police department but not to approach them or make any attempt to apprehend them. She watched as they carried their kayaks down to the beach. They were both tall and slim and had great bodies, which Sandy, herself short and a bit overweight, couldn't help but envy. The guy got their paddles and they pushed the kayaks into the water, got into them, and headed through the surf toward the rocks, the woman leading the way.

The station was only five minutes away and Sandy figured she could drive there, find the bulletin, and call the cops in Illinois before the couple got back from their kayak ride. It was seven in Oregon so it'd be nine back in Illinois and someone should be around to answer the phone.

She parked the cruiser near the station, unlocked the station door, and ran inside. No one was there of course. The chief and the other day shift cop didn't get in until eight and the chief was usually late. She found the bulletin in the stack on top of a file cabinet and looked at the pictures on it again. Yeah, the couple on the beach was definitely them.

She called the number in Illinois printed on the bulletin.

◻ ◻ ◻

The phone number on the bulletin didn't go to the Redemption police department. The Redemption cops, under the mayor's order, provided the manpower to distribute the bulletin but the phone number went to a cell phone carried by Mary White. When the phone rang Mary figured it had to be a wrong number; she'd never expected anyone to respond to the bulletin. The bulletin was the longest of long shots when it came to tracking down Gillian and Jamison.

She answered the phone saying: "Redemption PD."

"This is Officer Sandy Moran. I work for the police department in Dolphin Cove, Oregon. We got a bulletin saying that if anyone saw this couple wanted for embezzling to give you guys a call. Well, I just saw them. They're down on the beach here kayaking."

Mary emerged from the fog of grief that had surrounded her since Sam's death.

Forcing herself to speak calmly, she said, "Officer Moran, did you approach the couple?"

"No."

"Good. Have you told anyone about seeing them, other than me?"

"Not yet."

"Good, and it's imperative that you don't. You see, officer, this is a very complicated case and the FBI is now involved and before the FBI arrests them, they'll send in a surveillance team to gather more evidence and listen in on their calls and do whatever else they need to do to ensure a conviction. So the FBI won't want you talking to anybody about seeing them, not even your boss, as that might lead to them being alerted. What I'm saying is, the more people who know where they are, the greater the chance that a leak will occur. So can I trust you, Officer Moran, to keep this information to yourself?"

"I guess I can do that, but I need to know if they pose a danger to the community."

"They don't. They're a couple of smart thieves, not gangsters. They don't carry guns and they don't pose a physical danger to anyone. Now you said you saw this couple on the beach. Do they live in the town of Dolphin Cove?"

"I don't know. I've never seen them walking around town—and I think I would have noticed them—but I work the graveyard shift and spend most of the day sleeping. Do you want me to follow them when they leave the beach?"

Mary hesitated. "Do you think you can do that without being spotted? If they spot you following them—like I said, they're smart—they're likely to take off and we may never be able to find them again."

"I can do it. I'll follow them in my personal vehicle not my cruiser."

"Okay," Mary said. "Then do that. But we'd rather you lose them than have them see you tailing them. Now that we know the general area where they are, the FBI can send in a team to hunt for them. But Officer Moran, I need your word that you'll keep this information to yourself until after they've been arrested. After they've been apprehended, I'm sure the FBI will let your boss know what you've done and recommend that you get a commendation. So do I have your word?"

"Yes," Sandy said.

□ □ □

In spite of the fact that she'd spent four years as an army MP, the chief and the other two cops on the force treated her like some kind of joke. The only reason she'd been hired was to satisfy some kind of diversity requirement tied to state funding and they never let her forget it. Well, helping the FBI catch a couple of big-time embezzlers would show the chauvinistic assholes her worth.

Sandy said, "I need to go. I have to get back to the beach before they finish their kayak ride. I'll call you after I follow them."

Sandy went out to her car—a ten-year-old Prius—and grabbed a windbreaker she had on the backseat, put the windbreaker on over her uniform shirt, and took off for the beach. The chief would see her cruiser sitting in the parking lot but just think that she'd gotten off her shift and had gone home before he arrived and wouldn't give a shit.

When she got back to the beach, the couple's SUV was still parked there as she'd expected; she'd figured that they'd be out for at least an hour on their kayaks. Half an hour later, she watched as they pulled their kayaks onto the beach then secured them to the top of their car. They didn't take off their wetsuits; they just wiped the suits off with towels, used the towels to cover the seats, then hopped in and took off. Not taking off their wetsuits probably meant they lived or were staying someplace close by. The wetsuits would be uncomfortable on a long drive.

Sandy let them get a couple of blocks ahead of her and took off after them. They headed north out of town, then turned onto a paved road going east, one that headed up into the hills and the forest. Fortunately, at this time of day, people were going to work and there was traffic on the road and Sandy's car wasn't the only one behind them. But then they turned onto a narrow gravel road and Sandy had to hang way back to not be noticed. In fact, she hung so far back she lost sight of them when they rounded a couple of curves and when she sped up to spot them, she didn't see them.

She knew there were a few cabins out this way and she wondered if they'd gone to one of them. She drove two miles farther going fast, hoping to catch up with their car, and when she still didn't see them, she turned around and drove back the way she'd come. She passed four cabins but didn't see their car.

She came to a narrow, tree-lined driveway with a sign at the entrance that said PRIVATE DRIVEWAY, NO TRESPASSING but couldn't see a house at the end of the driveway. She decided to take a chance and drove up the driveway and stopped as soon as she saw the cabin, a huge, gorgeous place that she knew was owned by some fat cat who used to work for Microsoft. And there was their SUV with the kayaks still on top.

She backed down the driveway and headed back toward town. As she was driving, she called the Redemption cops' number again. The same woman she'd spoken to before answered.

Sandy said, "I know where they're staying."

36

Matt said, "I wonder if we ought to get some of those things you break open and stick under someone's nose to wake them up. What do they call those? Poppers?"

Judy, cranky from staying up all night waiting for Naomi to come to, said, "Where the hell would we get those, you dumb shit?"

At that moment, Naomi began to stir. Her hands twitched a couple of times and she started to cough. "Thank God," Judy said. "Get a chair."

Matt got a chair from the kitchen, picked up Naomi before she became fully awake, and placed her in the chair, then Judy wrapped duct tape around her arms to bind her to the chair. A moment later Naomi opened her eyes and seemed bewildered as she took in her surroundings—and then started *screaming*.

Judy said, "Shut up, shut up!" She wasn't worried about anyone hearing Naomi as there were no nearby neighbors, but Naomi's high-pitched screams made it impossible for her to think. When Naomi kept shrieking Judy slapped her, but all that did was make her scream louder. Judy took a piece of duct tape and placed it over Naomi's mouth then pinched her nostrils shut. She said, "I'm gonna suffocate you if you don't stop yelling."

But it didn't work. The whole time Judy was pinching her nose shut, Naomi kept thrashing in the chair and trying to scream through the duct tape. Judy didn't understand that being bound to a chair and being touched by a stranger was driving Naomi insane. Judy finally let go of Naomi's nostrils—she had to before the little twerp passed out—and when she did, Naomi stopped struggling. Now she just sat there staring straight ahead, her face expressionless.

Judy said, "That's better. Now I'm going to take the tape off your mouth but if you start screaming again, I'm going to really hurt you."

Judy ripped the duct tape off her mouth, which must have smarted, but Naomi didn't react. Her eyes were open, but vacant.

Judy said, "We just want to ask you a few questions and if you tell us the truth, we'll let you go."

Naomi didn't respond.

Judy took the file folder out of the steamer trunk, the folder she'd taken from Naomi's apartment, and showed it to Naomi. She said, "All we want to know about is this shit you sent your cousin."

Naomi still didn't respond, and although her eyes were open, Judy didn't think she was actually seeing the file folder being held in front of her face. The damn woman was there physically, but her mind had left the building.

Judy slapped her on the head with the file folder. "Hey! Say something."

No reaction.

Judy hit her again with the file folder. Naomi didn't even blink.

Judy yelled, "Say something, goddamnit, or I'm going to cut your fucking nose off."

Matt said, "Stop hitting her. It looks like she's gone into some kind trance or something. Just let her sit there for a while and see if she snaps out of it."

"Bullshit. I'm not gonna let her sit there," Judy said. She walked into the kitchen and found a carving knife with an eight-inch blade. She held it in front of Naomi's eyes and said, "I'm gonna cut off one of your fingers—then we'll see if you talk."

She grabbed Naomi's right hand but just then her phone rang. She looked at the caller ID and said to Matt, "It's Mom." She tapped the ACCEPT button on her phone and said to her mother: "We got her but—"

Her mother interrupted her. "We know where Gillian is."

Mary explained how a cop in an Oregon beach town called Dolphin Cove had spotted Gillian and Jamison and followed them to where they were living. Mary said, "You need to get out there right away. I've booked you seats on a flight to Portland that leaves Newark in three hours. You need to be on it."

"But what do you want us to do with this nut case we kidnapped? We haven't been able to question her because she wigged out on us and has gone into some kind of fucking trance. Should we kill her before we go?"

"No. We need to find out who she's talked to, but we'll deal with her later," Mary said. "She's not the priority. Can you tie her up and gag her and leave her where she is for a few hours?"

"I suppose so," Judy said. "This place is isolated, and I don't think anyone is going to come knocking on the door."

"Okay then leave her, and I'll send David out to watch her. He can get there in four hours."

Mary meant David Pine, her brother, the day shift security guard.

"Are you sure Uncle Dave is the right guy to send?" Judy said.

"He's the only one available. Ed is busy in D.C. and Claud has Steven working on some special project. And all he has to do is watch her for a few hours. After you deal with Gillian and Maddox, we'll figure out what to do with her. Plus keeping her alive might be good in case we need to use her for leverage, although I doubt we will. So get to the airport. I'll text you Gillian's address, and when you get to Dolphin Cove, call me and we'll talk about how to handle her."

Judy said, "Okay. We'll leave the key to the house in a lock box that's on the front door. That's where it was when we got here. I'll text you the combination to the box and the address."

Judy disconnected the call with her mother and said to her brother: "We gotta go. They found Gillian. Uncle Dave is going to come out here and watch this crazy bitch until we can get back here."

She walked over to Naomi who was still silent, staring straight ahead. She pressed a strip of duct tape over her mouth and said, "I'll be back, weirdo. You haven't seen the last of me."

37

After picking up a rental car and making the two-hour drive from Portland, it was ten p.m. when Matt and Judy arrived at Dolphin Cove. Judy called her mother, saying: "Okay, we're here. We'll check out the place where they're staying tonight to see what we're up against, then deal with them tomorrow."

"You need to do something first," Mary said. "You need to get rid of the cop who spotted them. I convinced her not to talk to anyone, but she has to be eliminated before she does and before you do anything else. Her name's Sandy Moran and she told me she works the graveyard shift. So get to the police station and hang around until she begins her shift and take care of her."

□ □ □

At eleven thirty, Judy watched a police cruiser pull up in front of the Dolphin Cove police station and an overweight male cop get out of the cruiser and walk into the station. Fifteen minutes later a woman wearing a police uniform parked a blue Prius next to the cruiser and entered the station.

Judy poked Matt who was sleeping in the passenger seat. "Wake up. She's here."

While they'd been waiting, Judy had checked out the police department's website and it showed photos of all four members of the force. Only one was a woman: Sandy Moran, a pleasant-looking woman with short dark hair.

Moran came out of the station ten minutes later, hopped into the cruiser, and drove off.

Judy followed her to a convenience store where she filled up a thermos with coffee and bought a sandwich. After that Moran just drove around the small town, which appeared to be completely locked up for the night. The only businesses open were the convenience store and a couple of taverns.

Moran cruised by one open bar, a place called the Crow's Nest located on the edge of the town. Two blocks later, the cruiser's light bar came to life, blue and red lights spinning. Judy could see that ahead of Moran was a pickup that had wandered over the center line. Moran got up close to the pickup's rear bumper and hit the siren for a moment, and the pickup pulled to the side of the road.

Judy stopped her car a block behind Moran's and turned off the headlights. She noticed that the only structure close to Moran was a feedstore that was closed. There were no houses nearby nor any other cars on the road.

Judy watched as Moran walked up to the driver's side of the pickup, amazed that Moran didn't put her hand on her weapon as she did. Most cops making a traffic stop these days were prepared for the possibility of a gunfight, but Judy figured that in a town this size Moran probably knew the driver. Moran made a motion for the pickup truck driver to roll down his window and a moment later an old white-haired coot wearing bib overalls got out of the pickup. He was visible in the cruiser's headlights. Moran administered a sobriety test, making the old guy walk a few paces to see if he could manage a straight line. She apparently decided he was sober enough to drive home because a moment later he got into his truck and took off, driving slowly. Moran got back in the cruiser—but then just sat there.

Judy said to Matt, "Switch places with me. Hurry! She's probably writing up a report."

Judy got out of the car, ran around to the passenger side, and Matt took her place behind the wheel. Judy said, "Drive up and park right next to her. Hurry, before she moves. And turn on the headlights."

Matt did as Judy ordered and drove up and parked next to the cruiser. Judy smiled at Moran and made a gesture for her to roll down her window. Moran did and said, "Yes, ma'am. What can I do for you? Are you lost?"

Judy raised the gun that she'd been holding in her lap and shot twenty-four-year-old Sandy Moran in the face.

38

Judy said, "Okay. Now let's check out the place where Gillian is staying."

Matt said, "We're not going to be able to see a damn thing."

He was right. It was one in the morning and pitch dark outside.

"I know," Judy said, "but I'm not planning to do anything tonight. I just want to see what the place looks like."

Half an hour later they arrived at an unlit driveway winding into the woods. The address on the rural mailbox was visible in the car's headlights. Judy thought for a moment then said, "I've changed my mind. I'm gonna go into the woods and wait until it's light enough to see. You go find a place to park so in case someone drives by they won't see the car sitting here. After it gets light and I've taken a look, I'll call you and you come back and get me."

"Jesus, Judy, I'm exhausted. We've been going since we snatched that woman."

The only sleep they'd gotten in the last two days was on the plane from New Jersey to Oregon. But Judy said, "Hey! Don't you want to get the people responsible for killing Sam?"

"Of course I do, but—"

"Then do what I'm telling you and quit whining."

Judy got out of the car and Matt drove off. She waited until her eyes adjusted to the darkness, and even though she could barely see, she walked slowly down the driveway. She just hoped the place wasn't guarded by motion detectors or that a fuckin' dog wasn't roaming around outside. As she neared the end of the driveway, she could see the outline of a large house and, thanks to a porch light that was on, an SUV parked in front of the house. The only impression she got was that the place was huge, which made her wonder how Gillian and Jamison could afford it.

She stepped off the driveway and into the thick woods surrounding the house, then sat down at the base of a tree and leaned her back against it. For the next four hours she sat, dozing off periodically, her head snapping back when her chin hit her chest. Finally, dawn came and it got light enough for her to see.

The house—a magnificent log cabin—was surrounded by forest on three sides and there were big picture windows that looked out into the woods. She noticed a couple of kayaks on the ground near the front porch. There was an attached two-car garage but for whatever reason the SUV was parked in front of the house and not in the garage.

She slowly circled the house, staying in the woods, the bushes and the trees making her mostly invisible to anyone inside the house. But she doubted anyone was watching. There wasn't a single light on inside the house, which was not surprising at five in the morning. She noticed the garage had a side door on the south end. It might be possible to pick open that door and then gain entry to the house through the garage. The south side of the garage also offered the advantage of not being visible from the house.

She completed her circuit of the house. There was a large deck on the backside with a patio table and a bunch of chairs and a sliding glass door that opened onto the deck. More big windows provided a view of the woods behind the house. On one corner of the deck was a hot tub. She could just picture Gillian and her fucking boyfriend drinking wine and sitting naked in the hot tub. Come to think of it, she'd never really liked Gillian.

The most important thing about the house was that it was completely isolated, surrounded by forest, and there were no nearby neighbors.

Judy walked quickly toward the road where Matt had dropped her off. On the way, she called him. His phone rang four times before he answered it and Judy figured he'd been sound asleep in the car. She said, "Come pick me up."

Back in the car, she said to her brother, "Let's go find a motel, but not in Dolphin Cove. There's another town about ten miles north of here called Lincoln Beach. We'll see if we can find something there."

Judy didn't want anyone in Dolphin Cove to see them, two strangers about to commit a double homicide.

Judy said, "We can sleep for five or six hours then I want to find a place that sells night vision goggles. We might have to drive back to Portland but I'm hoping we can find someplace closer.

"Then tonight, like around one or two in the morning, we'll come back here. With the goggles we'll be able to walk through the woods and see where we're going. The house has an attached garage with a side door that you can't see from the house. I'll pick open the side door if it's locked, then we'll go through the garage and into the house. And then we'll kill 'em."

39

When Jamison's laptop chirped that he had a Google alert, he'd been trying to decide if he should purchase two thousand dollars' worth of stock in a company that had come up with a new sleep apnea machine, one that was smaller than current models and didn't have all the tubing and other hardware that made wearers look like alien predators.

When he'd been at Goldman Sachs, he'd traded *millions* of dollars, but here he was agonizing over a 2K buy. He had to keep reminding himself that the day trading he was doing was just a fun way to spend some time, and not something he was doing to make serious money. Nor could he afford to blow his and Gillian's fortune just because he was bored.

He missed the rush of being a major player in the market. And he missed Manhattan more than ever; he needed the city that never slept. Gillian, however, was perfectly content in little Dolphin Cove, going on her daily kayak ride and sitting by a fire reading for hours. Her latest interest was baking, and although it amused him, he'd had to endure loafs of bread that didn't rise and lopsided cakes.

Oh, well. They had a good life, and as she'd said before, the life they were living was the one that most people wanted to retire to. He'd get used to it.

He tapped a button to get out of the trading program and went to the Safari screen on his laptop to see the Google alert.

When he saw the alert, he stood up and yelled, "No!"

The article in the *New York Post* said that Naomi Maddox, daughter of Jed Maddox, former owner and partner in the hedge fund firm of Maddox and Maddox, was missing and her father believed she'd been kidnapped. Jed had told the police that his daughter called him daily and she hadn't called for two days. He said she rarely left New York City, would never have left without telling him, and normally she stayed within a six-block area near her apartment.

Jed, however, had not received a ransom demand. He made an appeal to whoever took his daughter, begging them not to harm her, saying that he'd be willing to pay for her return, and wouldn't involve the police. The article contained a description of Naomi—five foot one, a hundred pounds—and a photograph showing Naomi's short, dark pageboy and her solemn, elfin face. (Naomi never smiled in photographs.)

Although Jamison knew it was possible that Naomi had been snatched off the street by some maniac, sexual predator, or serial killer, he didn't think that was the case. He believed that Claud Drexler was behind her abduction. Claud may have kidnapped her because he'd somehow learned about Naomi's research into Claud's extended family, but that seemed unlikely. How would Claud have known? Jamison hadn't left a copy of Naomi's letter in his apartment when he and Gillian left Redemption. He hadn't even told Gillian about Naomi's research. Although he was still curious about Gillian's inbred family, he'd seen no reason to question her about it after she'd told him the truth about what the family did, nor had he wanted to remind her of her troubled past.

So it seemed unlikely that Claud would have known about Naomi's research. A more likely possibility was that Claud had kidnapped Naomi—the most vulnerable member of Jamison's family—to use her as some sort of bargaining chip to force Gillian and him to return to Redemption.

Jamison paced the house waiting for Gillian to return home. She'd gone into Dolphin Cove to pick up a few groceries. As he waited, he tried to figure out what to do when it came to Naomi. The only thing he could think of was to call Claud and tell him that if he didn't release Naomi—immediately and unharmed—he was going to call the FBI and tell the Bureau about Drexler Limited and the criminal syndicate he worked for.

☐ ☐ ☐

Gillian walked into the house carrying a couple of bags of groceries, a long loaf of French bread protruding from one. She started to smile, but then saw the look on Jamison's face. "What's wrong?" she said.

Instead of answering her, he handed her the copy of the article from the *Post* that he'd printed out. Gillian read it, but before she could say anything, Jamison said, "Your goddamn family kidnapped her. I'm going to call Claud and tell him that if he doesn't release her—"

"Claud wouldn't have done this," Gillian said. "I sent him a letter after we left Redemption and told him that if he left us alone, we wouldn't talk about the company. He would know that doing something like this might cause us to go to the police."

"He sent a guy to kill my mother," Jamison said.

A few days after arriving in Oregon, Jamison had found out from the Internet that his mother had killed an intruder soon after he saw her in New Mexico. They didn't know who Vera had killed but Gillian was almost certain that it was one of Mary White's sons who had been sent to interrogate Vera.

Gillian said, "He sent someone to *question* your mother in an attempt to locate us, which at least makes sense. But kidnapping Naomi doesn't make sense. I almost called Claud after we found out about the attack on your mother but decided not to because she escaped unharmed. I guess I should have called him."

"Well, I'm going to call the old bastard now and tell him that if he doesn't let Naomi go—"

"No. I'll call him. I know how to contact him in a way that he won't be able to trace the call. And I'll be able to tell if he's lying."

Jamison stared at her for a long moment before saying, "Gillian, Naomi's a complete innocent. She's like a child and I love her and if anything happens to her it would destroy my uncle. If she's harmed, no matter what you say, I'm calling the FBI. I won't let Claud get away with this."

"I'm telling you, Jamison, if we go to the FBI we'll be dead before we have a chance to testify."

"I don't believe that," Jamison said. "No matter how connected this syndicate is, U.S. marshals will be able to protect us. That's their job and they're good at it. We may have to go into some sort of witness protection program but with the money we have, that won't be a problem."

"Let me just talk to Claud before you do anything drastic," Gillian said.

After that, and depending on what Claud said, she'd find a way to handle Jamison.

She had to.

40

Gillian told Jamison that she needed to go to Corvallis to call Claud. She said that even though it was unlikely that Claud would be able to trace the call, she didn't want to take any chances and Corvallis was about an hour from Dolphin Cove and on the I-5 corridor. The truth was that she could have made the call from the cabin, but she didn't want Jamison to hear what she was going to say.

"I'm coming with you," Jamison said.

"No, you're too emotional. I'll deal with this." Before Jamison could argue with her, she snatched her laptop off the desk where it had been sitting, jammed it into her laptop case, and walked out the door, saying, "I'll be back in a couple of hours. And I'm begging you, Jamison, for both our sakes, don't do anything until I get back. Let me handle this."

She didn't drive to Corvallis. She drove to the town of Lincoln Beach about ten miles north of Dolphin Cove. There was a Starbucks there and it would do. She didn't go into the Starbucks, however, because she didn't want anyone to overhear the call, but sitting in the Starbucks parking lot she could pick up the coffee shop's WiFi signal.

She booted up her computer and launched a program that would bounce the call she was about to make through a dozen cities and there would be no way anyone would be able to trace it back to the Starbucks where she was parked.

She plugged a headset into the computer but instead of calling Claud, she called Mary White.

She said: "Mary, it's Gillian."

There was a long pause, Mary obviously shocked to be hearing from her.

Mary said, "When we catch you, my daughter's going to cut your heart out."

"Mary, tell Claud I'm going to call the number in the comm room in ten minutes," Gillian said and hung up. Claud would be more open with her on the special phone in the communication room. As for the threat Mary had made, Gillian believed her. Judy White was a psychopath.

Gillian waited ten minutes, time enough for Claud to get from his office on the third floor to the comm room on the first floor, then made the call.

Claud answered the phone, saying, "Hello, Gillian." His voice, as usual, was low and calm.

She said: "Let Naomi Maddox go or I'll tell the FBI about you."

She thought Claud would deny having taken Naomi, but he didn't. He said, "No, you won't. You know we'll get you if you testify, and more likely before you testify."

Gillian knew that Claud was right, and that Jamison was wrong, thinking the FBI could protect them. If the FBI put her up in a hotel and surrounded her with federal marshals, the client would be willing to blow up the entire hotel to kill her. The client wouldn't care how many people had to die to stop her from talking.

Gillian said, "I don't have to testify. All I have to do is make a phone call. I'll tell the FBI about the hooker you placed in Cooper & Cooper to compromise Congressman Corcoran. I'll tell them the client's people are running a company in Virginia with a contract to produce machines for Merck. Once they investigate, the Corcoran and the Virginia Beach operations will be finished and I'll have credibility. And then I'll tell them about every operation you've ever done and about the ones you're planning. Like the cannery project. I don't want to do that, Claud, but I will. And you have to understand that when it comes to Naomi Maddox, I won't be able to control Jamison. The girl's like a sister to him and if you don't let her go or if you kill her, he'll go to the FBI on his own and I won't be able to stop him."

"Jamison doesn't know anything."

"No, but I do. Claud, let the girl go."

"I can't do that, Gillian. She learned something that poses a significant danger to me and she's told Jamison what she learned."

"What did she learn?"

"Ask Jamison and then you'll understand."

"Is Naomi already dead, Claud?"

"Gillian, forget about Naomi Maddox. There's nothing you can do about her. But there is a way out of this for you."

"What's that?"

"Kill Jamison Maddox. With him and his cousin both dead, I'm willing to overlook what you've done and I'll stop hunting for you. You know we'll find you eventually. It may take months or years, but we will find you and then you'll die a horrible death because we'll be forced to question you to find out who you've talked to. But kill Maddox and this whole thing ends. I know you have no desire to expose us because you're complicit in the things we've done. And if you wanted to expose us, you would have done so already. So kill Maddox and I promise that we'll stop hunting for you. Gillian, is Jamison Maddox worth your life? Do you love the man that much?"

Before Gillian could respond, Claud disconnected the call.

Gillian was stunned that he'd hung up on her. And he'd sounded confident that she'd do what he wanted when there was no reason for him to be confident. He should have been terrified of her calling the FBI and disrupting his ongoing operations, but he hadn't sounded the least bit concerned much less terrified. And why had he hung up on her before she could respond to the ultimatum that he'd given her?

As for what he'd told her—that he'd stop hunting for her if Jamison was dead—she was inclined to believe him. He may have wanted her back in the fold, doing the job she used to do, but he could live without her and, as he'd said, he wasn't concerned about her going to the authorities. Yes, if Jamison were dead, she could be truly free.

Killing Jamison was an option that had never occurred to her.

41

Gillian returned to the cabin to find Jamison pacing the front porch. She said, "Let's go inside and talk."

She led Jamison to the kitchen. Like everything else about the cabin, she loved the kitchen with its modern appliances and copper-bottomed pots hanging over granite countertops and an antique farm table big enough to seat eight. It was the kind of kitchen her husband would have wanted had their house in Redemption been big enough to accommodate one this size. What she particularly loved was that the kitchen windows looked out at a section of old-growth forest where some of the trees had to be over a hundred years old. It was like looking at a fairy tale forest, one that Hansel and Gretel might have wandered through. Just yesterday, she'd seen a stag with an enormous set of antlers; the only times she'd ever seen a deer with a rack that large had been in photos. If she wanted to stay living in this marvelous place, she needed to get Jamison under control.

Taking a seat at the kitchen table, she said, "Claud says that he didn't kidnap Naomi and I believe him."

"Well, I don't," Jamison said.

"Jamison, listen to me. Claud's a logical person and there's no logical reason for him to have kidnapped her. She doesn't know anything that could harm him. And if he had kidnapped her to force us do something, like return to Redemption, he would have said so."

She doubted that Claud would allow Naomi's body to be discovered and he certainly wouldn't have kidnapped the woman in a way that could be traced back to him. If she could convince Jamison that Claud had had nothing to do with her disappearance, Naomi would be just another one of the thousands of women who went missing every year.

On the other hand, she didn't know what Claud had meant when he'd said that Naomi had learned something that posed a significant danger to him and that she'd told Jamison what she'd learned. She could ask Jamison, but she didn't want to ask him. She wanted Jamison to believe that Claud would have had no reason to harm Naomi.

"So what did he tell you?" Jamison asked.

"He told me that if we returned to Redemption all would be forgiven." She laughed and added: "Now *that* I don't believe."

Jamison didn't respond. He turned his head away from her and looked out at the forest behind the house.

It occurred to her that the Jamison she was now looking at was a person she'd never seen before. Since she'd known him, she'd never seen him take anything really seriously. He'd certainly never taken his job at Drexler seriously, and even after they'd gone on the run, and even after she'd told him that they could be killed, he'd still acted as if life was one big game and he was confident that he could handle whatever the game threw at him. Maybe it was because of his wealthy upbringing, but he didn't really believe that any harm could ever come to him. He was handsome and he was young and he was smart—and he'd always been lucky. When he'd been convicted for insider trading, even then his luck had held. He didn't end up in prison, and he'd been certain that his ship would eventually right itself and his charmed existence would continue. But this thing with Naomi was different, and it was different because it wasn't about *him*. It was about two people he genuinely loved—Naomi and his uncle—and he'd gone from being an amused bystander to someone who was deadly serious and someone she might not be able to manipulate.

Finally, he looked back at her and said, "Gillian, I want the whole truth from you when it comes to Claud Drexler."

"I don't know what you mean. I have told you the truth," Gillian said.

"I don't think so. When we spent that weekend in New York, after you left, I went to see Naomi and asked her to investigate the people at Drexler."

"What are you talking about?"

"Naomi's very bright and she's a hell of a researcher, and I asked her to find out what she could about all the people at Drexler whose names I knew. I wanted to know more about who I was working with, particularly after you made it clear that you were afraid to leave the company."

"You shouldn't have done that."

"Well, I did."

"So what did she learn?"

"She found out that everyone at Drexler is the offspring of five couples who came to Redemption in 1961. The children of those five couples married each other and so did the children of the generation after that. Now that's pretty fucking weird all by itself, Gillian, but I suppose if you're all part of some criminal clan then maybe it makes sense. But the one thing Naomi learned that didn't make sense is that there's no record of the five original couples prior to 1961. So where did Claud Drexler come from, Gillian? For that matter, who is Claud Drexler?"

Gillian was too stunned to respond. But now she understood why Claud had kidnapped Naomi and why he would never stop hunting for

Jamison. Finding her was no longer Claud's priority. It was Jamison he had to silence.

Jamison said, "Gillian, answer me! Who is Claud Drexler?"

She said, "Jamison I have no idea what he did prior to 1961. I wasn't around then—I was born in 1990—and my grandparents died when I was just a kid and I barely remember them. And if my parents knew anything about Claud's past, they never told me. And maybe there's no record of the families prior to '61 because they changed their names for some reason, like maybe because they were running from the law. Claud's a criminal now and he was probably a criminal before he arrived in Redemption. All I know is that he didn't kidnap Naomi."

Jamison's eyes locked onto hers, studying her, assessing her.

She could tell that he didn't believe her.

Maybe Claud was right. Maybe the only way to end this was to kill Jamison. Only then would Claud stop chasing her, and only then would she be free.

42

While Judy and Matt were flying to Portland, David Pine, Mary's brother, arrived at the house near the marsh in New Jersey. He saw the lock box on the door and looked at the text message on his phone that provided the five-digit combination. He opened the lock box, took out the key, and let himself into the house.

Sitting in the living room, bound to a chair with gray duct tape, was a small woman with short dark hair. The woman's eyes were open, and she appeared to be looking right at him, but she didn't react in any way when she saw him. Mary had said that the girl had some type of disability, that she might be retarded or something, and that before Judy and Matt had left, she'd gone into some sort of stupor.

He walked over to her and said, "Hey."

She didn't respond.

He noticed a stain on her jeans and smelled urine. She must have wet her pants.

"Hey," he said again, and waved a hand in front of her eyes. "Can you hear me?" He pulled the duct tape off her mouth. "You want a drink of water or something?"

The woman didn't answer. Oh, well, what could he do?

All he'd been told was that he was supposed to stay with her and keep her where she was until Mary called and told him otherwise. So that's what he'd do. But he really wished he knew what the hell was going on.

David knew that Claud and his sister didn't think he was very bright—and he knew this to be true. He didn't have the brains of someone like Gillian who'd gone to college and understood computers. Nor was he as smart as Mary or his nieces and nephews. Most of the time he was only given simple jobs, like delivering something to someone when Claud decided it wasn't safe to use the mail. He picked up supplies; he ran errands for Claud that had nothing to do with the company. So he was surprised that he'd been given this particular job, which seemed important, and figured the only reason he'd been selected was because no one else had been available. He knew that Steven Lang hadn't been sent because he was working on a special project for Claud, one that had to do with the possibility of the family leaving Redemption, something he didn't even want to think about. Whatever the case, he'd been chosen and it really wasn't a hard job; all he had to do was keep a little woman in a house.

He hoped he wasn't told to hurt her. He'd do it if he had to, but he didn't want to.

He walked around the house and looked in the kitchen cabinets. There was some coffee and a bunch of condiments, like sugar and salt, and a couple of old cans of tuna fish in one of the cupboards, but that was about it. He'd been told he wouldn't have to watch the woman for very long, but he didn't know how long. He'd seen a grocery store on his way to the house. Maybe he should go there and buy a few things to eat; also, a six-pack of beer. The girl wasn't going anywhere and he'd only be gone for half an hour.

He said to her: "I'm going to the store to get some food. You want anything?"

She didn't answer. He put the duct tape back over her mouth and left.

43

Jamison left Gillian sitting in the kitchen and went outside and over to the woodshed on the north side of the house. He needed to think— and he needed to release all the anger and fear surging through him. He was terrified for Naomi and he was angry because he suspected that his lover was lying to him.

There were two cords of wood in the shed, the logs about twelve inches in diameter and twelve inches long. He put one of the logs on the tree stump near the woodshed, picked up an ax, and struck the log hard, splitting it in two. Then he split the two logs to make four—and reached for another log.

His gut told him that Gillian knew more about Claud's past than she claimed. She had to know more; her whole life had been devoted to Claud and her extended family. So how could she not know about their origins? And why would she withhold information from him? She'd already admitted that Claud ran an organization that committed crimes, including murder. If she'd be willing to tell him that, why not tell him everything she knew?

As for Claud not having kidnapped Naomi, he had to admit that that could be true. As Gillian had said, Claud had no reason to kidnap her—Claud didn't know about the research she'd done for Jamison—and if he had kidnapped her, he would have made some sort of demand and Gillian had said that he hadn't. But again, he had to wonder if Gillian was telling him the truth. All Gillian wanted was for Claud to leave them alone so they could continue their idyllic existence, but would she sacrifice Naomi to preserve what they had? He didn't think so—he didn't think she could be that heartless—but now he wasn't sure.

He still had the option of contacting the FBI and telling the Bureau what he knew about Claud and that Claud may have kidnapped his cousin. But what good would that do when it came to Naomi? If Claud hadn't kidnapped her, turning him in wouldn't help Naomi. If he had kidnapped her, he'd deny it and the FBI probably wouldn't be able to prove that an eighty-one-year-old man in Illinois, one with no criminal record, had kidnapped a woman in Manhattan. Then there was the problem that he had no proof that Claud had committed any crimes; all he knew was what Gillian had told him. In order to get the FBI to investigate Claud, Gillian would have to agree to testify against him and she was adamant she wouldn't do that, insisting that if they went to the Bureau they'd both be killed.

So what should he do? What *could* he do?

He reached for another log to split.

◻ ◻ ◻

Gillian watched Jamison split the logs. He'd split enough for two dozen fires and the T-shirt he was wearing on a cool October day was soaked with sweat.

She wondered what was going through his head. Was he thinking about the lies she'd told him or was he thinking only about Naomi?

If Naomi was found alive then Jamison probably wouldn't feel the need to do anything—but she knew Naomi was not going to be found alive. And when her body was found, *if* it was found, she was almost certain Jamison would call the FBI and she wouldn't be able to stop him—unless she killed him.

She didn't want to kill him. She really didn't. She just wanted their life to continue as it was.

She'd been suffocating in Redemption, trapped in a joyless existence, doing a job where the rewards never matched the risk. She wanted to be free to choose her own destiny. She wanted to live in a place where the view was something other than flat land and cornfields. She wanted to see oceans and mountains and all those places she'd read about. And she wanted to be with people other than those she was bound to by blood and an imposed sense of obligation. The only person in the family she liked was her sister-in-law, the mayor, who, like her, had dreams of leaving Redemption and her husband. They'd even talked about leaving together but she'd known that Agnes would never leave because she had a daughter.

As for the rest of the family, she didn't miss them at all: Claud, the domineering patriarch; the always watchful Mary White and her insane daughter; the subservient women married to Mary White's sons; her dour husband, whose only real ambition was to replace Claud. The person she missed the least was her father.

David Pine had never abused her or mistreated her in any way; he'd just allowed the abuse to happen. Her mother was the one who'd abused her, not physically, but emotionally. Her mother had been a zealot, one of Claud's most dedicated acolytes. Had cancer not killed her at the age of fifty, she might have been the one to replace Claud if he ever decided to step down. Her mother had also been the one responsible for ensuring

Gillian and the other children her age accepted the family's purpose and their roles in it. If Gillian questioned what she was being taught, her mother had responded with icy silences and belittlement and cruel, petty punishments. And her mother was the one who'd pushed her into marrying Steven. Her father, by comparison, had always been a passive figure in the background, doing whatever her mother told him, never once standing up for her. She'd never understood why her mother had married the man; although he'd been handsome when he was young, he'd always been as dull as dirt. Gillian imagined that the only reason her parents had married was that Gillian's grandmother, like her mother, insisted she take a partner in the family and then have children. And as best Gillian could tell, that was her father's greatest contribution to the clan: providing the seed that produced her.

Now she was free of all of them and happy for the first time in her life, but she had to get Jamison to quit obsessing over Claud's past and over his cousin Naomi. She may not have loved Jamison—she suspected that her upbringing had made it impossible for her to truly, unconditionally love anyone—but she liked him and liked being with him and didn't want to lose him and what they had together. And she really didn't want to lose the money they had.

❏ ❏ ❏

She walked outside the cabin and over to Jamison and said, "You've chopped enough wood to last the winter. Let's go for a kayak ride. All you're doing is driving yourself crazy, and you know your uncle is doing everything that can possibly be done to find Naomi. So come on, let's go for a ride. It'll make your head stop spinning for a while."

He stared at her for a moment, not speaking, and again she couldn't tell what he was thinking. But the look he gave her was one she'd never seen before. He was looking at her as if she were a stranger.

She thought he was going to refuse and tell her to leave him alone, but then he swung the ax, sinking the blade deep into the tree stump chopping block. "Okay," he said. He must have realized that she was right, that there was nothing he could do that his uncle wasn't already doing.

As they were driving to the beach, they passed what looked like a crime scene. There was a Dolphin Cove police cruiser on the side of the road surrounded by police tape and a couple of people in white coveralls were examining it. Nearby were three Oregon State Patrol cars and an ambulance; the red and blue lights on the patrol cars were spinning and there was one officer standing in the road waving cars by and telling them not to stop. Gillian wondered what had happened.

44

The kayak ride was exhilarating.

It had been windy and they were drenched with spray as they paddled past the rock formation off the coast—and then they saw the most amazing sight: a humpback whale breaching. Its enormous body came halfway out of the ocean and then it slapped its tail down as it dove, throwing up a ton of water. But even that hadn't been enough to alter Jamison's pensive mood as she'd been hoping. After they returned to the cabin, they took showers and Gillian made a seafood salad for dinner, but Jamison barely touched his food and didn't say more than a dozen words to her while they ate.

The only good thing was that he didn't ask her again about Claud's past.

The truth was that she really *didn't* know anything. Claud had never said anything about his past to her. Her grandparents most likely knew something, but she'd been a child when they passed away and, as she'd told Jamison, she could barely remember them. And if her parents knew something, they'd never said anything to her about the family's origins and the reason for this could have been because they didn't know anything either. Or it could have been because Claud forbade them to talk. Claud treated information like precious stones, stones that were to be kept hidden as long as possible and revealed only when necessary to those who had a need to know—and he'd apparently concluded that no one needed to know about his past. All she knew for sure was that everyone in the family who was alive today had lived in Redemption all their lives and they'd always worked for Claud. But where Claud came from and what he did prior to 1961—he would have been twenty-one at the time—she didn't know.

But she did have a theory. Although no one had told her anything specific, she could deduce Claud's past because of what Drexler Limited did in the present. But telling Jamison her theory wouldn't change their current situation and it wouldn't help Naomi. If anything, telling Jamison what she suspected could make it even more likely that he would insist on talking to the FBI. And that she wasn't going to permit.

Normally after dinner they would watch television or read but Jamison, without saying anything to her, took a bottle of brandy and a snifter and went out onto the back deck and sat down in a chaise lounge. Jamison wasn't a heavy drinker and normally didn't have more than a beer or two, but he sat there until it got dark, staring out into the woods, brooding as he sipped the brandy. Gillian could tell that he wanted to be alone and she couldn't think of what to say to him anyway—other than screaming: *Don't fuck up everything we have!*

Gillian watched TV for a couple of hours, and around eleven told Jamison that she was going to bed. "Why don't you join me?" she added, thinking that maybe sex would draw him out of his reverie. Without looking at her, he said, "I'll be up in a while." She noticed his words were a bit slurred and that the brandy bottle was almost half empty.

Gillian left on the small lights over the kitchen counter, turned off the rest of the lights in the house, went upstairs, and went to bed.

Jamison fell asleep—or passed out—in the patio lounge chair an hour later.

◻ ◻ ◻

At one a.m., Judy said, "Let's go."

She and Matt were dressed in dark clothes, wearing gloves, their new night vision goggles covering their eyes. The forest around them was an eerie gray-green color produced by the goggles. All the lights were out in the house except for some small ones toward the back in the kitchen that someone had probably forgotten to turn off. The SUV Judy had seen before was parked in front of the house.

They walked through the woods silently, Judy leading the way, circled around to the south side of the house, and approached the side door to the garage. Judy tried the doorknob, expecting it to be locked, but it turned. She thought: *Sometimes the angels just smile on you.*

They stepped into the garage. The garage was empty except for a work bench with some tools hanging on a pegboard, a snowblower, and a bunch of yard tools and she wondered again why they didn't park their car in the garage. Then she noticed the chain on the garage door opener hanging down. It appeared as if one of the links had broken.

They walked over to the door that led into the house and Judy again tried to turn the knob. This time it didn't turn; the door was locked. She took the lock picks out of her back pocket and less than a minute later had the door open.

She and Matt were both armed with Glocks machined for silencers. Matt was carrying his in his right hand. As soon as she got the door open, Judy took out her Glock, which had been stuck into the back of her pants, pulled the silencer from a pocket, and threaded it into the barrel.

The garage door opened into the kitchen and they stepped inside and were momentarily blinded by kitchen counter lights, their intensity magnified by the night vision goggles—and Judy bumped hard into a chair.

"Shit," she whispered. She whipped the goggles off her head; they were of no use to her in the lighted kitchen. Matt did the same thing. The sound of her bumping into the chair had been fairly loud in the silent house but Judy knew from checking out the house on the rental site that the master bedroom was upstairs, so maybe no one had heard it. She decided to just stand there for a moment to see if Gillian or Jamison would investigate the noise. If one of them did, she would shoot to wound and not to kill because her orders were to interrogate them before she killed them. But eventually she would kill them both.

口 口 口

Jamison didn't know what woke him up, then it took him a minute to realize where he was: sitting in a chair on the back deck. His head throbbed from the amount of brandy that he'd drunk, and his mouth tasted as if something had died in it. He rose unsteadily to his feet, still a bit drunk, and turned to walk back into the house and his knee hit one of the other chairs on the deck. He stumbled but didn't fall.

口 口 口

Judy heard a noise coming from outside the house and caught a motion in her peripheral vision. She turned and saw a man standing on the deck. It was Jamison. What the hell was he doing there?

Judy was about to tell her brother to get Jamison before he could run, but before she could speak, Matt fired. He'd panicked when he saw the man standing outside the house. The sound of the shot he fired was muted thanks to the silencer on his weapon, but the bullet shattered the glass in one of the large windows that looked toward the forest behind the house.

Judy saw Jamison fall to the deck after Matt shot and thought that Matt might have killed him. *Good.* But then Jamison got up and started running. She hissed at her brother: "Get him! I'll get Gillian."

What the hell had Jamison been doing outside on the deck? This was the sort of bad luck that could fuck up a perfectly planned operation.

□ □ □

When the bullet hit his leg, Jamison fell, but then he immediately got to his feet and started running away from the house. As he ran, he yelled "Gillian! Gillian!" as loud as he could. He ran to the edge of the deck, which was elevated about two feet off the ground. His left thigh was burning but the injury didn't seem severe. He jumped off the deck and headed toward the north corner of the house where the woodshed was.

□ □ □

Matt was delayed momentarily by the sliding glass door, which stuck in the lower rail as he pushed to open it. By the time he opened the door, Jamison was off the deck and halfway to the corner of the house. Matt fired a second shot at Jamison but missed. Matt was an excellent shot but hitting a running target in the dark isn't easy.

□ □ □

Jamison yelled a second time, "Gillian! There's guys with guns in the house!" He didn't know if she'd be able to hear him, but that was the only thing he could think to do to warn her. He rounded the corner and stopped. He was standing by the pile of logs that he'd split earlier in the day. He'd thought about running into the woods where he'd be able to hide but quickly dismissed that idea. He wasn't going to abandon Gillian. He grabbed the ax still stuck in the tree trunk chopping block.

□ □ □

Gillian hadn't been asleep. She couldn't sleep worrying about Jamison and what he might do next.

She didn't hear the silenced gunshots, but she did hear glass breaking. Then she thought she heard someone yell.

She rolled over in bed and opened the nightstand and pulled out the Beretta she'd taken with her when she left Redemption.

□ □ □

Matt sprinted toward the corner of the house to catch up with Jamison. There was no reason to be cautious; he was armed and Jamison wasn't. He had to get the damn guy before he ran into the woods.

He turned the corner.

The ax blade struck him on the top of the head, splitting his skull open.

◻ ◻ ◻

Gillian got out of bed and quickly slipped on a pair of jeans and tennis shoes. The Beretta in her hand, she opened the bedroom door, poked her head out, and looked down the hallway. There was no one there. She moved silently down the hall toward the stairs leading to the first floor.

As she turned the corner to go down the stairs, she saw a person at the bottom of the stairs, coming toward her.

Gillian and Judy saw each other at the same time.

They fired at the same time.

◻ ◻ ◻

Jamison had swung the ax as hard as he could, as hard as he had when he'd been splitting the logs.

He looked down at the man lying on the ground. He couldn't make out his features in the darkness, but he could tell the man wasn't dead. Yet. His limbs were twitching due to some aberrant motor function produced by his damaged brain as it shut down, and he was whimpering, making the final sounds of an animal dying in pain. But Jamison didn't have time to spend on him. He needed to get into the house and help Gillian.

He'd only taken a few steps toward the backdoor when he heard a single gunshot coming from inside the house.

Oh, Jesus.

He sprinted to the house, the ax in his hand. He ran across the deck, through the open sliding door, through the kitchen, and toward the staircase leading to the upstairs bedrooms, praying Gillian was still alive. As he ran, it occurred to him that the man he'd hit with the ax had a gun and he should have taken it. But he wasn't going to stop and go back and get it.

He stopped when he saw Gillian standing at the bottom of the stairs. She'd turned on the lights in the living room and was holding a gun in her hand, looking down at a body lying on its back. Jamison had forgotten about the Beretta that Gillian had taken with her when they left Redemption; that was the gun she was holding. He noticed then that the person on the floor was also holding a gun, but it had a silencer attached to the barrel. It was Gillian's weapon that he'd heard outside the house.

He looked down at the body. It was Judy White. Gillian's bullet had hit her in the center of the forehead. He knelt down next to Judy and felt for a pulse. There wasn't one.

He looked up at Gillian.

"She's dead."

"I know," Gillian said. "I can't believe she missed me. It was just luck that I killed her. I was aiming for her chest, not her head." She pointed at his leg. "My God, you're bleeding. Were you shot?"

With all the adrenaline surging through him, Jamison had forgotten about the wound to his leg. His pant leg was soaked with blood. "Yeah. There's a guy outside, near the woodpile. He shot me but I hit him with the ax. He might be dead by now."

Gillian said, "Let's go take a look."

He couldn't believe how calm she sounded; killing Judy didn't seem to have affected her at all. He wondered if she was in shock. He knew he was.

Gillian found a flashlight in one of the kitchen drawers and they walked outside together and over to the woodpile, the Beretta still in her right hand. She shined the light on the fallen man, and although blood covered half his face from the massive head wound, Jamison could see it was Matt White. He was alive, if just barely. He was still making that pitiful, whimpering sound.

Jamison knelt down next to him and said, "Did you kidnap Naomi Maddox?"

Matt's lips moved but no words came out.

Jamison said, "Tell me the truth and I'll call the medics. If you don't, I'm going to let you die. Did you kidnap Naomi?"

Matt croaked something. Jamison thought he may have said "Yes," but he wasn't sure. "What did he say?" he asked Gillian.

She said, "I don't know."

To Matt, Jamison said, "Where's my cousin?"

Matt didn't answer. He shuddered once and died.

Jamison stood up, looked down at the corpse, the realization dawning on him that he'd killed a man. He turned to Gillian and said, "We need to call the cops."

"Just take a breath," she said. "We need to think before we do anything. And we need to do something about your leg."

They started back toward the house when Jamison suddenly turned and went back and knelt next to Matt. He patted Matt's pockets and found and removed a cell phone.

With Gillian following, he went back into the house and searched Judy's pockets and found her cell phone. He said to Gillian, "I want to see who these people have been calling. I want to see if there's anything in their phones that might lead to Naomi."

"Let's look at your leg first," Gillian said.

They went to the bathroom and Jamison pulled down his pants. The wound was an angry, raw-looking groove on the outside of his left thigh above his knee. It was oozing blood but not bleeding badly and Jamison could see it wasn't a serious injury. He took a large bandage from the medicine cabinet, placed it over the wound, and pulled his pants back up. The wound might need stitches eventually, but the bandage would do for now.

Gillian said, "Jamison, we need to—"

"Not now," he said. "I want to look at their cell phones."

He sat down at the kitchen table, and with Gillian pacing behind him, watching, he looked at the recent-calls directory in both phones. On Matt's phone, the only calls were to and from the phone that Judy White had been carrying. Judy had called her brother's phone a couple of times, but she'd also called another phone several times.

He said to Gillian, "She called a number with an Illinois area code."

Gillian said, "They're burner phones and all the calls they made were to other burners. I know the way they work."

Jamison didn't know what that meant. He thought for a moment about calling the number Judy had called to see who answered but then it occurred to him that he should see if there were text messages in the phones. He looked at Judy's phone first.

In one text message *to* Judy was Gillian and Jamison's address in Oregon. He wondered how the sender had gotten their address. Another message to Judy gave a United Airlines flight number and a departure time. He looked up the flight on his phone and saw it was a nonstop from Newark to Portland. There was another message *from* Judy to the person who'd been texting her and it gave the address of a place in New Jersey and a five-digit number. Jamison didn't know what the numbers meant but he used his phone to look up the address on Google Maps. It was for a house on the Jersey shore. The satellite view showed that there were no other houses near the place.

The whole time Jamison was studying the phones, Gillian hadn't said anything. She just stood there watching him. He wondered why she was still holding the gun in her hand. Did she think they might be attacked again?

Jamison thought for a moment then picked up his phone and made a call.

"Who are you calling?" Gillian shrieked.

"My uncle."

"No! We need to talk before you do anything."

"No, we don't," he said.

His uncle came on the line, saying, "Yes, who is this?"

It was nearly two in the morning in Oregon meaning it was five in New York. At that time of day Jed should have been sleeping but he'd sounded alert when he answered the phone, which he did on the first ring. He'd probably been sitting there, wide awake, worrying about Naomi, hoping that whoever took her would call.

Jamison said, "Uncle Jed, it's Jamison."

"Did you hear about Naomi? Is that why you're calling?"

"Yes. Look, Uncle Jed, there isn't time right now for me to go into all the details, but I have an address where Naomi might be. I don't know if I'm right or not, but you need to get the cops to check it out right away."

"What?" Jed said. "How did you get an address?"

"Uncle Jed, there's no time to waste. You need to see if Naomi's at the address as fast as possible. The problem is that I don't have any information to pass on that will allow the cops to get a search warrant, but—"

"I'm not going to waste time on a search warrant. And I'm not going to call the cops. I've got a private security firm hunting for Naomi, and they won't give a damn about search warrants. Give me the address."

Jamison did.

Jed said, "Jamison, I don't know what the hell's going on here, but if you had something to do with Naomi being kidnapped . . . Never mind, I need to get moving on this. I'll deal with you later."

Jed hung up and Jamison thought: *Great*. Now his uncle, a man who'd always treated him like a son, thought Jamison was involved in Naomi's kidnapping—and he supposed that in a way he had been. Naomi wouldn't have been kidnapped if he hadn't left Redemption with Gillian.

Gillian said, "Okay, you've done what you can for your cousin, now we need to get out of here. Claud obviously knows where we are, and he'll be sending more people after us. We need to leave."

"Gillian, we killed two people. It may have been self-defense but the cops won't know that unless we're here to tell them. If we run, we'll not only be running from Claud but also from the law. No, Gillian, I'm through running and what I'm going to do is sic the FBI on fucking Claud. His people tried to kill us and I'm sure he was involved in kidnapping my cousin. I'm calling the FBI."

"What are you going to tell the FBI, Jamison? The only thing you know about Claud's operation are the jobs you did for him and you can't prove he did anything illegal."

"But you can."

"But I won't. I'm not going to testify against him. I told you if I do, he'll have me killed. He'll have both of us killed."

"Gillian, I don't know anything about this syndicate that Claud works for, but whoever they are, they're not some unstoppable force. The people Claud sent to kill us weren't even competent enough to do the job."

"They were competent. We just got lucky."

"That may be, but I'm going to put my faith in the FBI being able to protect us."

Jamison picked up his phone.

Gillian pointed the Beretta at his face and said, "Jamison, put down the phone."

He couldn't believe she was aiming a gun at him. "Jesus, Gillian. You're going to shoot me?"

"I can't let you call the FBI. Even if the FBI is able to protect us, once I tell them about Claud, I'll spend the rest of my life in prison. Don't make me kill you, Jamison. I don't want to kill you."

45

Jim Brady and Tom Kemper had spent twenty years in the army. They'd both been in special ops, meaning that they were two of the best killers the military produced. They'd served in Iraq and Afghanistan and also in a few places where United States soldiers weren't supposed to be, like Pakistan and Iran. They now operated a security company based in upstate New York where they had the acreage to train the people who worked for them and where they could maintain their skills. Their company occasionally did missions for some U.S. intelligence agencies when those agencies didn't consider it smart to use their own people. It also did security work for people who could afford them. Jed Maddox had hired them to find his daughter—and to deal with whoever had taken her.

They approached the house on the Jersey shore at six a.m., an hour after Jamison had given his uncle the address. The dawn sky was blue, tinged with pink; a low blanket of fog covered the marsh. They snuck up on the house from the backside, dressed as they'd often been when they were in the army: camouflaged clothing, bulletproof vests, their faces smeared with black streaks. They were armed with M4 rifles with sound suppressors and carried sidearms and combat knives.

Sixty-year-old David Pine never stood a chance.

They blew open the door with a small, shaped explosive charge and tossed a flash bang grenade into the house. It was the kind of entry they'd made dozens of times when entering the lairs of enemy combatants overseas.

Kemper entered the house first and in less than a second assessed the situation. He saw Naomi Maddox bound to a chair and a gray-haired man, blinded by the grenade, reaching for a pistol in the holster on his belt.

Kemper shot him twice in the chest.

◻ ◻ ◻

Mary White sat in her office going out of her mind with anxiety. Her face was haggard; there were deep, dark circles under her eyes. She'd lost ten pounds since her son Sam had been killed and she rarely slept more than two or three hours at night.

She put down the phone when the call again went to voice mail. She sat a moment, trying—*desperately* trying—to come up with a benign explanation for why her daughter and her son weren't answering her calls. She couldn't come up with one.

Finally, she trudged up the stairs to Claud's office on the third floor. She felt as if she were ascending Mount Everest.

She found Claud sitting behind his desk. He was wearing one of his black suits and a white shirt, but oddly he didn't have on a tie. He always wore a tie to work. She also noticed the white bristles on his chin and cheeks. He hadn't shaved that morning; she'd never seen him at the office unshaven. He was just sitting; he wasn't doing anything. His hands lay motionless on the desk in front of him and he appeared to be studying them as if he were puzzled, as if he couldn't understand how the large, powerful hands of his youth had turned into these swollen, gnarled appendages.

He looked up at Mary when she entered the office but didn't speak.

She said, "I still can't reach Judy and Matt. They were supposed to have taken care of Gillian and Jamison hours ago but they haven't called and they're not answering their phones. I know Judy would have called as soon as they were finished but she hasn't."

Claud didn't say anything.

Mary said, "And I can't reach David. He's not answering his phone either."

When Claud still didn't respond, she screamed, "Claud! One of my sons is dead and now I think something has happened to Judy and Matt and my brother. What should we do?"

Claud spoke at last.

"Mary, it's time for us to leave Redemption."

46

Gillian stood for what seemed an eternity aiming the gun at him, trying to make up her mind, trying to pull the trigger—but in the end, she didn't.

She said, "Give me your cell phone and the phones you took off Matt and Judy. And give me the keys to the car."

Jamison shook his head but placed the keys and phones on the kitchen table. She put the keys in a pocket, dropped the phones into her purse, and, while still pointing the gun at him, gathered up her purse and laptop case and backed toward the front door.

Jamison said, "Gillian, there are two dead bodies here. You have to stay and explain what happened."

"Well, I'm not."

"If we tell the cops the truth, and if we tell them about Claud, we'll be all right."

"*I* won't be all right," she said. She paused before she said, "If you really love me, Jamison, protect me. Find a way to explain all this without involving me."

He said, "I do love you and I promise that I'll protect you. I'll always protect you. You don't have to run."

"Goodbye, Jamison," she said. He was surprised to see that she had tears in her eyes. In the time he'd known her, he'd never seen her cry. The last thing she did before leaving the house was place the Beretta she'd been holding on the floor near the door. He immediately figured out why she did that; she couldn't take the gun that had been used to kill Judy with her.

Jamison stood there after she closed the door; he could see there was no point going after her. He heard the car start a minute later and watched through a window as his lover drove away.

After she left, he sat for ten minutes trying to figure out what to do. How could he explain the two dead bodies in the house without involving her? He could say that he didn't know who the killers were and that they'd tried to rob the house and he'd killed them in self-defense, whacking one with the ax and shooting the other with Gillian's gun. That's why she'd left the gun: it needed to remain in the cabin to explain Judy's death.

He'd partly tell the truth. He'd say he'd been sitting outside on the deck as he had been, that Matt saw him and took a shot at him, which he had, and then he ran over to the woodpile and killed Matt when Matt came after him. So he could start with the truth, but then what? What if he said he ran around the house, went in through the front door, got the gun from the upstairs bedroom, and shot Judy when she started to walk up the stairs? That could work, but then he'd have to explain what Judy had been doing when he'd been running to get the gun. He supposed he could say that she'd run after Matt and he just outran her.

But what would he say when they asked where Gillian was? All her clothes were still in the closets and it would be obvious that he hadn't been living in the house alone. And how would he explain why he didn't have a car or a cell phone. He couldn't say that Gillian had taken all the phones to prevent him from calling the cops right away.

Then there was the small problem that Gillian had pointed out: that Claud obviously knew where they'd been living and would send someone else to Oregon to kill them. Or now, since Gillian was gone, to kill him.

He made up his mind. No, he wasn't going to lie to the cops and he wasn't going to run from Claud. He was through running from Claud. He was going to end this whole thing. He was going to tell the truth about the killings—and he was going to tell the truth about Claud and Drexler Limited.

He'd done a lot of thinking while he'd been sitting on the deck drinking brandy and had come to the conclusion that Gillian had lied her lovely ass off when she'd told him about the activities of Drexler Limited. He was a finance guy, and in the end, the finances didn't make sense.

So he was going to tell the truth about everything but he was also going to protect Gillian as he'd promised—although he was certain she wouldn't approve of how he was going to protect her.

He walked over to Judy's body, and patted her pockets for a second time and this time removed a set of car keys from a pocket.

He took one last look at Judy's open eyes and the red hole in the center of her forehead and left the cabin.

◻ ◻ ◻

He couldn't find the car that Matt and Judy had been driving. He hit the key fob several times but never heard a beep or saw the lights flash. They must have hidden their car or parked it some distance from the cabin.

It took him over an hour to walk the five miles in the dark to Dolphin Cove, guiding his way with a flashlight. By the time he arrived it was four a.m. But he didn't go to the police station. He went into a 24-hour convenience store that also had tables where people could sit and drink coffee. Behind the counter was a young woman with streaks of blue in her blonde hair reading a Louise Penny novel. She smiled at him and said, "Good morning."

Jamison said, "Do you have a pay phone here?"

"No. And I'm not sure there's still a pay phone anywhere in town anymore. There used to be one at the gas station, but it's been gone for like two years."

"Can I use your cell phone?" Before she could answer, he said, "It's an emergency. I need to report a crime and I'm going to have to make several calls and I'm going to be on the phone for a long time, so I'll give you a hundred bucks if you'll let me use your phone."

She studied him briefly then said, "You don't have to do that. I can tell by your face that this is really serious."

□ □ □

Jamison took a table near a window, as far from the service counter as he could get. Through the window he could see the striking rock formation offshore. He couldn't believe it was only yesterday when he and Gillian had paddled past the rocks and seen the humpback whale. He imagined that the ride they took yesterday was the last one they would take together for some time to come. Or forever.

The first call he made was to his uncle. Jed didn't answer the call, maybe because he wasn't able to answer or maybe because he didn't recognize the number. Jamison left a message saying, "Uncle Jed, it's Jamison. I need to know what's happened with Naomi. Please call me back."

Less than a minute later, Jed called. Jamison answered, saying, "Was Naomi at the address I gave you?"

"Yes. Thank you. Now are you going to tell me how you got the address?"

"Not now, Uncle Jed. There isn't time now, but I will as soon as I can. I promise. Is Naomi all right?"

"She's pretty messed up mentally but physically she's fine. She wasn't hurt or raped or anything like that. She'll be okay eventually. But right now she's not talking so she wasn't able to say what happened. And the guy who kidnapped her is dead."

Jamison wondered who the guy was but didn't ask. It was undoubtedly someone who worked for Claud.

"Good," Jamison said. "I have to go now but I'll call you again as soon as I can."

Jamison hung up, relieved that Naomi was okay.

❑ ❑ ❑

Jamison glanced at his watch. It was ten after four, which meant it would be past seven in New York. He figured, relentless crusader that she was, that she'd already be in her office.

When Jamison had been prosecuted for insider trading the federal prosecutor was a woman named Jane Helmer and she'd gone after him and the others as if it had been personal for her, as if they'd stolen her grandmother's life savings. She'd reluctantly made the deal with Jamison, the deal where he wouldn't go to prison if he testified, but she'd insisted on him pleading guilty and then did everything she could to strip him of almost all the money he had.

Helmer was in her forties, a tall, stringy woman with almost zero body fat; it was as if the rage she felt toward the criminals she prosecuted burned away all the calories she ingested. But one thing about Helmer that Jamison was certain of. She was honest and if she gave her word, she would keep it. Plus, she was the only assistant U.S. district attorney he knew.

He called her office, gave her secretary his name, and she came on the line snarling: "What the hell do you want?"

"Before we get to what I want, let me tell you a few things. Right now, I'm sitting in a coffee shop in a town called Dolphin Cove, Oregon, and in the house where I've been staying are two dead people. I killed one of them and my girlfriend killed the other."

"What the hell? But why are you calling me? I don't have any jurisdiction when it comes to—"

"Just shut up and listen to me. We killed these people in self-defense but the thing that's important—and what you're going to want to know—is who these people worked for. These same people were also involved in the kidnapping of Naomi Maddox. I'm sure you've heard about that."

"Yeah, but—"

"The thing is, these people, the ones we killed, are part of a group that's been committing crimes for sixty years."

"Sixty years? What kind of crimes?"

"Well, now here's where it gets interesting and the reason why the FBI is going to want to round all these people up right away and why you're going to give me what I want. They've supposedly been committing fraud, stealing hundreds of millions of dollars from programs like Medicare and siphoning money off federal and state contracts."

"Why do you say *supposedly*? Does that mean you don't have any proof that they've done these things?"

"I'll answer the second question first. I don't actually have any evidence, or not much anyway. The person who has the evidence is my girlfriend who is now on the run and trying to get as far away from here as she can."

"Why did she run if she killed someone in self-defense?"

"She ran because she's afraid the people she used to work for will kill her."

"What's her name?"

"Not yet. Now I'll answer your first question. I said 'supposedly' because my girlfriend was the one who told me about the crimes these people committed. And I have no doubt that they've committed crimes but not the crimes she told me about. I think these people are involved in something much bigger than fraud."

"Like what?"

"Terrorism. They assisted with one terrorist attack that failed and I think they may be planning two more."

"Jesus Christ. Are they Muslims?"

Jamison laughed. "No, they're not Muslims. At least I don't think they are. They're all American citizens, born and raised in the good ol' US of A. Except for one guy. I'm not sure where he was born but I'm pretty sure it wasn't Saudi Arabia."

"Are these terrorist attacks they're planning imminent?"

"I don't know. But my girlfriend probably does. You just have to catch her to find out. But I won't tell you who she is or help you catch her unless you give me what I want."

"So what do you want?"

"Two things. I want my conviction voided, wiped off the books, whatever you call it, and I don't care what you have to do to make that happen. I'm not going to live the rest of my life with a felony conviction on my record and it's the kind of deal I should have gotten in the first place for testifying. The second thing I want is immunity for my girlfriend if she testifies against the people she used to work with. Now I'm going to hang up and call my lawyer, the guy who defended me when you were trying to put me in jail. I'm going to give him all the details and tell him to write up something for you to sign that will give me what I want. After he does that, and after you've signed it, I'll give you my girlfriend's name and tell you about the car she's driving. But the clock's ticking here, Jane. She has a two-hour head start on getting away and the longer you take to give me what I want, the farther away she'll be. And if I'm right about the terrorist attacks, well, who knows when they could happen."

"Hey! If you've got information about—"

"Jane, I'm hanging up and calling my lawyer. After that I'm gonna walk down to the police station here in Dolphin Cove and tell the cops about the two dead bodies in my house. I imagine they'll toss me in a cell, so you'll be able to find me there."

Jamison hung up on Jane and didn't answer the phone when she immediately called him back. He wondered how fast the FBI could get to Dolphin Cove. He figured the closest agent was probably in Portland, a couple of hours away. Well, unless they took a chopper instead of a car.

He walked up to the counter and said to the clerk, "Could I get a large coffee, please? And I need to use your phone for a while longer. I have one more call to make and it'll be a long one. Is that all right?"

"Yeah, sure," she said.

When she brought him his coffee, he placed a hundred-dollar bill on the counter and said, "Keep the change."

47

Gillian finally reached the head of the line of cars crossing the border into Canada.

She'd elected to cross over near the town of Blaine, Washington, the closest border crossing to Dolphin Cove, and only a six-and-a-half-hour drive. Once she crossed into Canada, she'd head to Vancouver. Vancouver was an international shipping port and she knew that a Hong Kong–based Chinese triad involved in drugs and smuggling in illegal Chinese immigrants operated there. Drexler Limited had taken advantage of the triad's smuggling skills a few times in the past and the gang would be able to get her a new identity, just as it provided new identities for those illegal immigrants who could afford its fees. So she'd become a Canadian citizen, and once she was a different person, she'd decide where she wanted to go next.

One of the Canadian customs agents approached her car and she rolled down her window. She smiled at the agent; he smiled at her in return. He asked to see her passport and she handed it to him. The name in the passport was Elizabeth Hall, and she'd obtained the passport and her driver's license using the birth certificate she'd obtained in El Paso. It was a valid, legitimate passport and she wasn't concerned about it.

The agent looked at the passport then at her face to make sure she matched the photo. He frowned momentarily, looked at her again, then walked to the front of her car and looked at the license plate. He came back to her and said, "Ma'am, would you please pull your car over to the outside lane. We need to search your vehicle and your luggage."

"Why?" she said.

"Merely a random security check, ma'am."

Concerned now—the look the guard had given her made her apprehensive—she pulled her car over to an area under an open shed where there were a couple of folding tables where people could place their luggage. Had she really been chosen at random? As she'd been wait-ing in line to cross the border, she'd noticed a couple of other vehicles pulled out of the line and had watched as agents looked into the vehicles' interiors and trunks and examined the passengers' luggage. There hadn't been anything unusual about the vehicles or their passengers, so maybe the luggage check actually was random, like maybe they picked every tenth car or something.

Another customs agent was standing near the tables. The agent, a woman, said to her, "Ma'am, please step out of your vehicle and place any luggage you have, including your purse, on the table."

Gillian said, "I don't have any luggage. Just my purse and a laptop case. I'm only planning to be in Canada for a couple of hours." There'd been no time for her to pack when she'd fled Dolphin Cove.

She stood watching, nervous and impatient, as the agent searched her car. She took forever, looking under the seats and into the space where the spare tire was stored.

As she was standing there, she saw the Canadian border guard that she'd initially spoken to, the one who had told her that her car had been selected for a random search. He was walking toward her accompanied by another man, a man wearing the uniform of an American customs agent. He had to be one of the agents who checked the people going into the United States from Canada. Why was the American agent with the Canadian?

The two men reached her and the American agent, a serious, hard-looking guy in his fifties, said, "Ma'am, I'm placing you under arrest."

"What?" Gillian said. "Why are you arresting me?"

"Ma'am, please turn around."

Gillian, having no choice, did as he said and he snapped handcuffs on her wrists. The female Canadian customs agent then patted her down for weapons.

"Why are you arresting me?" Gillian said to the American. "I have a right to know."

"Lady, I have no idea why you're being arrested. All I know is that there's a warrant out for your arrest. A federal warrant. I'm sure the FBI will explain the charges to you."

She should have killed Jamison.

48

Claud made one final pass through the silent building. As far as he knew, he was alone. He started on the third floor and worked his way down to the first, walking slowly from room to room, looking into every office, every closet, every desk. Two hours later, he was satisfied that everything had been taken care of.

When he'd passed Mary's office, he was surprised to see her sitting at her desk. She hadn't been there a few minutes earlier when he'd walked by her office to look into the comm room. She must have been in the restroom. She was looking at some framed photographs arrayed in front of her.

He'd said, "Mary, what are you doing here? You should have left town by now."

Mary didn't answer him or look at him. She continued to stare at the photographs.

He walked closer to her desk and saw the photographs were of her family. He looked down at the wastebasket next to her desk and saw an empty prescription drug vial. He knew then that Mary wasn't leaving.

He laid a heavy hand on her shoulder and said, "Mary, thank you for everything you've done. I'm going to miss you." He felt like he should have said more but couldn't think of anything else to say. Nor would anything he said at this point matter.

He left her office without looking back and trudged up the stairs to his office. At his age, taking those stairs every day was something he wouldn't miss.

A bit out of breath, he sat down in the chair behind his desk and looked at the picture of his late wife and smiled sadly. She'd been a good woman; it was a shame her mind had been so fragile and that she'd left him when she was so young. Like Mary, she just hadn't had the will to carry on.

He picked up the Sammy Sosa baseball and fondly rolled it in his hands. Catching Sammy's home run ball had been just one more lucky thing that had happened to him in a long and lucky life.

He had no regrets. None whatsoever.

◻ ◻ ◻

Mary was only vaguely aware that Claud had been in her office. She didn't hear whatever he'd said to her.

On her desk, arranged in a semicircle, were photographs of all the people she'd loved.

There was a photo of her parents, Aaron and Gloria. The photo had been taken when they were both in their twenties, only a couple of years after they'd arrived in Redemption. They looked like brand-new pennies, bright and shiny, her father handsome, her mother beautiful. This was the way she wanted to remember her father, as a young man with his whole life ahead of him and not as he'd been at the end, drooling, slack-jawed, no longer able to remember her name or where he was. She'd always be grateful to Claud for putting him out of his misery. That had been not only the smart thing to do but also the kind thing to do.

In the photo of her brother, David—poor, simple David—he was holding his newborn daughter, Gillian, in his arms, looking adoringly at her. He would always adore Gillian; she would never adore him in return. Gillian was made of ice. There was no photo of David's wife, Gillian's mother, Susan. Mary had never cared for Susan; she'd been a pushy, domineering woman and a terrible mother.

The photo of her and her husband, Mike, had been taken on the day they'd married. They hadn't been married in a church; a judge had pronounced them man and wife. Mike was wearing a double-breasted dark blue suit; she had on a cornflower-blue dress that reached below her knees and white high heels. She looked lovely, even if she said so herself. In the photo, Mike—a big, broad-shouldered man until the cancer ate him alive—looked indestructible. If only he had been.

The picture of her children was one taken when they were young. Sam had been ten, Matt nine, Judy only seven. They were all dressed in shorts and T-shirts, their knees smudged from playing on the grass. The photo had been taken on a summer day at a family picnic and Judy sat between her brothers, the center of attention as she'd always been. Mary had always gotten a kick out of how Judy used to boss her brothers around, something she started doing as a child and would continue to do all her life. Her Judy had been something special.

The final photo was of her grandchildren: Randy, Bobby, and her favorite, Carly. The boys looked mischievous and so much like her sons had looked at that age. Carly looked like a small, dark-haired angel— which she was. She knew, even if she'd been willing to live, that she'd never be reunited with her grandchildren again.

The photos blurred as the barbiturates began to stop her heart and cloud her vision.

What was the point of running when all the people she'd ever loved were gone?

◻ ◻ ◻

Claud decided it was time to go. He'd done all he could.

He stood up and put the photo of his late wife into his briefcase. Already in the briefcase was a driver's license and credit cards that identified him as James Garner, an easy name to remember as there'd been a handsome movie star who bore the same name. Steven, who he'd assigned to make preparations for the family's departure, had done an excellent job. Everyone in the family now had new identities and Steven had helped set up their itineraries. By now they should have all left Redemption. Well, except for Mary.

After he left his office, Claud would drive back to his house and pick up the bag he'd already packed, then drive to Chicago for a meeting with the client's man to discuss the future. The client, of course, had been informed that Drexler Limited was finished. Claud picked up the Sammy Sosa baseball and was about to put it into his briefcase when a small, mild-looking man stepped into his office.

It was the client's man.

Claud realized then that he wasn't going anywhere.

The client's man said, "Sorry, my friend, but we can't take the chance of you being arrested."

He raised a pistol and shot Claud in the heart.

The Sammy Sosa baseball fell from Claud's hand.

49

The day after Gillian was arrested at the Canadian border, she was escorted to a small, windowless room containing a battered table and two plain wooden chairs. There was a recording device on the table and a camera high up on one wall, but the recorder and the camera were both turned off.

The room was located in the basement of a building on the Bangor Submarine Base in Bangor, Washington. Trident ballistic missile and Seawolf-class attack submarines were moored and maintained on the sprawling base and some nuclear weapons were stored there as well. For this reason, the naval base was one of the most secure facilities on the planet, and not only was Gillian protected by all the military assets guarding the place, she also had six U.S. marshals assigned to her.

She hadn't yet been told why she'd been arrested. So far, the only one who had spoken to her was the customs agent who had handcuffed her at the border. The U.S. marshals who had escorted her from the border to the submarine base had made no attempt to interrogate her and she'd said nothing to them.

She'd spent the previous night in a locked room containing only a bed, a sink, and a toilet. In the morning, a female marshal provided her with a toothbrush and toothpaste and escorted her to a windowless restroom. Two marshals stood outside the restroom while she showered. As she had no other clothes to wear, she put on the clothes she'd worn the previous day. After her shower, she was offered coffee and an Egg McMuffin; she drank the coffee but didn't—couldn't—eat the sandwich. It wasn't long after that that she was taken to what she assumed was an interrogation room.

All she could think about as she sat there—all she'd been able to think about for the last twenty-four hours—was that she should have killed Jamison. She knew the only reason she'd been caught was because he had betrayed her. How else would the FBI have known the name on the passport she'd used when she'd attempted to cross the border? And he must have told them enough about the crimes she'd committed that they could get a warrant for her arrest.

But for reasons beyond her comprehension, she just hadn't been able to pull the trigger even though she knew it was the rational thing to do. She'd allowed emotion to override logic, something she thought would never happen. Was that love? Whatever the case, she'd been a fool.

The door to the room opened. She'd been expecting to see FBI agents, but it was Jamison who entered the room.

He looked at her for a moment, smiled sadly, and said, "I'm sorry about this, but it had to be done."

Gillian, her voice devoid of emotion, said, "I should have killed you."

"Well, I'm glad you didn't. And I told you I'd protect you and I have."

"You call this protecting me?"

"Yes. I've made a deal for you with an assistant U.S. attorney. You'll be given immunity from any crimes you've committed provided you tell the truth about Drexler Limited. The deal is in writing and it's been looked at by my lawyer and he's one of the best money can buy. And you don't have to worry about anyone trying to kill you, not on this base and not while you're being protected by a squad of marshals."

"We'll see about that. And if I'm killed you will be too."

"No one's going to die. But as soon as we've finished talking, you're going to be interviewed by a couple of agents from the Bureau's anti-terrorism branch."

"Anti-terrorism?"

"Yeah. I told them Drexler was involved in at least one terrorism attempt and is maybe involved in planning two more. I told them about how I found the perfect guy in Michigan for the terrorists to buy detonators from and I also told them about the cannery project and the company that makes the vaccine machines. The truth is, I'm not exactly sure what Claud's planning but I had to tell them something that was big enough to get you the deal I got you, and terrorism is a big deal."

"Claud isn't a terrorist; he's a thief."

"No, he isn't Gillian. If all Claud had been was a thief, I never would have told the FBI how to catch you. But what Claud's involved in—and what you were involved in—goes way beyond fraud. I'm also fairly sure that Claud isn't a terrorist, or at least not in the conventional sense. He isn't some religious fanatic who wants to kill people who don't share his beliefs. There's more to Claud that I don't understand but I know you do."

"The only thing I know about Claud is what I've told you. He helps the syndicate commit fraud."

"That's a lie, Gillian. And I know it's a lie because I'm a finance guy, and the money, the finances, never made sense."

"What are you talking about?"

"When you told me about all the ways Claud helped the syndicate commit fraud, I bought the story mainly because of the details you provided, most of which I think you made up on the fly. The details made the lies plausible. Like when I asked about the canneries and you explained how canneries could be tied to food stamp fraud. That was a good one. When you said that Don Steward's company gave the syndicate an inside position for overbilling on a government contract, what made that lie particularly convincing was what you said about how legitimate contractors overbilled all the time, so imagine what an illegitimate one could do. You described how nursing homes could be used to commit Medicare fraud and how a gang of con men committed insurance fraud. For every project I worked on at the company or knew about, you had a reasonable explanation for how a clever group of criminals could make money."

Gillian just stared at him. Those pale blue eyes that he loved were as cold as chips of ice.

He kept going. "So the details you provided fit the lies but the big picture never made sense to me. That's what I was thinking about that night when I was sitting on the deck, right before your fucking cousins tried to kill us. Gillian, thieves work for money and you said the syndicate made millions. So why weren't the people at Drexler Limited rich? At first, I thought it was because Claud made sure there were no flashy displays of wealth that might attract unwanted attention. Eventually I realized that no one at Drexler had any money because Claud wasn't working for money. I thought about the client offering Don Steward seven million for his share of the company. That never made sense to me, offering the guy so much. What thief would make a seven-million-dollar upfront investment in a company? Thieves don't invest; they steal. They might put in a little money to salt a deal but not seven million, and not unless it was someone else's money. I thought about the guys that I researched at the canneries. The client was supposedly trying to get one of those guys to relocate but I kept thinking who in the hell would hire one of these losers? The amount of money it would have taken to pay off their debts could easily have been used to hire someone who wasn't carrying the baggage those guys were."

Gillian remained mute.

"Gillian, Claud Drexler isn't a thief. But someone has been giving him money. Someone was paying Drexler Limited's bills, and someone didn't mind spending seven million bucks to buy into Don Steward's company. Who has that kind of money, Gillian?"

"The client, the syndicate," Gillian said.

Jamison shook his head. "No. Stop lying. Lying isn't going to help you. Like I said, in a little while you're going to be interviewed by federal agents and it's in your own best interest to tell them the truth. If you tell the truth, you'll be free eventually. That's the deal. But before you tell them the truth, you're going to tell me."

50

Two armored personnel carriers pulled up to the front entrance of the building as the citizens of Redemption stood on the street watching. Twelve agents in body armor, wearing helmets with face shields, holding machine guns and shotguns, burst out of the vehicles and ran up the steps. One of the agents was carrying a doorknocker—a four-inch-diameter carbon steel pipe with handles welded to the top—and he slammed it into the front door. The remainder of the team ran inside the building and the people on the street could hear them yelling "Clear!" every couple of minutes.

The agents would work their way methodically upward from the ground floor to the third floor, prepared to fight their way into any locked space and ready to kill anyone who offered resistance. On the ground floor they found a plump, gray-haired woman with her head down on a desk. The woman was dead. In a semicircle in front of her were several framed photos. On the credenza behind her desk was a laptop computer that looked as if it had been melted by someone pouring a highly corrosive substance on it.

Outside the woman's office they found a room filled with monitors that they suspected were connected to the security cameras they'd seen on the exterior of the building. The screens of the monitors were dark. The computer connected to the cameras had been destroyed in the same way the computer on the woman's credenza had been: some highly corrosive liquid had been poured into it. In another room they found a bank of servers, the guts of the servers had been ripped out and also drenched in acid.

They found a room containing file cabinets; the drawers were empty. In one room was an industrial shredder. The room was filled with shredded paper, enough to fill several pickup trucks. In another room was a state-of-the-art phone for making encrypted phone calls and another laptop computer. The internals had been ripped from the phone, placed on top of the computer, and then both had been melted into a lump of wire and plastic. One agent touched a gloved hand to the melted material and immediately jerked his hand back and ripped off his glove. A hole had burned through his glove and a blister was already forming on his finger.

On the second and third floors they found more offices; the file cabinets in all the offices were empty and on almost every desk was a melted-down computer. A forensic team would later spend six months examining everything in the building, but the entry team didn't see anything that provided a single clue as to who had occupied the building or what they had been working on. The forensic team wouldn't find anything either.

In the last office they entered on the third floor they found an old man with white hair lying on the floor. He'd been shot in the heart. Near his outstretched hand was a baseball signed by Sammy Sosa.

□ □ □

Ralph Finney was sitting in his living room, watching a game show on TV. Scattered around him were beer cans and empty pizza boxes. He'd been sitting in pretty much the same spot for two days, mindlessly eating and watching television, unable to decide what he should do.

Two days ago, Mary White had assembled all the people on the second floor and told them they were being "let go."

Mary, the most cheerful person that Ralph knew at Drexler Limited, had looked haggard, as if she'd lost weight and hadn't slept for days. Her eyes were red, as if she'd been weeping nonstop. She delivered her message in a monotone, not looking anyone in the eye. After she'd told them they were all fired, she said that they were to leave immediately and not to take anything from their offices, not even personal things. She said, barely audible, that all their personal belongings would be boxed up and mailed to them later. Ralph's things would never be mailed to him.

Standing next to Mary while she spoke had been two men from the third floor, Steven Lang and Ed Pine. The weird thing was that they were wearing sidearms in holsters on their belts. When one of the guys, one of the lawyers, asked about severance pay, Mary didn't answer. Ralph wasn't sure she'd even heard the question, but Steven Lang said, "You'll get a severance check along with the other things we'll mail to you. Now get out of here."

Ralph had gotten the distinct impression that if anyone had argued and didn't leave immediately, Steven Lang had been prepared to use the gun on his hip. After the meeting, Ralph had walked back to his apartment in a state of shock. He had no idea what he was going to do next; all he knew was that he didn't want to leave Redemption and didn't want another job.

Ralph had been just sitting there, trying to avoid thinking about his future, when someone knocked on his door.

He opened his door to find two men in suits. One of them said, "Are you Ralph Finney?"

"Yes," Ralph said. "Who are you?"

"FBI. You're coming with us."

Ralph said, "What? Why?"

The agents ignored the questions; one of them gripped Ralph's right arm and walked him to an unmarked black van that looked like those armored vehicles used by banks. Already in the van were three people he'd worked with on the second floor.

Ralph and his former coworkers were taken to the Rock Island Arsenal, a U.S. Army facility located on a nine-hundred-acre island in the Mississippi River. They would spend a month there being interrogated by FBI agents regarding everything they had ever done at Drexler Limited. They were told that they were not under arrest and charges hadn't been filed against them. Yet. Charges would be filed, however, if they refused to cooperate. When people demanded to see a lawyer, they were told that due to certain provisions in the Patriot Act they wouldn't be allowed one unless they were arrested and formally charged, something that would happen if they refused to cooperate. As far as Ralph knew, everyone cooperated. He certainly did.

□ □ □

The FBI couldn't locate Heather Fine. Security camera footage showed that she hadn't been at her apartment in Arlington in two weeks, nor had she used her phone or a credit card in that same period. The agents suspected, based on what Gillian Lang had told them, that Heather Fine was dead.

The FBI easily found Congressman John Corcoran. He was sitting in his office in the Rayburn Building. When the agents walked into his office, he stood and smiled. "What can I do for you gentlemen?" he said. "It's always a pleasure to assist the Bureau."

The lead agent said, "Congressman, you were videotaped having sex with a woman known to you as Maria Alverez. Maria's real name is, or was, Heather Fine, and she worked for an escort service in Los Angeles before taking a job at the lobbying firm of Cooper & Cooper. After you were shown the video, you began to divulge information on various government programs to a man named Edward Pine. Most of this information was classified."

Corcoran, a onetime college wrestler, a big, blustery man who normally projected an aura of strength and confidence, looked as if he was about to deny the accusation, then his face slumped and he dropped into his chair and begin to cry.

Congressman Corcoran did not receive his party's nomination to become the next vice president.

◻ ◻ ◻

When the FBI tactical team burst into Robert Coolidge's home, the agents found him sitting in a battered recliner, drunk, an almost empty bottle of bourbon on the floor near his chair. When the agents pointed assault rifles at him and screamed that he was under arrest, Robert Coolidge wet his pants.

Technicians dressed in biohazard suits searched Coolidge's home and the cannery where he worked. At the cannery, hidden inside a box containing oil-stained rags, they found five two-ounce vials containing a clear liquid. The vials were small enough that they could easily be hidden in the palm of a man's hand.

The vials contained a form of botulism that had been manipulated in a laboratory. Coolidge had been told to pour the vials into one of the vats used in the canning process before the cans were sealed. He was to pour one vial into the vat every day for five days. It would take approximately a week for people who ate the corn in the cans to become sick and some would die the week after that. Had Coolidge been successful, five hundred thousand cans of corn would have been contaminated and distributed to stores in a dozen southern states. The only reason Coolidge hadn't yet completed his mission was that the cannery had been shut down for a week for periodic maintenance and as soon as it began operating again—which would have been two days after the FBI raid—Coolidge would have accomplished his task.

Coolidge had been led to believe that although the poison would cause people to become sick, the worst symptoms would be only diarrhea and nausea. When asked why he agreed to contaminate half a million cans of corn, he said a man had told him that he was going to kill his seven-year-old son if he didn't cooperate. Coolidge didn't mention that the mortgage on his house and all his credit card debt had been paid off, but the FBI knew this before they raided his house.

As for the man who had coerced/paid Coolidge, Coolidge didn't know his name, didn't know where he lived, and the description of the man he provided was useless. The FBI never located this individual.

□ □ □

Six people working at the vial-filling-machine manufacturer in Virginia Beach—six people all new to the firm—were arrested. The FBI agent in charge of the arrest—a woman who had three small children—broke down and cried with relief when she learned that none of the new machines had yet been delivered to Merck. She couldn't even imagine the number of children who might have died or become ill had a hundred million doses of contaminated measles vaccine been distributed, not to mention all the children who would die in the future when parents would have no faith whatsoever in the safety of vaccines.

□ □ □

Agnes Pine, the mayor of Redemption, and Sarah White and Connie White, the wives of the late Sam and Matt White, were arrested but never charged. The FBI had no evidence that these widows, these mothers of young children, these pillars of the community of Redemption, had ever committed a crime. Gillian Lang claimed that they'd done nothing wrong that she knew of and Jamison Maddox had never had any interaction with these women at all.

Ed Pine, Agnes's husband, was killed in Niagara Falls, New York, near the border crossing. Like Gillian, he'd decided to head to Canada and when he was surrounded by half a dozen FBI agents and told to put up his hands, instead of doing so, he pulled out a pistol. He was struck by fourteen bullets before he could fire a shot. He'd elected to commit suicide by cop rather than be captured.

Steven Lang was arrested in a bar at the Miami International Airport, sitting with six other people who were all part of a small tour group venturing to Cuba. Steven didn't put up a fight. The only thing Steven said when an agent snapped handcuffs on his wrists was: "That bitch."

Steven would spend the remainder of his life at the supermax prison in Florence, Colorado.

51

Gillian and the two marshals jogging with her stopped at the halfway point on their morning run. From where they were standing, they could see a body of water called Dabob Bay and the jagged peaks of the snow-covered Olympic Mountains. One of the marshals, a female, pointed at the bay and said, "Look. Orcas. I had no idea they came this far into Hood Canal. I wonder if they're lost or something." The female marshal walked a few paces away from Gillian to get a closer look at the killer whales and when she did, Gillian briefly squeezed the hand of the other marshal, a man named Danny O'Brien.

After four months at the submarine base, Gillian had settled into a routine. She would wake at six and, rain or shine, go for a three-mile run accompanied by two of the six marshals assigned to protect her. Part of the submarine base was devoted to the moorage and repair of the nuclear submarines homeported at Bangor, and Gillian was not allowed near these areas. But vast sections of the huge base—sections where nuclear warheads were reportedly stored underground—were like a nature preserve and deer and other wildlife were everywhere. The shoreline near the base, which was patrolled by boats armed with large-caliber machine guns, had magnificent views of Hood Canal; seals and sea lions were often visible and eagles could be seen soaring overhead. It was through these areas that Gillian and her guards would run.

One of the guards always assigned to accompany her was handsome Danny O'Brien. He was one of her running partners in part because he was fit enough to keep up with her. The other reason was that he'd asked for the job, saying he liked to keep in shape. Danny was twenty-nine years old—the same age as Jamison now—and had a wife and two kids who lived in Seattle that he only saw occasionally because of his current assignment. Danny O'Brien was in love with Gillian Lang.

After her run, Gillian would shower and have breakfast in a nearby mess hall where sailors also dined, but she had to wait until the sailors had eaten before she and the marshals guarding her could eat. From the mess hall, always accompanied by two marshals, she would walk over to a small two-story building that at one time had been used for training navy personnel; the building had been commandeered by the FBI. The FBI was getting so much information from Gillian that twenty agents and six lawyers had been assigned to follow up on everything she'd told her interrogators. More than forty criminal investigations had been initiated in the time she'd been at Bangor and more were certain to follow.

She walked into the FBI command center and down a hallway to the interrogation room, the room where she'd spent almost every day since arriving at Bangor. There were cameras and recording equipment in the room and a large conference table where papers could be spread out, but because Gillian and her interrogators spent so much time there, it had been made into a comfortable space with a couch and armchairs surrounding a coffee table. There was a Keurig coffee maker and a refrigerator where soft drinks and bottles of water and snacks were stored.

One of her interrogators, an FBI agent who also had a law degree, was already in the room when Gillian arrived. The agent's name was Amy Murdock and she was about Gillian's age.

Amy said, "Good morning. How was your run?"

"Wonderful," Gillian said. "We saw a pod of orcas in the bay. Someone said they don't usually come into this area."

"I've never seen an orca," Amy said, "and I've lived in this state for ten years."

"Amy, you need to get a life."

Gillian had developed a cordial relationship with her primary inquisitor. Amy had told her about her perpetually unemployed husband who thought he was an artist; her belligerent teenage daughter; her meddlesome, annoying mother-in-law. Whereas Amy, although she thought otherwise, knew very little about Gillian's personal life and certainly knew nothing about the way she felt.

"Would you like a cup of coffee?" Amy said.

"No, I'm fine."

"Okay, then. We might as well get started."

Amy took a seat on the couch, placed a manila file folder crammed with paper on the coffee table in front of her, and turned on the recorder. Gillian took a seat in one of the armchairs, the chair where she normally sat, and crossed her legs. Amy said, "I want to go back over the Indianapolis operation we discussed yesterday. You said a man named—"

In the four months Gillian had been on the base she'd told Amy and the other FBI agents about every operation that she knew about or had taken part in at Drexler Limited. In the first few days she'd talked about the ongoing operations—the cannery project, the blackmailing of Congressman Corcoran, the takeover of the Virginia Beach company that built vial-filling machines—which allowed the FBI to get warrants to invade Claud Drexler's building in Redemption and start rounding up the people associated with those schemes. Unfortunately, by the time the FBI got to Redemption, Claud was dead and all the information in the building had been destroyed or disappeared.

After discussing the current operations, Gillian then began to talk about everything she'd done or knew about since 2012. In 2012, she had been twenty-two years old, recently married to Steven, and that was the year she began to take an active role in the company. It was as if she threw a large rock into a pond and the ripples expanded outward in concentric ring after ring as the FBI begin to learn about Drexler Limited's accomplishments. And it was because she was providing so much information—about ten years' worth of crimes, including several murders—that twenty-six agents and lawyers had been brought to Bangor to follow up on what she told them. She would often spend days going over the same operation and would be questioned by multiple agents, not all of them working for the FBI, and would have to repeat everything she said several times. She'd been talking about the Indianapolis operation, one that occurred in 2015, for three days and had been interviewed by six different agents, two of them from Homeland Security, one of them from the CIA.

Gillian fully expected that she would spend at least a year at Bangor being debriefed by the FBI. After that she would spend the next four or five years testifying in courtrooms once the FBI had arrested all the people associated with the crimes she'd revealed. Then she would disappear into a witness protection program, but she had no idea where she'd end up.

That is, that's what would happen unless Gillian did something to change the vector of her life. U.S. Marshal Danny O'Brien was instrumental in changing that vector.

□ □ □

One of the conditions that Jamison had negotiated as part of Gillian's deal was that she be treated like a witness and not a prisoner. She wasn't required to wear an orange jail jumpsuit; she dressed in normal civilian clothes. She didn't sleep in a cell. She slept in a building that at one time had been occupied by unmarried junior naval officers. She had a one-bedroom apartment with a small kitchen and a seating area with a television set. She wasn't locked in her room at night.

Although she wasn't permitted to leave the naval base and was always accompanied by two to four marshals, she was allowed to enjoy all the amenities available to military personnel and their families. She would go shopping at the base exchange, use the gym, see movies at the base cinema, bowl at the bowling lanes. And although the marshals believed that the people Gillian had once worked for would try to kill her as she'd told Jamison, after four months the marshals had become somewhat relaxed when it came to her security. For one thing, the likelihood of anyone being able to get to her on the base was small. Furthermore, she wasn't a prisoner who would be inclined to escape; her future freedom depended on her cooperating with the FBI and were she to escape, she'd become a fugitive, and if captured she would spend the rest of her life in prison.

It was for this reason she wasn't locked into her room at night. At first the marshals had stood guard outside her room but after a month, they decided that this wasn't necessary. She was told to lock her door, not to open it to anyone other than a marshal, and if she wanted to go outside, she was instructed to call the marshal on duty and he or she would accompany her. The marshals eventually became more like companions than bodyguards and would enjoy seeing a movie or bowling with her. Danny O'Brien in particular.

Gillian began her seduction of Danny O'Brien two months after arriving at Bangor. And seducing him had been as easy as seducing Jamison. It helped that Danny hadn't always been faithful to his wife and that he'd been unfaithful with women much less attractive than Gillian. Like Jamison, he was fascinated by her; not only was she beautiful but he felt sorry for her and wanted to protect her. By the end of her third month at the naval base, Gillian would go to her room at night and, an hour or so later, Danny would knock quietly on her door and she'd let him in.

As for Jamison, she hadn't seen him since the time she'd told him the complete truth about Drexler Limited. She'd made it clear that she never wanted to see him or speak to him again—and she hadn't. He had betrayed her, and it was his fault that she was in her current predicament. She had no idea where he was today, nor did she care—although she wasn't yet through with Jamison Maddox.

The last night Gillian spent on the submarine base, Danny came to her room and they had sex. As Danny was sleeping in her bed—his phone alarm set to wake him at five so he could sneak back to his room— Gillian took the credit cards out of his wallet and his car keys and left the building.

It was almost impossible for an unauthorized person to get on the submarine base. The base was constantly patrolled and all the entrances were guarded and people entering had to show credentials, such as badges and stickers on their cars that permitted them to enter the facility. But the security was designed to keep unauthorized personnel from *entering* the base, not from exiting. All Gillian had to do was drive Danny O'Brien's car through the main gate.

When Gillian didn't come out of her apartment for her morning run, the marshals just assumed that she'd decided to sleep in. (Danny didn't mention that she wasn't in bed when he'd left her room at five.) When she didn't join the marshals for breakfast, no one was alarmed; she periodically skipped breakfast. At eight, when she was due to resume her interrogation sessions with Amy Murdock, a marshal was sent to knock on her door and see if she'd overslept or was feeling ill. The marshal found her room empty. But no one panicked at this point.

The marshals all believed that she wouldn't try to escape as escaping was not in her best interest. They thought that maybe she'd gone for an early morning walk even though doing so by herself was a violation of the requirement to notify the on-duty marshal if she wanted to leave the building. The marshals, still not overly concerned, walked around the area near Gillian's apartment. There were a couple of nearby walking trails and benches where it was pleasant to sit in the morning and have a cup of coffee and enjoy the mountain view. But she wasn't on the trails or sitting on the benches.

Now panic began to set in, and the marshals notified the FBI agents and decided to get into their vehicles and drive around the base to see if they could spot her—and that's when Danny O'Brien, a man who would soon be unemployed, noticed that his car was missing.

The last known sighting of Gillian Lang was at a Best Buy in Spokane, Washington, where she purchased a laptop computer fifteen minutes after the store opened. She used one of Danny O'Brien's credit cards to buy the computer. Danny O'Brien's car was found in the parking lot.

Gillian Lang was never seen again.

52

Jamison looked down at the snarled Manhattan traffic. Fortunately, from his Wall Street office on the forty-second floor, he couldn't hear the constant blare of the horns produced by New York's thirteen thousand perpetually angry cabdrivers. He sat there with a wry smile on his face, although he had no reason to smile after seeing the statement on his computer. But he just couldn't help himself.

He was no longer a convicted felon; records showed instead that he'd been a cooperating witness in a trial hardly anyone could remember. How the Justice Department was able to make this happen, he had no idea. Nor did he care.

He was now employed by a boutique hedge fund. The firm's partners had decided, now that Jamison didn't have an embarrassing criminal blemish, to overlook his prior transgressions, knowing that he had the talent to make them rich. Or richer. His salary was a modest two hundred thousand dollars per annum, but he was sure that with time it would increase.

His uncle Jed had forgiven him regarding Naomi's kidnapping once he understood what had happened at Drexler Limited and how Jamison had assisted the FBI. His cousin, Naomi, was once again fully functional—or as functional as she would ever get. She was back in her apartment in Tribeca and working for not one but two polling companies. She'd doubled her income and could almost pay the rent on her apartment without any under-the-table contributions to the landlord from her father.

It had taken Naomi two months to recover from the trauma of being kidnapped. She spent those months not with mental health care professionals but with her father, who slowly and patiently made her whole again. When Jamison was able to talk to her and tell her how she'd been instrumental in bringing down Drexler Limited he could tell, even though her face was expressionless, how proud and pleased she was.

An hour earlier, two FBI agents had visited Jamison and informed him that Gillian Lang had escaped. They wanted to know if he'd been contacted by her or had any idea where she might be. The agents, skeptical by nature and inclination, eventually accepted that he couldn't help them. He was certain, however, that someone would be watching him and monitoring his phone calls for some time to come.

He sat thinking about Gillian—beautiful, damaged Gillian—after the agents left, wondering where she could be. But mostly he thought about the time they'd spent together, particularly those few weeks in Oregon, where she'd been the happiest he'd ever seen her. He wondered if she'd eventually settle in someplace similar to Dolphin Cove, although he suspected she wouldn't stay in the United States.

But it was an hour before something occurred to him—and that's when he'd checked his computer.

Thus, the wry smile on his face.

□ □ □

The last time he saw Gillian in the small interrogation room on the sub base and demanded that she tell him the truth, she eventually did.

She began with: "I wasn't lying when I said that I didn't know where Claud came from or who he was prior to 1961. He never discussed his past and like I told you, my grandparents died when I was very young but I'm sure they wouldn't have talked about their pasts either. But based on the things the family did and the things I was taught, it's pretty obvious where he came from."

"What do you mean?" Jamison asked.

Gillian said, "1961—the year Claud came to Redemption—was the height of the Cold War. The Cuban missile crisis occurred a year later. There was an arms race and a space race going on and cells of sleeper agents were trained and placed in various countries, not just the United States."

"Trained by who?" Jamison said.

"Who do you think?" Gillian said. "In 1961 there were only two superpowers. Anyway, the agents were expected to remain in place until they were called home or captured. They were also expected to marry and have families and become an integral part of their communities. I have no idea how many cells were placed in the United States. If Claud was ever told, he never told anyone else, but my guess would be that he didn't know.

"I think the five couples placed in Redemption were the Midwest cell. There are numerous military bases and government facilities and universities doing cutting-edge research within a four-hundred-mile radius of Redemption. There are twenty military facilities in Illinois alone. The Argonne National Laboratory operated by the Department of Energy is located in Chicago. The Rock Island Arsenal is ninety minutes from Redemption. I imagine other sleeper cells were placed on both coasts and in strategic places like maybe near Los Alamos or Colorado Springs where NORAD is headquartered, but I don't know.

"I do know that sleeper agents have been captured over the years. I know that from the media. Ten agents on the East Coast, some of them married and with children, were captured as late as 2010. That television show *The Americans*? I read it was based in part on that cell. I also know agents have penetrated numerous government organizations and one of the reasons I didn't want you going to the FBI is that I know the FBI has been penetrated several times. A man named Robert Hanssen was a double agent in the FBI for over twenty years before he was finally caught and there have been at least three other FBI double agents that I know about who've been arrested. But I only know about the ones who were caught and I have no doubt that there are others who haven't been caught. As far as I know, Claud was never able to penetrate the FBI."

"So let's talk about what you do know," Jamison said. "Let's talk about Claud and your fucked-up family. What have they been doing the last sixty years?"

"I know from my mother that the initial mission of the five couples who came to Redemption was basic espionage. They spied on government facilities. They paid and blackmailed people to obtain information. They listened in on the phone calls of people discussing classified subjects. They did what spies do. This mission—basic espionage—went on for almost thirty years. But in 1989 the mission changed."

"What happened in 1989?"

"The Berlin Wall fell and two years later the Soviet Union disintegrated. And the world changed in other ways. Economies became more global and interconnected. China rose to a dominant position. Technology changed. Hackers could obtain information sitting in an office thousands of miles away. You no longer needed to break into a building; you only had to break into a computer. Satellites looking down from the sky could learn more than any spy on the ground using binoculars. And so the mission, Claud's mission, changed. Although he was still engaged in espionage, by the time I was born in 1990, espionage was no longer the primary focus. Instead the focus became disruption."

"Disruption?"

"Yes. The goal became to weaken the United States through any means possible. Racial unrest. Casting doubt on institutions and the validity of elections. Driving political and ideological wedges between people. Causing fear and economic instability. Anything and everything that could be done to make the country less stable and more difficult to govern. Claud's masters didn't want a nuclear war. Nobody wanted war. Instead they wanted a weakened United States, and Claud established Drexler Limited to carry out this mission.

"When 9/11 happened, it had a huge short-term effect on the stock market and a much bigger long-term effect on travel and security in general. One of Claud's jobs was to create 9/11–like events that would damage the economy or cause dissension or generate fear. That man Crane that you researched? The objective was to help white supremacists blow up the federal building in Detroit. That would have increased racial tension and money would have been wasted on increasing the security of government facilities, as if enough hadn't already been wasted. Disruption. Your friend Ralph Finney was part of a project to cast doubt on the accuracy of elections in Florida, a critical swing state. Disruption."

"The cannery project?"

"In 1982, someone in Chicago put cyanide in a bunch of Tylenol bottles. They never caught who did it. It may have been Claud, although I don't know for sure. Only seven people died, but because of that and other cases of product tampering, items like food and pills are now double sealed whenever possible. How do you double seal a can? And what if everyone was afraid to eat canned food for some period? Do you remember the mad cow scare?"

"What about Don Steward's company?"

"The people inserted into Steward's company were to make a modification to the machines that would have contaminated the vaccine doses put into the vials. The intent wasn't to kill children, but to cause them to become ill. In a country which already has a large contingent of people opposed to vaccines in general, the disruptive factor would have been enormous."

"Jesus Christ," Jamison said, sickened by the thought of kids being targeted. "How in the hell were you and the others, I don't know, *brainwashed* into doing what you did?"

"The second generation, my mother's generation, was steeped in the superiority of communism as a political and economic system. With my generation it was the need to maintain a weakened United States to prevent imperialism and maintain some sort of balance in the world. As a child, I was no different than other children who are molded and browbeat into following a particular religion or ideology. We were taught that what we were doing was for the greater good of the world as a whole and people like my mother and my husband bought in to this completely. I did for a while, but eventually, as you know, I just wanted to live my own life."

"But why would Claud hire people like me?"

"Because the family couldn't do everything on its own. There weren't enough of us and we didn't have sufficient education or expertise in some areas. The people like you, the people on the second floor, were only given small parts in Claud's projects, mostly doing research, and were never allowed to see the big picture. And if you ever had, Mary White's children would have dealt with you. There have been several people who worked on the second floor that have disappeared."

Jamison couldn't help but wonder if Mary's kids might have eventually disappeared him. Considering some of the things he'd worked on, that seemed a likely possibility.

"Who did Claud report to?" Jamison asked.

"I have no idea and in sixty years I imagine there were several different people. All I know is what I told you before, that Claud worked with someone in Chicago. He called him the client's man. But who he was, I have no idea."

She paused before she said, "Claud Drexler ruined my life, but he was an amazing man. They should erect a monument to him in Red Square."

□ □ □

And that was the last time he saw her, sitting in the interrogation room, the trapped, haunted look back in her eyes. The lioness was again in her cage.

Why she'd decided to escape, he didn't know. Eventually she would have been freed and placed into a witness protection program where she could have begun a new life. Maybe she didn't believe that the FBI could protect her. Or, more likely, she didn't want to be under anyone's control again.

He didn't know if she'd be able to elude capture, but he suspected, as brilliant as she was, that she would. And one thing she wouldn't have to worry about was money.

She'd set up the account where they'd placed the three million dollars his mother had given him. After Gillian was arrested and he'd been debriefed by the FBI and allowed to return to New York, he moved the money to another account, one that only he had access to. Or so he thought. That account now had only a hundred dollars in it, the minimum amount needed to keep the account open.

Still, he couldn't help but smile.

Good luck, Gillian, wherever you are.

Acknowledgments

I especially want to thank Morgan Entrekin, publisher and CEO of Grove Atlantic, for taking a chance on this book. Grove Atlantic has published thirteen of my fifteen Joe DeMarco novels, for which I'll always be grateful, but this is the first stand-alone of mine the company has released. A departure from the norm always entails some risk for both the writer and the publisher, so I'm particularly grateful to Morgan for giving me this opportunity.

I've been extremely lucky when it's come to the editors assigned to my books at Grove Atlantic. For this book, as well as several others, Sara Vitale was the editor. Sara has not only improved my books, she's also made the whole publishing process enjoyable and has been a pleasure to work with. The other thing that Grove Atlantic has consistently done is assign good copyeditors to work on my books; without these copyeditors, my books would be riddled with errors and typos. On this book, I'm grateful for the work done by Maria Zerafa who did the copyediting, and Donald Kennison who did the proofreading, and to Julia Berner-Tobin who, among other things, has overseen the copyediting process on many of my books.

There are many other people at Grove who have helped me over the years—it takes the work of a lot of good people to publish a book—and I also want to acknowledge the efforts of Deb Seager, Kait Astrella, Bill Weinberg, Mary Flower, Peter Blackstock, Judy Hottensen, who, among many others, have all worked hard on my behalf.

Lastly, I want to thank my agent, David Gernert. Without him, I imagine none of my books, including this one, would have been published. Like Morgan Entrekin, I owe David more than I'll ever be able to repay.